The redhead Plays Her Hand

The
redhead
Plays
Her Hand

Alice Clayton

GALLERY BOOKS

New York   London   Toronto   Sydney   New Delhi

G

A Division of Simon & Schuster, Inc.
1230 Avenue of the Americas
New York, NY 10020

First Gallery Books trade paperback edition December 2013

GALLERY BOOKS and colophon are registered trademarks of Simon & Schuster, Inc.

For information about special discounts for bulk purchases, please contact Simon & Schuster Special Sales at 1-866-506-1949 or business@simonandschuster.com.

The Simon & Schuster Speakers Bureau can bring authors to your live event. For more information or to book an event contact the Simon & Schuster Speakers Bureau at 1-866-248-3049 or visit our website at www.simonspeakers.com.

Design by Aline C. Pace

Manufactured in the United States of America

10 9 8 7 6 5 4 3 2 1

Library of Congress Cataloging-in-Publication Data is available.

ISBN 978-1-4767-4125-3
ISBN 978-1-4767-4131-4 (ebook)

This book is dedicated to Professor Jim Miller, who taught me that it can never be too big, it can never be too splashy, and that life is infinitely better with a tap-dancing chorus. Thank you for being the first adult to see my funny, and give me a home and a stage to let my funny fly.

acknowledgments

The family that helped to bring the Redhead series is large, loyal, and amazing in their dedication. Not only to me and my craziness as I finished this book but in their dedication to you, the fantastic Redhead Reader. Everyone that helped put this book together always kept you in their mind, and in their hearts, while working to make sure that Grace and Jack got to tell their story, their way.

Thank you to Micki Nuding, the most amazing editor and superhero. This is the first book we got to work on together, and I'm blessed beyond measure to have someone like her at the beginning of my career. Thank you for believing in me and making this my new life.

Thank you to the entire team at Simon & Schuster/Gallery Books, the coolest group of ladies I've ever had the privilege of working with. To know that I have your support and your backing means the world.

Thank you to my agent Karen Solem for being as patient and as kind as you have been to a newbie like me. It means so much to have someone like you alongside for this journey.

Thank you to Lauren, Deb, and Sarah for reading patiently and persistently, letting me send you pages at 2 a.m. and then giving me notes, sometimes within twenty minutes. I literally could not have finished this book without you and I'm grateful beyond words to have you all as my sounding board.

Thank you to Jessica, for being my friend since 4th grade and taking this crazy trip with me, for never failing to support and challenge me, and making my new career a dream come true.

Thank you to Nina, one of the best friends and biggest cheerleaders a girl could ask for. When I say this would not have been possible without you, I ain't just whistling "Dixie." Even though I can't whistle . . .

Thank you to my bestie since college and the *voice* of the Redhead series audiobooks, Keili Lefkovitz. When I found out there was going to be an audio version of these books, I knew immediately that I had to have my girl do the narration. For any of you who love the character of Holly, then you will *love* Keili's.

Thank you to my family. To my mom, who knew this was going to happen way before it did, and to my dad, who still can't believe this has happened but is pleased as punch that it did. To my sister, who bought as many copies of my books as she could and then pimped me to her friends like it was her job.

Thank you to the bloggers, the incredible women who do this because you love it and because you feel the way I do when I read a book I love, that we *must* tell everyone about it! Thank you for supporting me when no one knew who Jack and Grace were, and made it your business to tell the world.

Thank you to the Nuts Girls, to the readers who have been there since this was one chapter, one idea, one weird take on a giant phenomenon, and have let me be true to my own inner Nuts Girl.

And as always, thank you to Peter, who I've been in love with since I was sixteen years old. Thank you for always telling me how cute I am, and for being the only person on the planet who could possibly take me on and live to tell about it. I adore you.

Jack Hamilton was spotted today shopping at a vintage furniture store on La Brea, pausing over shower fixtures and an antique coffeepot. With the sales of *Time* cementing him as a leading man in Hollywood and the offers pouring in, we think he can afford some new appliances.

Superstar Jack Hamilton seen having dinner at Chin Chin on Sunset Boulevard with the now-identified redhead Grace Sheridan. The two continue to say nothing about their relationship, with their manager affirming again, "They're friends. That's all." Someone should tell them friends don't usually feed each other pot stickers, do they?

Production begins next month on the new dramedy *Mabel's Unstable?* by writer-creator Michael O'Connell. Directed by David Lancaster, this marks the first show of the kind to premiere on Venue. Leading the cast is actress Grace Sheridan, who is perhaps best known as the other half of the are-they-or-aren't-they couple with actor Jack Hamilton. Grace, 33, originated the role of Mabel in New York in a staged workshop production. Billed as a cross between a comedy, drama, and variety/reality show, the series is likely slated for a fall premiere.

one

*N*o, I can't do this."

"You have to do this. You promised you'd try."

"I know what I said, but now that it's time, I'm too nervous."

"A promise is a promise."

"You can't make me do something I don't want to, you know . . ."

"Okay, we're going to try this again . . . We can go as slow as you need. Ready, love?"

"Jesus, I guess . . . I still can't believe I agreed to this . . . This hurts so much."

"You'll feel better once we get going, I promise."

I closed my eyes, took a breath, opened them once more, and nodded. His eyes met mine in the mirror, and he grinned that grin he knew always won me over.

I dug my hands into his hair, running my fingers through the silky curls and scratching at his scalp. I blinked back tears. I lifted a chunk straight up, picked up the scissors . . . and cut.

And cut.

And cut.

And cut some more.

He kept encouraging me because he wanted it short.

When he'd first asked me to cut his hair, I'd refused. I told him no way. He reminded me that if he got this done at a salon, it would be on Twitter within minutes, and the paparazzi would surround the place.

"But I love your curls. I need your curls! Please don't make me cut it. I-I-I'll do anything!" I begged, kneeling at his feet dramatically. We may have been in the shower at the time.

"Would you not make such a big deal about this? But as long as you're down there . . ." He grinned, and I stood up immediately.

"Hell no. You cut that hair, and you can wave good-bye to any kind of oral action. Your Mr. Hamilton will not be very happy about that," I threatened, picking up the shower gel. The scent of coconuts filled the air.

"Bollocks, I can play that game too. You want to go without? I can remove certain things from the menu as well."

You can't let him take that *off the menu . . .*

Dammit. He had me. A day without oral is simply a day not worth living.

So here we were, in the guest bathroom, inches and inches of glorious shaggy blond hair on the floor around us, as his grin got bigger and bigger.

And my frown got, well, frownier and frownier.

By the time he felt I had butchered it successfully, I was almost in a full-on meltdown.

"Jesus, George, I ruined it!"

It was sticking up in places, flat in others, and just generally a disaster area. It looked like a five-year-old had cut it.

"Hmm, it does have a sort of whacked look to it, doesn't it, love?" He laughed, running his hands through it, throwing an errant curl to the floor.

"I may vomit," I whined, setting down the scissors.

"Come on, Crazy, finish it." He pressed the clippers into my hand.

Clippers? "Finish it?"

"How many grunts do you know without a buzz cut?" he asked, trying on his new southern accent. Alabama by way of London, interesting combo.

"When you said you needed to get ready for this movie, I had no idea I was going to have to bear the brunt of it." I sighed and picked up the clippers after he adjusted the setting. He'd dialed it way down. This was gonna be short.

"How exactly are you bearing the brunt of this?" he asked, pulling me between his legs as I stood before him.

"I'm the one who has to look at you, Sweet Nuts." I winked.

3

"Buzz me," he commanded, eyes twinkling.

I buzzed away. As the hair continued to fall, we talked about our schedules, all the changes that were to come.

Jack's name was on every woman's lips across the world, in every woman's dreams, and on every casting director's hot list. Holly, my best friend and Jack's agent as well as mine, had been flooded with offers. Directors, producers, talk-show hosts—everyone wanted a piece of him.

And I *had* a piece of him. Frequently.

Before the success of *Time*, a movie based on a series of popular erotic short stories that had been released this past fall, Jack Hamilton had been your average, ordinary British-guy-about-Hollywood. At only twenty-four, he had been in a few small, independent films and acted a bit in repertory theater, but once he was cast as Joshua, the Super Sexy Scientist Guy who traveled through time, seducing women across the centuries, his life changed. He was now one of the hottest young actors in Hollywood, and Holly was determined that he would not just be another flash in the pan.

Holly Newman was a great friend and a great agent. She had a killer instinct and was known for finding new talent. She had carefully crafted the careers of several of the most respected actors currently working, and she was poised to do the same for Jack. Declining several big-budget action films, she now guided Jack to a smaller film: a gritty, documentary-style picture about soldiers in Afghanistan. Jack could easily have headlined a huge summer blockbuster, but instead he chose to work in an ensemble cast, where the story was important.

And what was really important right now was shaving his head. He was a young soldier from Alabama, and he needed to look the part. *Sigh.*

"Did you just sigh, Grace?"

"I did." I took one last pass with the clippers and smoothed my hand over his shorn scalp.

"Is it really that bad?" he asked, nerves flitting over his face.

I smiled and scratched at his head. He leaned into it, just as he always had, and I looked carefully at him. The green eyes were the same, beginning to darken just the tiniest bit as my hand stroked the back of his neck. His hands tightened on my hips, drawing me close again. His hair was gone, but the heat was still there. In fact, his features seemed even stronger now. Cheekbones, jaw, everything even more chiseled, and his two days' worth of scruff even sexier than usual. His tongue dipped out of his mouth just so, teeth then nibbling on that lower lip in the way he knew would evoke a response.

"I have to admit, now that I can truly appreciate it, it's kind of . . . hmmm," I ventured.

"Kind of . . ."

"Sexy?"

"Sexy. Really?" His thumbs traced a tiny pattern along

the skin just above my drawstring. Which he was now tugging on.

"Yes, yes, it's true. Even with my butchering your hair,
you're still the sexiest man in America." I sighed again, this
time in a different way, as his thumbs fumbled apart the
buttons on my shirt.

"Only America?" He laughed, his newly cropped fuzzy
head tickling at the skin below my jaw as he nuzzled into
my neck.

"You're pushing it, George," I warned, my stern voice
giving way to giggles that broke free as he pushed me up
against the bathroom door.

"Only America?" he insisted, raising my hands and
holding them over my head.

"Okay, the Ameri*cas*. North and South combined." I
bumped my hips into his as he pressed into me.

"Speaking of south," he breathed into my ear, one hand
slipping slowly beneath my . . .

Ding dong.

"Who the hell is that?" he muttered, keeping me
pushed against the door, hand continuing its path toward
my . . .

Ding dong. Ding dong.

"It might be Michael. He said he might stop by tonight."
I slid out from in between Jack's body and the door and
looked at myself in the mirror. Rumpled, flushed, happy.

"Bloody Michael," he grumbled, grabbing for me as I
made for the door.

"Bloody nothing. You two are friends now. Behave yourself." I laughed, dancing away from his grab as I headed out into the hallway and toward the front door.

"Finishing this later!" he called after me, and my heart skipped a little.

"I'll hold you to that," I called back, thinking of all the ways he could and would finish this. And how I would most certainly let him. Since Jack and I had started seeing each other last year, the chemistry between us had been and remained off the charts. He'd finish it. He'd finish me right off a cliff.

I laughed as I heard him groan, knowing he was adjusting himself not so discreetly now. I straightened myself up a bit, then opened the door to see my friend Michael smiling back at me.

"Sure took you long enough," he chided.

"I was detained." I gestured for him to come in as he looked at my feet and laughed.

"You look like the missing link. Something you want to tell me?" He pointed down.

I looked and noticed I had clumps of Jack's hair between my polished toes.

"Ah, well, haircut gone bad," I explained, waving him inside as I went to the kitchen to get a broom. I had left a trail.

"Haircut gone great, you mean," Jack corrected, coming into the kitchen and running his hand over his head.

"Wow, what happened to you?" Michael chuckled, brown eyes full of mischief.

alice Clayton

Michael and I had gone to college with Holly and had been friends for years. Well, we *had* been friends, until a one-night stand clouded everything that had been good and made it ugly. We didn't speak for years, and then through a series of coincidences, he ended up casting me in his new musical a few months ago. This time another near miss of a one-night stand had almost ruined everything, but we came to our senses and remained great friends.

And more. While the musical we had worked on together in New York didn't go anywhere, there was enough interest in the project to keep it alive in a new way. Right after the holidays we found out that there was a production company interested in developing it into a TV show. In the vein of HBO and Showtime, Venue was the new cable channel everyone was watching. Edgy comedies, dark dramas—their TV lineup was making a lot of waves. We brought a few of the original cast in from New York, shot a quick pilot, and Venue bought it. And they were putting Michael's new show right in the middle of their fall lineup.

Michael's original concept was a traditional musical, with a modern twist. Staged workshop style, we had worked with a live band. Now the story of Mabel, an aging beauty queen going through a divorce and redefining her life on her own terms, was set against the backdrop of Los Angeles—a perfect town for reflecting back the warped way our culture views women and aging. The show was now a cross between *Glee*,

The Real Housewives of Beverly Hills, and *Sex and the City*. It was witty, it was sexy, and I was the star. Wait, I was the star?

Yes, Grace, you are the star.

I shook my head to clear it, still waiting for the other shoe to drop.

"You got water in your ear, love?" Jack asked me, watching me shake my head.

"Shut it, you," I warned as he gave my behind a pat on his way to the fridge. I settled on a bar stool and watched two of my favorite people in the world circle each other. It was true: they were friends now but tentatively. Jack knew Michael and I had almost, well, *almost* while I was in New York. And while Michael and I were friends and only friends, I knew it was tough for Jack. But true to form, he was more of a grown-up than I was, even nine years my junior. And they were now easing into this weird guy friendship.

"No seriously, man, what's with the skin?" Michael asked again, catching the beer Jack threw at him. Without asking. Again, weird guy thing.

"Movie. I start shooting next week. Couldn't put it off any longer," Jack explained, taking a long pull on his beer.

"That's right, the new Daniel Richards picture. Afghanistan? There's some great buzz about that already. A writer friend of mine consulted on it. Looks like it's gonna be intense. You're shooting out in the Mojave, right?"

"Yeah, we're doing some here, then out to the desert. Should be a good time." Jack smiled, tipping back his bottle and draining it. Grabbing another from the fridge, he sat down on the bar stool across from me, still rubbing his head absently.

"What's a good time?" I heard a new voice from the hall chime in, with heels clicking on the floor. My other favorite person in the world.

Holly came into the kitchen, appraised the crew assembled, and sighed dramatically. She nodded to me. "Asshead,"

"Dillweed." I nodded back, pointing to the bottle of vodka I had removed from the freezer and raising an eyebrow in her direction.

"Yes. God, yes. You would not believe the day I had. I hate this town! Remind me never to work with anyone who used to be on the CW ever again," she cried.

I busied myself making dirty martinis. Holly pulled herself onto the counter, kicked off her heels, and put her feet in Michael's lap, pointing at them.

"Rub. And you, Buzzy, get behind me. Work on these shoulders," she instructed, gesturing Jack over. With a grin he obliged, and Michael's surprised face gave over to sheepish as he began working on Holly's heels. Stacked like a porn star, Holly's natural good looks tended to make all men a little gooey around her, present company included. I handed her the cocktail, grimacing as she sucked it back quickly, presenting me with an empty glass.

"Seriously, fruitcake, it was a dilly of a day. I'm gonna need a double. And harder, please, Michael." She moaned as he hit a spot in the middle of her instep. I laughed as she began to tell us about her day, and I made her another cocktail. I caught Jack's eye over Holly's shoulder, and he winked at me.

Life was good.

An impromptu dinner party ensued, and after dinner was over, we all ended up on the cushiony chairs in the backyard. Winter in Los Angeles was chilly at nighttime, at least enough that the cashmere throws I brought out were necessary. Snuggled into a large love seat, Jack played with my hair as we laughed and chatted with our friends. Strings of white lights dotted the fig and plum trees out back, and the potted lemon trees that framed the patio threw off their fragrance into the night. I leaned into Jack's warmth, his breath heady and thick with brandy as he and Holly went back and forth about his shooting schedule. He'd be leaving in a few weeks, but this was different from when we'd been apart in the past. This time I got to stay here, in my home that I'd worked so hard on and barely gotten to enjoy before heading off to New York. Now I was able to work where I lived, and I relished my surroundings.

I had created a space for myself exactly the way I wanted. Built into the hillsides of Los Angeles there were certainly bigger and grander homes, but my Laurel Canyon bungalow was exactly what I wanted. And having Jack move into it with me? Well, that made it all the more homey.

As Holly and Jack got louder and louder, trying to hammer down some interview she had planned for him, I leaned across to Michael.

"You still looking to rent a new place?"

"Yep, the corporate housing has been fine, but now that I'm setting down some roots I think I want something a bit more distinct. This agent I have, though, is showing me all these rentals on Wilshire—in the corridor, all those high-rises. They're great, but I just left New York. I'd like something a little closer to the ground."

"I can see that. Roots, hmm . . . Do you want to buy? Great time to buy," I prodded.

"Not quite that rooty. I still want to rent. I want rental roots," he answered, causing Holly to stop midstream in her conversation with Jack.

"I've got a great rental agent. I'll have her send over some listings. You want a house? Pool? Standard L.A. bachelor pad?"

"House, yes. Pool, perhaps. Bachelor pad, no. No neon." He grinned.

"I can totally find you that. I'll go with you to look at houses next week if you want," she offered, sipping at her brandy.

"That'd be great. You sure you have time?"

I snuggled closer to Jack.

"Of course. I can take an afternoon off. The business will still be there. And speaking of business, Jack, we need to talk about—"

"Holly, don't you ever quit? Enough for tonight, okay?" Jack snapped, surprising us all. We turned to look at him as he ran his hands through his nonexistent hair. He sighed, then gulped the rest of his brandy. With heavy eyes, he looked at Holly.

"Sorry. I think I'm just tired," he muttered, eyes falling back down to his glass.

"No worries, Jack. We can talk tomorrow. Call me in the morning?" she asked, pushing herself out of her chair with a quick glance at me.

I shrugged my shoulders and stood as well. "You're leaving?"

"I should get going—early meeting tomorrow with some kid with three names. When did everyone decide to name their children with such long names? If I see one more Noah Jonathan Blahblah I will lose my mind. Truly," she exclaimed, pulling Michael out of his chair. "Come on, you can walk me to my car."

"Okay, sure, yeah, of course. Um . . . 'night, Grace! See you later, Jack," Michael called back over his shoulder as they made their way into the house.

"'Night," Jack said, wrapping the blanket more firmly around himself. I waved at the two of them, then turned to stand in front of him.

"You okay?" I asked, taking his empty glass and setting it down on the table. I was pulled quickly into his lap, his strong arms wrapping around me suddenly and completely. I was pressed against him, his body caging me in, close to him.

"Sometimes, I swear, she just doesn't know when to quit!" he exclaimed, sighing into my neck as he clutched me closer.

"She's just doing her job, Sweet Nuts. Don't take it personally." I snuggled further into his arms.

"How can I not take it personally? It's my *life* she's managing, not just my career. I just— Fucking hell, I don't know."

"Hey, hey. I know, shush," I soothed, scratching his scalp and feeling him relax into me. His brandy breath was heavy around us, and I was reminded once again of how young he truly was. No one could possibly have prepared him for the life and all its trimmings that had been thrust upon him when he took his defining role. He held up remarkably well, all things considered.

We quietly rocked for a moment, the canyon still and quiet around us.

"Hey, did I tell you the good news?"

"What's that, Crazy?" he asked, his lips tickling now at the edge of my shirt. Apparently he had rallied.

"I get my own trailer! Can you believe that?"

"Of course you get your own trailer. You're the star of the show, love," he reminded me.

That still did not seem real to me.

"Listen, it's a pretty big deal. Not all of us are big film stars," I reminded him, settling more firmly on his lap.

"Now when you say *big*, what exactly were you referring to?" he asked, gently but firmly thrusting up against me.

"Oh, please." I laughed as he buried his face into my neck, blowing brandy-scented raspberries.

"I'm proud of you," he whispered, his hands now roaming freely across my back, familiar yet still very much capable of making me shiver. "Are you cold?"

"No, George, I'm all kinds of warm," I breathed into his ear, shivering once more as he literally swept me off my feet and inside to our bed.

two

$\mathcal{S}$o tonight, I'm heading to this club and I thought—" he said the following morning.

At least I think that's what he said. I was under the shower spray, and someone had his hands all over my breasts. Keeping me steady, of course, just for balance.

"You're going out again tonight?" I spluttered.

"Again? I was home last night," he answered, leaning underneath his own showerhead. The shower he had installed boasted his and hers nozzles. Although more often than not we ended up on one side or the other.

"True, but you were out almost every night last week."

"Is this where you turn into a nagging girlfriend?" He winked, letting the water stream off his face and down onto his chest and tummy, making the happy trail stand out even more. It sure made me happy.

"I think so. Hang on, let me put on my nag face," I said sternly, frowning in an exaggerated way. "Honey, don't you think you should stay home and clean out the gutters?" I whined, putting my hands on my hips and stomping my foot. An action that would have been more forceful had I not slipped as I did it. He caught me, laughing as I struggled to stay upright. He gave me a light smack on the bottom as he put me back on my feet.

"As it happens, I was going to ask if you wanted to come out with me tonight."

"Me? Go out with the boys club? Seriously?" I teased, handing him a washcloth.

Jack had been spending more and more time with some of the guys from his new film, something I initially encouraged him to do. For all the lip service he gave me about loving *The Golden Girls*, I reminded him often that he was a young guy about town and needed to live it up. Lately he had taken me up on my offer, almost too willingly at times.

"Sure, why not? I figured it was about time you met these guys. These are the guys I'm supposed to be willing to die for, right?"

"In a movie, love. Die for them in a movie. Will there be dancing?" I asked.

"I imagine so."

"Will you be dancing?"

"I'm British. We don't dance."

"Can I dance?"

"I'm counting on it. Jesus, Grace, you should see your-self right now." He sighed. I was leaning back under the spray, and was I making sure my breasts were pushed up high and perky? Yep.

Nice. Posing for your man?

Can't hurt.

I felt his mouth beginning to drag down the side of my neck, and I came up for air.

"Hey, we can't do this now, Sweet Nuts. I'm meeting Holly in forty-five minutes, and she gets testy when I'm late."

"I only need five minutes; just hold still, Crazy."

I laughed as he slid his body up mine, every nerve end-ing sparking to life. But water and sparks don't play well together, and I held him at arm's length.

"Seriously, I can't. Holly won't let me use sex with you as an excuse to be late."

"How do you know? Try it."

"Shush, you. Shower gel, please," I instructed, pointing. He handed it to me, we lathered, and I tried to go about the business of washing up. Which was hard.

Because so was he . . .

Because so was he.

Twenty minutes later, he sat on the bench at the end of the bed while I got ready.

"So tonight? Yes?" he asked, handing me my bra. Which he held with reverence. I think he was jealous that it got to hold my boobies all day, something he would prefer to do.

"Yes, tonight. Can I bring Holly? She's been dying to go out dancing. We can make a night of it!" I said excitedly, standing in front of him and running my hands over his scruff. It was taking some getting used to, but I was kind of digging it. He looked older and younger all at the same time. It was mesmerizing.

"Bring everyone you want, love. Just text me the names, and I'll tell Adam."

"Adam?"

"Adam Kasen, from the film? He'll make sure whoever we want is on the list," he replied, nuzzling into my palm.

"'On the list'? You going Hollywood on me, George?"

"This from the girl taking a meeting today to discuss her shooting schedule for her new TV series, right?"

"Wow, my new TV series. Can you say that again?"

"'My new TV series'?"

"Nope, *my* new TV series."

"That's what I said, exactly." He grinned as I threw my towel at him. He growled as I danced away from his grabbing hands.

"You better go to your meeting, you little tease, before I keep you here all day."

"Okay, I'll see you later tonight then?"

"Yep, I'll be the one in the corner with the posse behind the velvet rope." He nodded, laying back on the bed, the sheets still tussled from our previous activities.

"Perfect. This pussy loves a posse," I teased as he rolled his eyes at me.

"You have five seconds to get out of here, Grace."

"Leaving," I yelled as I headed toward the kitchen, grabbing my water bottle off the counter.

"Hey, Crazy?" I heard his feet slapping behind me on the hardwood.

"Yes?" I smiled as he stuck his head around the corner.

"I saw a couple cars that looked really familiar yesterday down the hill. Watch yourself out there, okay?" He smiled, his eyes burning into mine.

"No pics. Got it." I mock saluted.

"Don't let them make us into the next Ashton and Demi. People love to see a couple fall apart."

"Did you really just compare me to Demi?"

"Sorry. I guess you're a little older, right?" he teased, tugging on my ponytail as I slid a ball cap on.

I used to tease him so much about wearing his ball cap, and now I hardly went anywhere without one, especially when driving in my neighborhood. I was fanatical about making sure no one knew where we lived. I knew it couldn't last much longer, but I wanted to keep our bubble around us as long as possible.

"Seriously, George? How often do these little jabs work out in your favor in the long run?" I glared, letting him smooth out my ponytail.

"Just be careful out there, 'kay?" he said, his eyes concerned.

"I will, love. See you later." I nodded, blowing him a kiss.

"I got something for you to blow . . ." I heard him muttering as he headed back into the bedroom.

I giggled, grabbing my keys and heading out into the sunshine.

Even in winter, Los Angeles was golden. I smiled to myself as I crossed to my car, pausing a moment to take in the lemon trees, the thick carpet of pine needles on the lawn, the beige Taurus driving not too slow but not too fast either— Wait, what? I hurried behind the steering wheel, getting in just as it drove past the large pine at the edge of the property. Most of the houses on this part of Laurel were set back from the road but not too far.

Paranoid much?

Paparazzi were almost a daily concern. Running into them was no longer an occasional surprise, it was borderline becoming a nuisance. Jack's new car had been spotted multiple times, although somehow we'd been able to avoid being tracked back to the house. But it was getting dicey. Once, when he was being followed very closely on Robertson, a car in front of him stopped so quickly he almost ran right into it. Shots were taken of him looking grimly over the steering wheel, ball cap pulled down low. This was beginning to take its toll on Jack. It was a side of his fame that no one could prepare for.

I'd managed to avoid getting my picture taken with him again, although we both knew it would happen sooner or later. But that was part of it, being the girlfriend of the new It Boy.

Girlfriend.

I was his girlfriend, and along with that came all kinds of stuff we were both barely equipped to handle. When we came back from our vacation in the Seychelles in January, I had to stay behind with the luggage when we landed at LAX. The paparazzi who camped at the airport just waiting for celebrities to come off an airplane tired and bedraggled and less than were there to trail Jack. Someone, always someone, had tipped them off that he would be arriving, and they swarmed as soon as he showed up. And they took tons of pictures. He later told me he could barely keep hold of his duffel bag, they were so close and so tight on him as he made his way to the car we'd arranged to pick *us* up. In the meantime, I was waiting by the baggage carousel, watching and waiting. And paying a porter to help me quietly schlep all our stuff into a taxi.

Since we'd been back we kept a pretty low profile. We didn't run a ton of errands together, and if we did go out, we kept it off the beaten path and low-key. We lived together, we loved together, but we kept things as private as we could. Holly was still very much in favor of this tactic. Since *Time*, his female fan base had grown considerably, and there was an online presence that continued to grow.

This was a fan base still very much on the fence about whether they wanted their Jack Hamilton involved with anyone, much less a woman quite a bit older than he was. After the pictures of me taken at the premiere came out, and subsequently died down, his adoring fans had moved on from me. But I was about to embark on my own high-profile job. The TV series would bring those pictures, and more like them, back up and into the spotlight.

I kept this in mind as I opted to keep the convertible top up. I cinched the ball cap down tighter on my head and turned out onto the canyon to make my way to Holly's office. With my eyes peeled, I looked for those seemingly random tan sedans. That's where the flashbulbs tended to come from. It was amazing how quickly you could get used to looking behind you when you were moving forward.

three

*O*kay, so we have the first three scripts done, shooting
schedule in place, read-through next week. What else
do we need to talk about? You know us TV stars, we have
places to go, people to see." I winked, stretching from my
chair in front of Holly's desk. The two of us, along with Michael, had been hashing over details for the better part of
an hour.

Michael had fought for and managed to retain creative
control from the network. This was his show, his creation,
and while being funded solely by the network, he was still
steering the ship. He was working closely with the director,
making sure that as his show twisted and turned naturally
from stage production to the small screen it retained its
initial soul. David Lancaster was a well-known and well-
respected director, who had worked on some of the best

and most commercially successful series in the last ten years. He was also known for being a bit hardheaded, tough, and unyielding. He'd already shared some specific notes with Michael, and they were in agreement about the overall tone and content of the show. While Michael had experience in writing and directing, he'd never done it at this level, and he was understandably a bit nervous.

"Almost done. Just a few more things to talk about, and then we can call it a day." Holly shuffled some notes on her desk.

"Thank God. I'm starving," I moaned, standing and grabbing at some candy she had stashed on a shelf underneath her award for Manager of the Year. Which she had awarded herself.

I sat back down, offering a handful of jelly beans to Holly, which she shook her head at. She and Michael exchanged a glance, and Michael nodded at her slightly. She took a deep breath and then sighed. Then she brightened into her All-Business Face. All of this happened in about 2.7 seconds, none of which was lost on me. I gulped. Holly turned to face me now, and I heard the voice I had heard often but rarely directed toward me.

"So we got some notes from the producers after they watched the pilot. All good things, but I do have some feedback for you that they were pretty specific on, before we start shooting," she said—Holly Newman the agent now speaking, not Holly Dillweed, best friend and gal about town.

I swallowed my jelly beans. "Okay, what's up?" I asked, wondering what was about to go down.

Michael fidgeted.

"So you know you're fabulous; we all do. I think you're amazing. I mean it, really," she said, not totally meeting my eyes.

"Okay, you're amazing too?" I volleyed back, looking at Michael, who had stopped fidgeting and was now not moving at all. He was frozen, in fact.

Holly smiled a bit, then continued. "This show has a very specific look, very stylized, very Hollywood. Everything about this show will be over the top. You know this."

"I do know this. Jeez, spit it out, Holly." I popped another handful of jelly beans into my mouth.

"We need you to drop about fifteen pounds, Grace."

The jelly beans congealed in my throat and lodged there.

"Or *I* should spit it out," I joked, swallowing hard.

"Here's the thing. This is very common. Producers are looking at the overall package—everything, right? They have tons of notes, from what kind of car you should be driving to whether the hardwood floors in your on-set home should be lighter or darker. Perhaps your hair should be a little more red. And, well . . ."

"My ass should be a little smaller," I completed for her, placing the jelly beans back on the shelf and straightening up, lengthening my frame and pulling in my tummy.

"No, we actually got great notes on your ass," she replied, shuffling through papers on her desk. I looked in horror at Michael.

"I was kidding!" I laughed, forcing my hands to unclench from the fists that had formed.

"Grace, come on, you're beautiful, I—" Michael started, and Holly interrupted him.

"Here it is. The exact note is: 'We need her to have a little more cheekbone, a little more jawline,'" she read, looking over her glasses at me as she finished.

"A little more cheekbone," I repeated, mentally tallying how many miles I was already running in a week and wondering how many more I could squeeze in.

"Grace, look. Do you know how many times I've had this conversation with someone I represent? I honestly can't count at this point," she began tiredly.

"This sucks," I succinctly pointed out.

"It *does* suck, but that's the industry you've chosen. The good and bad, you get it all. You want less cheekbone, you move into the best friend category, okay?" she said, eyes blazing.

"Let's look at this a different way, maybe—" Michael started, and I held up my hand.

"I'm a big girl—literally, apparently. I can handle this," I said, and Holly sighed.

"I love you, ya little fruitcake, but this is the way it is. You've been given an amazing opportunity, one that other actors in this industry have been working toward for years and would live on lettuce and Diet Coke for months to get. You've got it. This is just part of the gig." Her eyes softened a bit. "This is totally something you can do. I know you can." She smiled.

"Hey, if that's what I need to do, that's what I need to do, right? Not a problem," I assured her, smiling through my teeth.

"You sure?" Michael asked, clearly uncomfortable with this entire conversation.

"I got this." I nodded.

"We good?" Holly asked.

"We're good." I nodded again.

We all sat together, quiet. Three friends who had found one another in a college theater class and were now working in their chosen industry, in positions most could only dream about. What a strange world this was.

"So, I hear we're going dancing tonight? Tell me more," Holly said, leaning back in her chair and putting her feet up on the desk, indicating that the business portion of our meeting was over.

I started to tell her all about the plans for the evening, but all I could think about were those damn jelly beans.

☆　☆　☆

Driving home I put the top down, no matter who could see. My mind was whirling. I needed some air. With the stereo cranked up, I navigated the streets of the city I loved, the city I worked so hard to get back to.

After leaving Los Angeles the first time, I spent several years—the better part of a decade really—smothering my feelings in smothered chicken. And burgers. And lots and lots of Doritos. I felt such shame that I hadn't managed to even last a year in L.A. that when I came home I licked my wounds, and the inside of more than one Klondike bar wrapper. Then I cocooned. Years went by, and I found a great job that allowed me some creativity but all behind a computer. I didn't go out much, didn't date at all, and as the pounds packed on and my sadness grew, I lost so much of what was me, what Jack had so quickly identified as his Nuts Girl. I eventually pulled myself out of it, rallying bigtime to come back to L.A. and try again. And within the span of a year, I was about to live out every dream I'd ever had, and the dream of actors everywhere. This would be my breakout role, one way or another.

So what's fifteen pounds, really?

Nothing, except I already managed what I ate so carefully. And exercised religiously. Dating a younger man initially brought back so many of my fears—not good enough, not young enough, not thin enough—but it was finally good. It was really good with Jack, and I was content with how I looked. For the first time in a long time, I felt good when I looked in the mirror.

So they need fifteen pounds. If they asked you to dye your hair a deeper shade of red, would you do it?

Yep.

If they said your character should have blue eyes, would you get contacts?

I'm afraid of touching my eyeballs.

And yet . . .

Yes, I would do it.

So what's fifteen pounds? It's certainly not going to stand in your way of this . . . is it?

It really shouldn't.

My phone interrupted my inner monologue. It was Holly.

"Stop it."

"Stop what?"

"Stop whatever it is you're doing. Don't let this freak you out."

"Wow, you're good,"

"That's why I get fifteen percent. Which, based on the contract I negotiated for you, is significant. So trust me, okay?"

"I do; I do."

"So stop it. Go home, get prettied up, and we'll shake our asses all over town tonight. Now that's an order."

I smiled into the phone, giving up the fight even before it began. I pulled to a stop on Beverly, leaning my head back against the seat. Closing my eyes for a moment, I could feel the good sunshine soaking into my pores, the scent of the canyons ahead thick in the air. Smog, perhaps, but definite canyon mixed in.

31

"I'll pick you up at eleven, dillweed."

"So late? My God are we old." Holly laughed.

"You said it." I hung up the phone and headed home. To the home I shared with a twenty-four-year-old.

Fifteen pounds. I got this.

Atta girl . . .

☆ ☆ ☆

"Jesus, look at that line!" I yawned, as we pulled up in front of Bar the Door later that night. Very much later that night. It was eleven thirty, and young Hollywood was out in force. Holly and I stepped out of the car to valet and made our way toward the front of the line. I looked down at my little black dress, glad Holly had talked me into dressing up a bit. Her instincts, as usual, were correct, as the ladies waiting to get in were dressed to the nines. Eyes—irritated eyes—pored over me as we walked up to the front. Eyes that said, *Bitch, you better not get in before me* . . .

Yes, every now and again it was nice to be dating the new It Boy. And also a Brit Boy.

"Jack said our names would be on the list," I whispered to Holly as we approached the giant bouncer. His eyes were more appreciative than the ladies in line. He smiled as we walked up.

"Hi, we're guests of Adam Kasen's." Holly grinned, blond hair swinging over her shoulder, swinging down low into her cleavage. She was looking good. Velvet ropes were pushed aside, smiles were bestowed, and we were ushered in.

In to a different world. Black walls, mirrored ceiling, bars everywhere, and music. Thick, screaming house music. Industrial, heavy, it pounded in my ears and got inside my brain. Everything about this place was sexy, and it was packed with sexy people. Dancing, mingling, kissing, this was no longer Los Angeles. This was Hollywood. And it was hot.

A bouncer inside immediately brought us to the VIP area, and there behind a double round of more velvet ropes was Jack. Reclining into a plush red leather banquette, he was drinking a Heineken and watching the scene. He was surrounded by young Hollywood hipsters. I recognized most of NBC's fall lineup. It was a unique opportunity to see him in his element but unnaturally so.

He had no idea how strong his personality was, the innate star quality he possessed. The fact that he was un-aware of it made him even more appealing. He was the only one who was unaware of it, however, and as we got closer I saw the girls, all the girls. But how could I blame them?

Some of the other guys from his film were there, hang-ing around but not hanging on. These guys were actors too, and they were in the same position Jack was in just two years ago: breaking in but not breaking big yet.

And there was Adam Kasen. He *was* the It Boy, the It Boy this town had bet everything on a few years ago. He'd been in Jack's position back then: the one everyone wanted to work with. But rather than being smart like Jack, Adam rushed into big-budget after big-budget, huge movies that cost a ton and flopped miserably. A few bad reviews, a few scandals in the tabloids, and his star had fallen fast. He had a reputation for being difficult to work with, showing up late and, throwing tantrums—a nightmare on the set. A nightmare wrapped up in a very handsome package. Dark hair, deep-set brooding eyes, he was stunning. And a little bit dangerous, which explained why even though he was not nearly as in demand as he was a few years ago, he still had a blonde on each arm.

Jack was laughing at something Adam was saying. When the two first met, Jack had taken an instant liking to Adam, telling me how he had gotten a bad rap, that the stories told about him were exaggerated, that he was not the bad boy everyone had made him out to be. I hoped so.

Jack caught my eye as we approached, and a slow grin spread across his face. Draining his beer, he gestured for the bouncer to let us behind the ropes, and just like that, we were VIPs. He stood to hug Holly and then let his arm fall around my waist. A little too familiarly. I gently nudged back against him. I shook my head at him slightly, and he rolled his eyes. The last thing he needed was a picture of the two of us manhandling each other at a high-profile bar on Twitter in two minutes. He started to step back to a respectable distance but couldn't resist dropping a quick kiss on my cheek, one that could have been interpreted as friendly, except for what he whispered in my ear as he let me go.

"Your tits look fabulous in that, Crazy,"

"Behave, George," I admonished, slapping him in the chest and achieving a safe separation. The girls in the banquette were quickly ushered aside to make room for Holly and me, and we sat down.

"You must be Grace. My man has been watching the door all night," Adam said, dropping down next to us and taking my hand.

"Yes, and you're Adam. Thanks so much for the invite tonight. This place is incredible!" I gushed, shaking his hand and noticing that up close, he was just as attractive as he was from far away. This guy must be lethal.

"I can't believe you haven't been here before. I'm always telling Jack to get you to come out too," he answered, still holding my hand.

"Just a homebody, I guess. Have you met Holly?" I asked, gesturing to my best friend. "This is Jack's manager."

"Sure, sure, I know Holly. We've met before. If I'd been smart, I would have hired her ages ago. She might have been able to keep me in line." He smiled, dropping my hand and taking hers.

"Doubtful. But it's good to see you again. I was surprised when I heard you'd signed on to this project," she answered, shaking his hand.

"Surprised? Why?"

"Don't get me wrong, I think it's a great move on your

part. I was just surprised to see you in a movie without an action figure," she replied, smiling genuinely when she saw Adam's jaw clench.

As I watched the two of them, Jack's hand kept wandering over to my knee. He was handsy tonight. Must have been the Heineken. I nudged him back, spotting several girls in the crowd just beyond the VIP section taking it all in.

"Well, let's just say I've learned my lesson. I'm a fucking Boy Scout nowadays," Adam answered, pulling one of the blondes down onto his lap and gesturing for a waiter to bring over another bottle of champagne. He raised a glass as Holly laughed, taking her own when it was offered.

"To the Boy Scouts," she toasted, and rolled her eyes at me over the rim. I bit back a laugh, pulling Jack's hand once more off my knee. The music was pounding, and I was dying to dance.

"Shall we?" I asked Holly, nodding toward the dance floor.

"Hell yes, I need to shake my ass," she affirmed, draining her glass and moving beyond the velvet ropes. Adam was busying himself with the blondes and had already lost interest in us.

"You coming?" I asked Jack.

"I'm watching." He smirked, leaning back against the leather and taking another bottle off the waiter's tray as he passed by.

"That's no fun, George," I teased, backing away.

"Depends on what you're watching." He winked, taking a sip of his beer and licking his lips as a shudder ran through me.

I continued to back away, turning around at the velvet ropes and making sure to add a little extra sexy to my hips, knowing he was watching. I joined Holly on the dance floor as the music changed to a new song, heavy bass pumping through the club. I threw back my head and gave myself over to the beat. Holly and I carved out our own dance space, losing ourselves in the song and the vibe. Screaming synthesizers and angry guitar buffeted everyone on the floor, hands groping and hips bumping as collectively we thrashed. Song after song we danced, energy spiking and spiraling throughout.

Sex poured through the speakers, oozed onto the floor, and inflamed everyone as we danced. It was dark and enveloping, hot and sticky, sweaty. I pulled my hair back from my face and felt hands on my hips, pulling me back against another body. I smiled, looking over my shoulder at who belonged to the hands. Just another guy at a club, looking for someone to dance with. Tall and handsome, his hands moved me, and I looked over his shoulder to find Jack.

Still sitting against the red leather, his eyes burned into mine as he took in the sight of me dancing with another man. I raised my arms up, the hem of my little black dress sliding farther up my legs. I let my hands tangle into his hair, feeling my body press along his, sliding low and then back up again, my fingers now tangling behind his neck as we moved together. I turned to grin at my partner, noticing that his boyfriend had appeared and was dancing behind him. Moving slightly, I slid in between the two, feeling both men encircle me, one leg sliding inside my own, grinding me hard. I let my head fall back against my new partner, feeling the beat of the music slip inside and pound my brain.

I closed my eyes and could feel the bass drugging me, relaxing me more than alcohol ever could. I was spun quickly, and as I smiled at Holly, lost in her own world with a very good-looking guy who couldn't be older than twenty, I glanced at the VIP section, wondering if Jack was still enjoying the view. I felt hands dipping lower on my legs and dragging my dress higher than was probably appropriate, and I was pulled back suddenly, a very wet mouth finding my neck and sucking hard at my shoulder. I began to turn when that very mouth was pressed against my ear.

"Fucking Nuts Girl, do you know what you do to me?" my Brit whispered, teeth sinking into my skin and shocking me still. My eyes rolled back in my head as I felt him, hard and thick against my back. I reached up, but he grabbed at my hand, turning it and pinning it behind me, holding me tightly. He pressed my hand against him, letting me feel exactly what I had done to him. I moaned, the beat pulsing and continuing to assault as he turned my face to the side. Kissing the side of my neck, he thrust himself against my hand, and I couldn't resist giving him a squeeze.

He groaned low in his throat, and he released my hand,

encircling my waist with his strong arms, pulling me even more flush against him, moving now with the music. I wrapped my arms around his neck, and one of his hands came up to tweak my nipple, causing me to gasp.

"I thought you didn't dance," I said, pushing my hips into his, relishing in the lust that was cooking on this dance floor.

He turned me roughly in his arms, hitching one of my legs up high around his hip, his fingers dangerously close to my panties. He played with the lace, slipping underneath and grazing me, watching as my eyes grew wide.

"I'm not dancing," he breathed, then crushed his mouth to mine. In the middle of the dance floor in the middle of Hollywood, Jack Hamilton pressed his fingers against me, hidden from the crowd and only known to me. Working to the beat, he thrust, the green on fire in his eyes as I struggled to keep upright.

"Jesus, what are you— Ohhh," I moaned. Knowing how dangerous this was made it sweeter, and I was on the verge within seconds of his skin meeting mine.

"I love watching you," he panted, keeping me pulled tightly into him, totally at his mercy, his hand hidden between our bodies.

"Yes, yes! God, Jack, yes," I panted, riding his hand shamelessly, my nails digging into the back of his neck as he hissed in pain.

"You ready?" he asked, his eyes on mine as I got close, so close, so very close. I nodded, incapable of speech, lost.

"Great, let's go," he grinned, removing his hand and straightening my dress. I stumbled slightly, and he grasped my hand, pulling me through the club. Waving at Holly, he motioned toward the door as she smiled back, mouthing to me, "Call you tomorrow."

I was stunned, my skin still warm from his touch, still tingling from what had just happened. I shook my head to clear it, not believing I had let things get carried so far away. I let him guide me to the door, and he released my hand as we neared the entrance. "I can't wait to get you home," he whispered in my ear, that grin that always made me smile stretching back across his face.

"I'm gonna get you for that, George," I warned, sighing as he pursed his lips in a silent kiss.

"Counting on it." He winked and leaned back into the door.

Which opened into a barrage of flashbulbs.

four

*J*ack pushed back against me, slamming me into the wall as the paparazzi surged, flashes going off from every direction. My head hit the brick, and I let out a gasp as I fumbled for my balance. People were screaming his name, shouting and yelling and trying to get their shots.

"Jack! Jack! Over here!"

"Hey, Hamilton, who you got with you there?"

"Hey, Jack, right here! Can you smile? Come on, right here!"

A bouncer had us back inside within seconds, but it was minutes before I could see clearly. Jack clutched at me, shielding me as another member of security ushered us back to another part of the club, quieter and more secluded.

"Jesus, Grace, you okay? Shit!" he exclaimed. I blinked back the flashes I was still seeing and accepted a bottle of water from someone.

"I'm fine. I'm fine!" I told him as he looked me over. "Come on, I mean it. I'm fine." I tried to smile, patting the back of my head.

"Where the hell is the security in this place? Dammit, why wasn't someone at that door?" Jack yelled as a manager hurried over.

"Sir, Mr. Hamilton, I'm so sorry," he tried to explain. "I didn't realize you were heading out that way, I thought—"

"Are you bloody kidding? What's the point of having a VIP section if you can't even keep those fucking animals away from my girlfriend?" he exploded, pulling his phone out of his pocket and dialing angrily.

I crossed to him, placing my hand on his arm. "Who are you calling?"

He held up a finger. "Yeah, Bryan? Hey, can you pick us up? Right, we're at Bar the Door. Great, twenty minutes? Thanks, man," he finished, putting his phone away and grabbing for my hand.

Bryan. His new security guy he used for public appearances.

Your boyfriend has his own bodyguard . . .

Wow, did I just have a hit of Hollywood.

"Bryan's on his way, he's going to take you home." Jack kissed my forehead and kept me close against him.

"Why don't you let me take her home?" I heard a familiar voice say. I looked around and saw Holly walk up behind Jack. He closed his eyes, biting down on his lip—not in the way I was used to seeing it, though.

"Yeah, why don't I go with Holly?" I scratched at his scalp and prodded him to open his eyes.

"I'd really prefer you go with Bryan. He can get you in and out of here without—"

"Without what, Jack? Paparazzi?" Holly interjected. "It'll be easier if she and I leave together. They've already seen you. They're only looking for her if she's with you. You go out with Bryan, and we'll head out another entrance."

"I don't know. I'd feel better if—"

"Jack. You're famous. She isn't yet, but she's gonna be. You two wanna go out dancing? This is gonna happen. Let me take her home," Holly interrupted, her voice taking on the tone that was not to be messed with.

"I'll see you there, okay?" I said, leaning in and squeezing his hand before starting after Holly.

"I'm sorry, Grace," he called after me.

"Hush. *You* be careful," I called back, meeting his eyes, which now looked red and tired. Letting Holly lead me back into the crowded club, I took one last look at Jack, head hanging.

This was not good.

☆ ☆ ☆

"So that was weird," I said twenty minutes later. Holly and I were packed into her car and speeding up Robertson toward the canyons.

"That? That was nothing. This was just your first real taste of it. It's gonna get worse. You remember what it was like at his premiere, don't you?" She passed me her bottle of water. Now that I was outside the club, I could feel my dress sticking to me. I rolled down the window and let the breeze fluff out my hair and clear my brain a little. On the way back out of the club, I had noticed how packed that dance floor really was.

Holy shit, did I really let Jack almost give me an orgasm in the middle of that club? Hollywood . . . Damn, it's a powerful drug.

"I remember. They barely paid Nick and me any attention at first. They sure went crazy when Jack showed up, though." I winced, thinking of that night.

"Pfft, they barely paid any attention to you until one of them figured out you were the unidentified redhead. I was doing damage control all night! Gimme that." She gestured for the water.

I winced again, remembering when a photographer had made the connection that I'd been the one connecting with Jack for months. There weren't many pictures of us together, but before *Time* had come out, we'd had a few weeks of relative anonymity early in our relationship. We didn't really think too much about showing affection in public, and the pictures were still out there.

"That was a bad night all around." I grimaced. Many cocktails and a shaky sense of self combined into not one of my better moments. I'd almost lost Jack for good.

"Listen, I know he doesn't always want to listen to me, but my job—in fact, my only job—is to make his life work for him. That's it. He needs to remember that." She turned onto Laurel Canyon.

I thought about what she said carefully before I answered. Soon she'd be doing that job for me. Maybe. Possibly. "He knows, Holly. He's just having a little trouble with all this. It's so much to get used to. I think he's doing pretty great, all things considered."

"Sure, but it's my job to consider *all things*, and we still have to figure out what we're going to do about you two."

"What about us?"

"Asshead, listen. When you two first got together, it was manageable. He hadn't really hit yet, and you, well, you were nobody."

"Thanks."

"You know what I mean." She laughed, turning into my drive. She killed the car and the lights, and we sat for a moment in the quiet. "Now he's the guy everyone is clamoring for, and you're about to take off on your own path. The same rules don't apply."

"So what are you suggesting? That we go public? I thought you said his fans wouldn't stand for that." I sighed, running my fingers through my hair and crinkling my nose at the club smell that lingered.

"They won't. They definitely won't," she said, worrying at a fingernail. "Eh, let me think on it. Let me figure out a few things. Don't worry about it." She grinned.

"You coming in?" I asked, gesturing toward the house.

"Hell no. I'm exhausted. I've got meetings all day tomorrow. Say good night to Jack for me, will you?"

"Will do." I slid out of the car but turned back toward her as she called my name. "Yes?" I asked through the window.

"He won't want to hear it from me, but Jack needs to be careful with Adam, okay?"

"Adam? Why?"

"Just tell him to watch it."

"Anything I need to be worried about?"

"I don't think so. Not yet anyway. Just mention it?"

"Sure thing. Call me tomorrow."

"'Night, asshead."

"'Night, dillweed." I snorted as she pulled away.

I walked into the house, the weight of the evening hitting me like a ton of bricks and making me very tired.

Watch out for Adam?

Hmmm.

☆ ☆ ☆

I showered the club stink off, and as I thought back over the night, I was still glad I'd gone out. Did things go a bit far? Yep. But damn that Jack, when he wanted something, he got it. And that included an almost peep show on the

dance floor. Images of what could have happened if someone had gotten that on their cell phone made me shiver,
even under the hot water. Images of how he'd made me
feel made me shiver again, for a very different reason.

I wrapped my hair up in a towel, threw on a cotton
nightie, and padded around the house while I waited for
Jack to come home. I was a bit surprised he was still not
here, but I knew Bryan would get him home safely. It was
not uncommon for him to drive around for a while if he
thought someone was following him. A sad but true com-
mentary on our lives together.

And you want this career too?

I do.

As I passed a mirror on my way to the kitchen, I
stopped and scrutinized a bit. I saw where there could be a
bit more cheekbone. I made a mental note to find a trainer
this week.

Tomorrow.

I made another mental note to find a trainer tomorrow.
Damn.

I went into the kitchen, poured myself a glass of red,
and headed out to the patio to wait for Jack. Curling up on
the love seat, I let myself relax into the night. I had barely
started to worry again about what was taking him so long
when I heard a car pull into the driveway. Moments later
I saw him walking through the house via the big windows
that lined the living room. He made a weavy sort of path
toward the patio. He knew where I'd be.

"How'd everything go?" I asked as he stepped out onto the flagstone. His eyes were bloodshot, his feet heavy as he went to the chair opposite mine. He sat down heavily, slipping off his jacket and turning to me.

"C'mere," he said, his voice quiet but his eyes beginning to darken.

"So . . . I take it everything went okay?" I pulled the towel off my head and shook my hair out a bit. "I was getting a bit worried, but I figured Bryan had you stay for a bit so you could—"

"Grace?" he interrupted.

"Yeah?"

"C'mere," he repeated, beckoning me forward with two fingers. I let myself be beckoned. As soon as I was close enough, he pulled me down onto his lap, pressing the entire length of his body to mine. Whiskey heat poured from his skin, dark and the tiniest bit dangerous.

"I don't want to talk about tonight," he whispered into my skin, his jaw sandpapering my neck in a very good way.

"Don't you think we should? I mean, what happens if—"

"No more talking tonight," he muttered, his mouth crashing down onto mine.

His lips were sure and insistent, his tongue exploring my mouth with a need that was answered quickly by my own.

His hands pushed up my shift, searching, needing, finding my skin. I shivered at his touch, not just from the chill of the night but because his hands on me always caused the same effect. I needed him, always.

"I need . . . Christ, I just need," he stammered between rough kisses on my lips, my cheeks, just under my ear.

"What, love, what do you need?" I asked, arching into him, holding him to me.

"Fuck, Grace, I need this." He groaned, his hands strong and not at all gentle. I didn't always need gentle. And he needed me.

Deft hands made short work of my nightie, and he bent his head to my breasts, dragging his warm tongue across me, making me pant, making me need him even more. I straddled him, legs parting on either side of his. He brought me closer, pressing my heat against his as he rocked upward, nudging me farther apart as I groaned shamelessly. His eyes were wild as he gazed up at me, biting down on that lower lip in a way designed to make every thought I ever had about sexing it up outside melt away. Neighbors? Who cared, this was the canyon. Canyon sex was the best.

I pushed up his shirt, hissing as I felt his warm skin along my own. Heat bloomed between us, wrapping us in our own little hot pocket of lust.

Strong hands and calloused fingers shoved open my thighs. He found me instantly, being well acquainted with the landscape. My own hands scrambled to unbutton his jeans, raising up on my knees. This brought my breasts within reach of his lips again, nipples hardening beneath the work of his glorious tongue. I found him, hard and wanting in my hands. I twisted this way and that, seeking friction, any friction I could get, pressing his hands hard into my soft skin.

"Fuck, Grace, I can't wait," he groaned, pulling me down on top of him, pushing inside me. I moaned loudly as he filled me, thick and wonderful. His mouth opened at my neck, teeth grazing and nibbling, then biting down hard as he pushed farther into me. I threw my head back, riding him, reveling in the strength he was using on me, his body owning my own, completely and totally. His thrusts were punctuated by his voice, delicious and dirty, raining down obscenities as he guided my hips into his, pushing and pulling me on top of him, impaling me with his body. I let his arms hold my weight, arching back. His hands imprinted into my skin, fingers grasping and leading me in his pace, fast and furious.

"Mmm, Jack," I sighed, my eyes opening to take in the dark night, the stars above me twinkling, as the star below me thrust, low and deep.

I gasped as he pulled me up flush against him, my hands clasped behind his neck, his arms locked around me as I stared down into his eyes. His brow furrowed, and he was frantic, groaning as he drove on and on, not stopping, my cries echoing throughout the night as he ravaged me. He angled his hips suddenly, and then he was there, pressed perfectly against the spot, that spot that he alone knew and knew well enough to coax out something so intense.

What Jack Hamilton was capable of doing to my body could not be defined. I came apart in the Southern California night, strung out and unaware of anything in the universe other than the feeling of him inside me, exactly where he should be, his own body taut and tight as he groaned through his own little piece of pleasure. The star had exploded.

He clutched at me, shaking as I shattered, face nuzzled into my breasts as his breath came as heavy as he did.

"Love you, Grace. Love you . . . so much," he sighed moments later, eyes sleepy and sex filled as he gazed up at me. I kissed him again and again, brushing my lips across his nose and eyelids, feeling the stubble of his new haircut rough against my mouth.

"Love you too, Jack," I murmured as he gathered me closer still, unwilling to leave my body.

The canyon was finally quiet. I put my star to bed.

five

I woke up the next morning pleasantly sore and rolled away from the wall of man who made me so. He grabbed for my breasts in his sleep, finally searching out a pillow instead and settling back. I perched on my hip, watching him as the morning sun danced across his frame, highlighting the red in his slight beard. I ran my hand across his newly shorn hair, delighting in the feel of it against my palm as he leaned into me, even in his sleep.

I thought back to the night before, color flooding my cheeks as I remembered how out of control we both were on the dance floor. Usually the voice of reason when it came to public displays of affection, I'd thrown all caution—and very nearly my dress—into the wind last night. Steps away from where the paparazzi had been waiting, I'd let the most beautiful man into my knickers. I had to be more careful. But when his hands were on me, it was hard to remain in control. Still, the thought of all those Hollywood chippies surrounding us last night—all of whom had fast phone fingers and could have tweeted our soft-core porn shots around the world . . .

You're in the right town if porn is what you're into.

I shuddered again at the could-haves and the close calls and continued my survey of Jack's sleeping self. I found those green eyes locked on me.

"What are you thinking about, Crazy?" he purred, his voice still thick with whiskey and sleep.

"When did you wake up?" I asked, curling into his side and relishing in his warmth.

"Just a minute or so ago. What are you working yourself over about so early in the morning?"

"Early? It's almost noon, Jack."

"I'm an actor. That's early." He grinned, pinching my bottom. "What's got you so twisted up already?"

"What do you mean?"

"You're worrying. You've got frown lines on your forehead."

"Remind me to tell you about things to never talk about with your older girlfriend." I winked before he pushed me back against the pillows and nuzzled his way into my neck. I scratched at his head while he played absently with my breasts, sending the tiniest of shock waves down to the tips of my toes.

"Just thinking about last night. Kind of strange, huh?"

He hummed Jack's Happy Sound into my skin. "You mean when you let me get into your knickers?"

"Which time?" I laughed as his hands became less absent and more determined.

"You were quite the bad girl, Gracie," he whispered into my neck, hands beginning to dip lower and lower.

"Hey, handsy, don't you think we need to talk about last night?" I asked, trying to distract him, which was never easy to do.

"About what?"

"Um, let's see, we were almost attacked by photographers." I laughed, lacing my fingers through his and bringing them safely above the covers.

He stilled. "What is there to talk about?"

"Listen, I know you're more used to it than I am, but I still think it's a bad idea for us to be photographed together. Holly says—"

"Oh bollocks what Holly says. It's ridiculous that I can't even go out dancing with my girlfriend without it becoming a major event."

"Major event?" I asked as he rolled away.

He grabbed his phone from his nightstand and scrolled through. Finding what he wanted, he handed it to me, sitting up in bed.

I looked and drew in a breath.

TMZ. Pictures of us first from when we tried to leave together. I was mostly hidden behind him, but you could see the red hair.

Hearthrob Jack Hamilton seen at Bar the Door last night. Is this the elusive redhead? Later that same night, he was snapped leaving the same nightclub with frequent party boy Adam Kasen, a blonde, and a brunette. Way to go, Sexy Scientist Guy . . .

He looked irritated in the first shot, drunk in the second.

"You left with Adam?" I asked, placing my hand on his back.

"It made sense at the time. Bryan thought it was a good time to go, Adam needed a ride, and we thought it would pull the focus from the earlier shots. Guess I was wrong. Now I'm leaving a nightclub with star fuckers." He groaned.

Interesting. He's never called himself a star before.

But he is. He's a bona fide Hollywood movie star.

"I think I'm going to stay home next time you go out on the town, Jack. Not really my scene anyway." I sighed, handing him his phone back.

"Probably best until your series premieres. Then you'll have people trying to take a shot at you too," he said over his shoulder.

"I doubt that's going to happen. I'm lucky to have this job, but my career is never going to go in the direction of yours."

"You don't know that. Why would you say that?" He turned around so he could see me.

"I just mean that, well, you're Super Sexy Scientist Guy.

Women love you. They go insane when you show up somewhere. That's not really the same thing as having a new series no one has even seen yet." I leaned up on one shoulder
so I could touch him. "Besides, if I get too famous and we
come out publicly, that means they'll come up with one of
those combo names for us, like Grack or Jace." I grinned as
I watched his face clear.

"Or George and Gracie." He smiled, reaching out to
sweep his fingers across the necklace he gave me, the word
schmaltz facing out, but our secret names facing in. George
loves Gracie.

"No one knows about that," I whispered, his hands
sweet and gentle now. He leaned in and kissed me quietly,
succinctly, our foreheads coming to rest together. We sat
for a moment, just breathing each other in.

"Okay, Sweet Nuts, as much as I would love to schmaltz
around this bed all day, I have to get my ass to the gym.
Mama needs to hire a trainer," I announced, moving away
from his hands as he lay back down. I slipped into my nightie
on the end of the bed and ran my hands through my hair.

"Wait, what? A trainer?"

"Oh, yes. Operation Cheekbone is in full effect. We
start shooting next week, and I need to lose about fifteen
pounds by yesterday, so say good-bye to this, mister." I
pulled up my nightie and slapped my tummy. I used to be
so shy about my body being on display, but falling in love
with Jack had been the best confidence booster ever. If he
loved my body, shouldn't I?

You'd think so . . .

"Operation Cheekbone? What in bloody hell is that?" he exclaimed from his place against the pillows.

I took a moment to take in the sight. Long and lean, tanned and sprawling, he could be shooting a magazine cover as we spoke.

"Well, the producers have been watching the pilot we shot, and it would seem that I need a little more cheekbone, which translates to about fifteen pounds or so. So I'm hiring a trainer to kick some ass."

"That's a bunch of crap, Grace."

"Yes, well, be that as it may, it's different for women in this town—especially at my age. So I'll do what I need to do. No biggie." I leaned over him to give him a kiss.

"I'm making a shit ton of money with this next movie, Crazy. Let's quit working and move to London. We'd never need to leave the bedroom." He winked at me as I moved toward the bathroom.

"Love, it took me years to get back here. I'm not letting fifteen pounds stand in my way. Now get your British ass in here." I laughed, dodging the pillow he threw at me.

We showered. It took more time than I planned.

It always does . . .

☆ ☆ ☆

I was on my way to the gym when my conscience called.

"Did you see the pictures?"

"Yes, Holly, I saw the pictures. What can I do about it?" I asked as I rolled my eyes.

"Nothing now, asshead, but we do need to work on the deer-in-headlights look you always seem to have going. Doesn't fly now that you have your own TV show."

My heart still fluttered when I heard her say that.

"I was totally caught off guard. Lay off."

"You're dating Jack Hamilton. You can't ever be off guard."

"I know, I know. What's up?"

"Just talked to David. They're moving the shooting schedule up, and they want you on set at the end of next week."

"What?"

"Yep, everything has been accelerated. They fast-tracked the show for a summer slot, which means they need to get all six episodes shot yesterday. This isn't a problem, is it?"

"No, but Operation Cheekbone hasn't even started yet!"

"I love it when you talk like someone from *The Bourne Supremacy*. What's even stranger is that I totally got that."

"I'm serious! I'm on my way to the gym right now."

"Don't worry about it. It'll be fine. Are you getting a trainer?"

"Yes, but I don't know how fast I can do this. Now I'm worried, although I suppose we can just shoot scenes with me walking with a large purse in front of me," I joked.

"Exactly. They will work with what they have. Not a problem."

Wow, that was a joke . . .

"Um, I was kidding about the large purse."

"That's funny because I wasn't kidding at all," Holly countered. "We talked about this."

"Yeah, yeah, I know, but—"

"But nothing, Grace. I love you. Is this weird for you? Yes. But not for me. This is my job. Does it suck that I have to tell girls all the time to fucking lose weight? Yep. Do I have to tell girls who just a year ago were voted Best Looking in their high school yearbook that they're too generic to make it in this town? All the time. I hate it, but this industry isn't changing any time soon, and other than that I love what I do. So suck it up."

I breathed in and out.

"You scared of me now?" she asked, her voice worried.

"I'm more scared that you just carried on an entire conversation by yourself, actually."

She laughed. "Don't hate me because you're beautiful."

"Okay, it's getting a little thick around here." I pulled into the gym parking lot. I saw three stunning girls walking in, sports bras and tiny shorts, legs for days and boobs for hire. Sigh.

"Love you, ya little fruitcake."

"Fruit I can have. Cake has gone bye-bye." I snorted, hanging up on her as she laughed. I watched the stunnings as they headed inside. I hated the gym. Even when I was losing all my weight, I'd worked out as much as I could from home or outside. But gyms were where the trainers were, so when in Rome . . .

Can't eat pasta . . .

Yeah, yeah, yeah.

I repeated the words *my own TV show, my own TV show* as I headed in.

☆ ☆ ☆

"I can't go anywhere. I can't even move." I moaned.

"Not even to run and get something to eat? We need groceries, love. There's nothing in the house," Jack whined, pulling at my shoe.

I had collapsed when I returned from the gym, my entire body a wet noodle. I had been worked out. Hollywood style. When my trainer wasn't admiring his abs in the mirror, he was sending me into another round of sprints or down to the floor to do kill-me-now crunches. He was good, no doubt. But clearly the devil.

"Get in your car and go get something. Leave me. I'm no good to you," I cried, trying to lift my head off the couch and giving up immediately.

"Gracie, come on, walk it off," he teased, pulling at both shoes now. I could feel myself sliding down the couch.

"Take your ass down the hill to the canyon store and get yourself a sandwich. Let me die," I instructed, trying to kick him as he pulled me farther off the couch. Kicking used muscles, though, and that was impossible. Every muscle I possessed was now on strike.

"Oh, love, I won't let you die," he pronounced dramatically, finally succeeding in pulling me clear of the couch and thumping me into his lap.

"Ow! Ow! Ow!" I yelled as he wrapped his arms around me. Once I was settled, he ran his hands up and down my back, his fingers pressing into my skin in a soothing way. My muscles relaxed, albeit slightly.

"How many days are you on this crazy workout plan?"

"Chip has me coming in twice a day every day this week."

"Your trainer's name is Chip?" He laughed into my neck.

"Of course his name is Chip. Chip's also an actor, you'll be glad to know."

"Is he good-looking? Do I need to be worried here?"

"He's a juicehead, Jack. You have nothing to worry about. Besides, as sore as I am, I'm not even going to have the energy to keep up with you for a while, to say nothing of the likes of Chip Chip the Devil Man."

"Oh, I'll get you sorted out all right. I can't have my girl-friend so tired she can't service me properly." He sighed, sitting back against the wall and bringing me farther into his lap. I snuggled in and yawned.

"I know. It's in my contract that I keep you satisfied. You might have to do it while I'm sleeping, though."

"Certainly makes it easier for me when you're unconscious." He laughed.

"I promise I'm mentally laughing, George. I just don't have the abdominal strength to manage it right now." I yawned again. We sat in the quiet for a moment as he stroked my hair until I heard his tummy growl.

"Okay, you run to the market and get something to eat. I'm going to try and make it to the bed," I said, trying to extricate myself from his lap. He stood with me, picking me up and throwing me over his shoulder like a bag of overexercised potatoes.

"You nap. I'll sort out the sandwiches. You want the chicken salad?" he asked.

"Yeah, sounds good, and get me a bag of Chex Mix and— Wait! No, get me a cucumber. And some air. I can have as much air as I want." I sighed as he eased me down onto the bed. He chuckled as I put my arms in the air, gesturing for him to remove my sweatshirt.

"Cucumber and air, got it. How long are you on the all-air diet?"

"Until I don't have to carry a big purse." I snorted as my head hit the pillow. The last thing I heard before I slipped into sleep was his asking me what the bloody hell a big purse had to do with it.

☆　☆　☆

I woke up to the sound of my phone ringing shrilly. I blinked, looking around, confused. It was dark out. Jesus. How long had I been asleep?

"Jack?" I called out, but no answer. I looked at the clock. I'd been sleeping for a few hours. Where was he? I jumped as the phone rang again and winced as I reached across the bed for it. It was the Brit.

"Hey, you get lost?" I smiled into the phone.

"Yeah, something like that," he mumbled, and I stopped midstretch. He sounded weird.

"What's wrong, where are you?"

"Somewhere on Santa Monica. I'm stuck in traffic."

"What the hell are you doing on Santa Monica?"

"Bloody photographer at the market . . . I pulled out and started heading back up the hill, and he followed me. Followed me no matter where I went, and I didn't want to come home yet, so I kept driving. And so did he. And I ended up getting turned around in the hills and came back down and then—"

"Jack, hey, slow down. It's okay. Where are you now?"

"It's not okay! This is fucking ridiculous! Grace, you should have seen how close this guy was behind me. He was a maniac—just to get a picture? It's insane! I—"

"Okay, love, just come back home. Is he still following you?"

"I don't think so. I'm not sure. He's— Dammit! He's still back there, and now there's another one. Shit!"

A prickle of fear began to work its way from the base of my spine all the way to the top. I started pacing around the room, not noticing my muscles cramping up.

"Jack? Hey, Jack?"

"I'm pulling over. This is crazy. Hey! Look out—"

I heard tires squealing. I heard metal crunching. The phone went dead.

"Jack? Jack? Hey, are you there?"

Six

Movie star Jack Hamilton was involved in an altercation today at the corner of Santa Monica Blvd. and Doheny Dr. Several cars were impacted when Hamilton swerved into oncoming traffic, allegedly to avoid a car driven by a photographer. No one was seriously injured, although Hamilton was treated for "minor scrapes" at the scene.

Was the Scientist Mad?

New heartthrob and sexy scientist Jack Hamilton from the hit movie *Time* crashed his car into a signpost, causing an accident that involved three other vehicles yesterday in Beverly Hills. Onlookers report that Hamilton ran off the road causing fender benders. Paparazzi flooded the scene, capturing the star sitting on the side of the road with his head in his hands. It's unclear at the time whether authorities suspect foul play.

Doheny Dr. turned into a media circus yesterday when movie star Jack Hamilton ran off the road trying to get away from intrusive photographers. No one was seriously hurt in the accident, but it took more than 45 minutes to get the street cleared, and additional police had to be called to the scene to handle the crowd after it was reported on Twitter that the one and only Sexy Scientist Guy was sitting on the side of the road in Beverly Hills. Hamilton rose to fame late last year with the success of the movie *Time*, the first in the series that has grossed more than $300 million worldwide. Hamilton's fans call themselves Jack's Pack, and they are devout in their devotion to their favorite actor. "He is, like, so freaking hot," one of them gushed. She then screamed her love to Jack as he talked with police after the accident. After being treated for a minor cut on his forehead, Hamilton was bundled into an SUV and whisked away by security. His car was towed. No word on whether any charges have been filed.

☆ ☆ ☆

I sat back in my chair, breathing in through the nose and out through the mouth. My heart was pounding, my pulse was racing, and my palms currently were more clammy than a bowl of chowder.

To calm myself and take the attention off my nerves, I

allowed my eyes to sweep across the room, taking note of the congratulations balloons in the corner, the tastefully beautiful bouquet of sugar-pink peonies on the table in front of the sofa, and the strategically placed bowls of hard candy scattered about. As my eyes roamed, they landed back in the mirror directly in front of me. I studied my face as I continued to work through my breathing.

Hey, fruitcake, you got this. No sweat.

I do have this. That's true.

I glanced down at the stack of magazines next to me, grinning when I saw my boy on almost all the covers, smiling rakishly into the camera, casting that pure sex vibe across the entire country. Jack was on location out in the Mojave with the rest of the cast for his movie. The paparazzi had been relentless since the accident, catching him at all hours of the night and day. The green eyes, the closely cropped hair, his deadly grin—yep, he was a movie star now, pure and simple. He'd finally been officially anointed the Sexiest Man Alive, even after the terrible haircut I gave him. Oh, well, duh I'd known this for a while now. As always, when my thoughts drifted to Jack, a little flutter ran through my tummy on its way to setting up shop somewhere decidedly south. Before my thoughts could go full gutter, I heard a loud knock on the door, and my heart once more began to pound.

"Ms. Sheridan, you're wanted on set," the second AD called through the door.

First day on the set of my new series. No big thing.

Really big thing.

That's what she said.

I grabbed my script, gave a final tousle to my curls, and thunked down the steps of my trailer, giving a big smile to the woman who knocked on the door. "No Ms. Sheridan. Call me Grace."

As I made my way to the set, I saw Michael waving me over. Winking at the assistant director, I made a beeline for him, grasping his hand and squeezing it tightly. "I see you're not wearing Adidas today. Good call." I laughed, looking down.

"No way. I know how you like to puke on them." He laughed as well as we looked at each other nervously. Years of history, months of rekindled friendship, and weeks of frenzied work had brought us to this moment. We were about to start shooting our TV series, and it was a little surreal.

"Can I tell you something?" I whispered as we walked toward the set.

"Sure," he whispered back, nodding at PAs as they scurried by.

It was a hot set, and there was activity everywhere. I'd been there since early this morning, getting hair and makeup just so. This was the world I'd been dreaming of since I was little, and it was all here now, right in front of me. Since we'd shot the pilot and everyone finally figured out how green I was, I'd been sent to "acting for the camera" class. I finally knew how much work went into television production, after taking it for granted all those years as a viewer.

"I kind of can't believe this!" I quietly squealed, resisting the urge to shout and scream. I was here! I was doing this! Holy Lord, I was doing this!

"I kind of can't believe it either, but we're cool. We're cool. Nothing to see here, just two industry professionals." He squeezed my hand even harder as we caught sight of a chair with my name on the back.

"Wow," I said, dropping his hand to run my fingers along the back, tracing the letters in my name. "I have to take a picture of this. I don't care how dorky it is." I snapped a quick shot with my phone and immediately texted Jack.

Look look! They gave me my own chair!

"Did you send that to Jack?" Michael asked as I settled in my chair. *My* chair!

"I did. I wanted to document the beginning of the diva." I laughed, posing as he took a picture as well.

"Oh, please. I think I have an actual Polaroid of that moment somewhere in my parents' basement." He snorted as he texted furiously. "How's he doing, by the way? That accident with the photographers looked intense."

"Who are you sending that to?"

"Holly. She has to see this too."

"Of course. You know, he's doing okay. We circled the

wagons a bit. We had Bryan come to the house and check things out, increased the security system, that kind of thing."

"He's okay then?"

"He's as well as can be expected. Normally when someone has a little car accident, it doesn't end up on the nightly news." I sighed, looking down as my phone chirped.

Looks great, Crazy! As long as you're taking pictures, I need a new one of you. Sparkly boobies?

I smiled. He was pretty freaked out after everything that had happened, to say nothing of the accident I almost caused trying to get to him. When his phone went dead I had damn near come out of my skin. My mind went through the worst possibilities, calming only when Holly was able to get through to Bryan and find out where he was. Bryan was able to track him with his cell phone—how weird was this world? When your boyfriend's bodyguard could find him just by tapping a few buttons on his phone?

As weird as a world where you have your name on a chair and people asking you if the right kind of bottled water is in your trailer.

Touché.

Jack had been glad to get out of town and to the desert for this new film. His mind was already in character, and he'd been working closely with the other guys in the cast. They had a week of boot camp before they started shoot-

70

ing, and he was really getting into it. Boys. They liked to run and jump in the mud. They just don't always look so good doing it . . .

My own boot camp had consisted of cucumber and air, twice daily workouts, new hair extensions, a deeper shade of red, and a spray tan or two. I was down nine pounds, but luckily I had kept the girls. Jack would be grateful.

I may have also bought new boots for the boot camp.

"Hey, how's the new house, by the way?" I asked Michael.

"It's great. Moving in next week. That Holly, she really has this town on lockdown, doesn't she? She found that house in one afternoon. Everything I wanted, she found it."

"I'm glad she's on our team. She is not someone I'd want to mess with." I laughed, straightening in my chair as David, the director, approached. David Lancaster was known for being hard on newcomers. So far he'd been easygoing, nice . . . funny even. But I knew he'd had something to do with the notes the producers had given about my weight, and I hadn't been able to get a good read on him yet.

"Grace, you ready to shoot?"

You got this; you got this; you got this. You. Got. This.

"Good to go, David," I answered, my voice coming out in a squeak, which quickly turned into nervous giggles. "Might be a little nervous."

"No problem. We're going to start off slow today. We're set up to start with the kitchen scene: your ex has papers for you to sign, and he brings along his new girlfriend. You got the rewrites last night, right?"

"Yep. They're great," I answered, winking at Michael.

"Okay, let's get set up on your first mark. We changed the blocking a bit. We're going to have you behind this potted plant to start with, okay?"

Behind a potted plant, huh?

My first day on the set of my own series I learned that craft services can do a lot with cucumbers and air.

☆ ☆ ☆

That night I went to bed early. Being a TV star was hard work.

Did you really just say that out loud in your own head?

Totally. Danced around a bit too.

Before bed I walked through the house, closing blinds and double-checking the locks. I always did, but now I was extra careful. As I was sliding between the sheets, Jack called.

"Hey, sweet girl, how was your first day?"

"It was exhausting! But awesome. How was the mud run?"

"Also exhausting, but awesome. But really, how did it go?"

"What do you know about potted plants?"

"What?"

He laughed as I flipped out the light and snuggled

down to recap my day with my Sweet Nuts. I talked shop, and he wisely let me fumble when trying to explain what a key grip was. As we were winding down, I heard someone in the background.

"Who's that I hear? Another one of the grunts?" I yawned. He and the other guys in the cast called one another grunts. It was so hard for me to control my eye rolling.

I think you just did . . .

"Right. Adam and I are heading into town to this dive bar. Apparently lots of bikers hang out there!"

I heard Adam laugh. Jack was obsessed with American culture and dying to take a road trip.

"You and Adam, huh?" I asked, twisting the sheets in my hand.

"Sure, why?"

"Nothing. I was just hoping for a little phone action with my Brit tonight," I whispered, my skin dancing with just the idea of it.

"Oh, you were, huh? What exactly did you have in mind, Grace? What's got your knickers in a twist?"

"Fuck. You had to say knickers, didn't you?" I moaned into the phone.

"I know it makes you crazy, Crazy. Wish I could get you sorted, but I've got company and—"

I could hear Adam laughing again. "I can't hear this! Get off the phone and let's go!"

Jack told him to shut up.

"No, it's okay. You go," I told him. "Get in a biker brawl.

Just make sure you stay away from the assless chaps, okay?"
I frowned slightly.

Calm down. He's twenty-four. Of course he's going out.

"Call you when I get home?"

"No, call me tomorrow. I've got an early call time, and I need to fit in a run before I head to the studio."

"Listen to you, you're like an old pro."

"That's five."

"What's five?" he asked.

"You called me old. Every time you say something about frown lines or being old in general, that's five orgasms you owe me, got it?"

"Fucking hell, Grace," he groaned.

"'Night, love," I whispered, and hung up as he was protesting.

Well played . . .

I chuckled to myself as I rolled over in bed, letting one hand linger on his pillow. Out with Adam. Huh.

I sent him a text.

Be careful, George. Love you xoxo

☆ ☆ ☆

And so it went. I was on set most days and even some nights, and loving every second of it. Shooting was going well, and the cast was settling in with one another. Leslie had signed on to reprise her role as my nemesis, and it was nice having someone else around from the original New York crew. She had pictures of Jack up in her trailer and made no bones about the fact that if I were ever done with him, she would absolutely swoop right in. I didn't blame her one bit. But no one was getting ahold of my Brit.

A little more press was written about the series being in production, and I was starting to notice a trend. Whenever I was mentioned, Jack was mentioned. These were just trade magazines, *Variety*, *Deadline*, but still. I wasn't fooling myself. I knew I was damn lucky to have this job. It was rare that producers would sign an unknown like myself for the lead in a series like this. In fact, it was almost unheard of. So I got it, but still.

"Don't worry about it, asshead. It comes with the territory. People want to know who you are, why you got this part. It's natural—in a town where nothing is," Holly informed me one day. We rolled around on the bed in my trailer until we were dizzy, enjoying the spoils that came with a large production budget. She'd stopped by to inform me she was hiring me a stylist.

"What? You mean I can't continue to run around in yoga pants every day?" I laughed, pulling myself off the bed and picking up a plate of cucumbers. My first sex scene was scheduled in a few days, and while the potted plant was no longer, I did seem to have a lot of scenes where I was holding a book. I'd be dropping the cucumbers soon and just sticking with the air. Big, yummy gulps of air.

"No, dear, you need a look. I'm sending someone over tomorrow. She's bringing lots of great things. Let her dress you. You'll love it. And make sure she picks out something for the party next week," Holly instructed, leaning into the mirror and inspecting her face.

Looking at her, it was hard to tell she was on the business side of show business. She always looked flawless. But she'd brought studio heads to their knees when working out a deal—figuratively speaking, of course—and she loved her job. Part of her job was combining work with fun, and she was having one of her famous parties. Jack and I had met at her last one.

"Yeah, yeah, is Lane coming?" I asked, watching her face carefully. She was always vague about Lane, who'd played Jack's assistant in the *Time* movie. Tall and impossibly good-looking, built like a god and capable of making her see God as well, the two had been engaging in a purely sexual relationship for months now. It was on; it was off. It was on; it was *really* on; it was off. Lane was great—sweet as can be—but I think they both knew it was just about getting an itch scratched.

Gross.

"I think so. Rebecca too. Nick's going to try to make it. He's supposed to be back from Oregon sometime next week," she answered, her cheeks barely flushing.

Hmmm. Off again?

Wow, the whole gang. We knew Rebecca through Jack as well. She was a part of the *Time* cast. Nick was, well, Nick.

"Is he still working on that series?"

"Trying to. He wanted so badly to go legit, but he misses Hollywood too much." She snorted as she stood up to leave. Nick was a screenwriter and had been working on a documentary for PBS. He was on location most of the time now. It would be good to see him. He texted me all the time, telling me how much he missed me, but I know secretly he just wanted to look at the pretty. He had a major crush on Jack, and he loved to make it as obvious as he could. Which was pretty obvious.

After Holly left, I looked at myself critically in the mirror. I could see a difference. I could definitely see more "cheekbone," but did that mean I was ready to sex it up for the camera? I twisted this way and that, checking it out from all angles. I thought I looked pretty good, but that damn camera. They say it adds ten pounds, but I think that's when you're under thirty. Over thirty, I think it was a few more than that. David made sure I was watching the dailies and could see what I really looked like.

I texted Chip Chip the Devil Man and added an extra workout for tonight.

Air is good.

☆　☆　☆

In the end, I tried like hell to give them the cheekbone they asked for. I barely ate for three days, ran my ass up and down the canyon like I was getting paid to, which I was, and worked out more than I had ever worked out in my life. I moved that scale two pounds. Two pounds! And don't think I didn't hear about it, everyone had their two cents to say about my two pounds. Diet tips, weight-loss books, fasting schedules, everyone had an opinion. But we also had a tight shooting schedule to stick to, so when SS Day (Sex Scene Day) came, I breathed deep and went for it.

We had blocked the scene earlier that morning, the actor who I had been working with on this particular story arc was great, supersweet and very good-looking. Relatively new to the industry, he was just as nervous as I was, so we psyched each other up.

It was strange, rolling around on a bed with another actor and trying to make it seem natural, when it was more choreographed than my high school pom-pom routines. Hand here, knee bent here, stick your butt out here, but keep it covered with the sheet, it was like a grown-up game of Twister. Mabel, my character, was having a one-night stand, and when I met the actor I could understand why.

A few minutes before we were ready to shoot, I headed over to the craft table for a bottle of water, my throat suddenly dry at the thought that I'd be rolling around on said bed in my skivvies, otherwise known as pasties and a thong. Mumbling a cheekbone mantra in my head, I turned a corner and overheard David talking to the assistant director. Really wished I hadn't.

"It's fine, wardrobe's sending over a bunch of those

teddy things, just tell her it'll be sexier to have her covered up, more suggestive that way," the AD said.

"Suggestive, sure, that's a good word for it. I've got a lead actress who's got no business being naked on-screen and can't do something simple like lose twenty pounds."

Twenty pounds?

"I'm telling you, the teddy will work out fine."

"More like teddy bear." David snorted, and the two walked back toward the set. I stood there for a moment, in shock.

"You cold?" I heard from behind me. Michael.

"Cold?" I asked, closing my eyes to blink back the tears.

"Yeah, you're shaking," he said, walking in front of me and rubbing my arms. I could tell him. I could tell him what I had just heard; he was my friend and he'd likely intercede on my behalf.

Not sure this is the kind of thing one wants to draw attention to, is it?

No, no it wasn't.

"Nerves I guess," I muttered, opening my eyes just in time to see the wardrobe consultant walk up to me.

"Grace? We're making a last-minute change. David thought it might be sexier to have you in one of these, give the audience more to think about, right?" she asked, waving a bunch of black lace in front of me. Michael, clueless, smiled and blushed.

"Sure, let's give them something to think about," I agreed, beginning a slow burn.

That poor actor, I threw him all over that bed. Rolling

around in my black lace and my curves, I made damn sure David saw just how sexy a teddy bear could be. Something that would have made Last-Year Grace shrink up and curl into a ball made This-Year Grace pissed off and ballsy. When they called wrap for the day, I crawled off the bed after giving my costar a high five, ignored the robe someone tried to give me, walked past David while meeting his eyes the entire time, and strolled the rest of the way to my trailer. Across the lot. In my teddy. And Adidas soccer sandals. To a chorus of catcalls and whistles from every single male crew member I passed.

By the time I walked up the steps to my trailer, I was smiling big and laughing out loud. After I banged open the door, my eyes fell on the only thing that could have made me smile bigger. Jack.

☆　☆　☆

"What are you doing here?" I grinned, walking over toward where he was relaxing on the couch.

"Christ, Grace, what are you wearing?"

"Just shot my first sex scene," I said proudly as he pulled me down onto his lap.

"And you walked across the entire lot like that?" he asked, his eyes everywhere, hands quickly to follow.

"Proving a point, but more to the point, what are you doing here? I didn't think you were coming in till tomorrow?" I squealed as he pressed a kiss under my ear.

"They didn't need me anymore, so I caught an earlier flight and headed straight here. If I'd known there were garters involved, I would have been here sooner." He grinned appreciatively, snapping one and making me bounce a bit.

"And they just let you on set? Into my trailer?"

"Thank god all the PAs read *People*." He laughed, leaning back to look at me. I blushed, reminded again of my state of undress. I took the opportunity to look at him as well. Christ, he looked good. Deeply tanned and his eyes were emerald green but darkening by the second. He still had the short hair, made even more blond by the sun. Beautiful.

I tried to think through all the implications of having him here, on set. Anyone could talk; anyone could sell this story to the tabloids.

Jack Hamilton meets Grace Sheridan on set of new TV show for a quickie . . .

He could see me overthinking it, knowing exactly what I was worrying about when I chewed my lip.

"Hey, Crazy. It's okay. We're adults, for Christ's sake, they all know exactly what we're doing in here." He chuckled, his laughs dying down as his lips searched out my skin. I sighed without thinking, my hands coming up to his hair and tucking in.

"But what if someone talks? What if . . . Jesus that feels good." I tried to focus my brain scrambling and coherent thought becoming more and more difficult. It wasn't that I didn't trust the cast and crew, and while we were deliberate with our behavior in public, we were much less so in a professional setting like this. Just because we didn't comment publicly, and allowed Holly to tell the press we were just friends, didn't mean that we were not every bit a couple when alone or with people we knew. And I felt like I knew everyone on this set. However, it still made me feel exposed a bit. Speaking of feeling exposed . . .

"I just spent two weeks in the desert with a bunch of guys, and if I'm not inside you immediately, I can't be held responsible for what I might do otherwise, you hear me?" he murmured into my ear, kissing and nipping at my shoulder, my collarbone, my jaw.

"Mother-of-pearl that's good," I moaned as he lifted me up onto the table.

"Please don't talk like one of the Golden Girls right now; it might be the only thing that could stop me at this point," he pleaded. Giggling, I wrapped my arms around him and gave in to what I was feeling, skin heating as his hands swept over me, taking in the black lace and sassiness. With a wicked grin he sent my panties sailing across the room, and I gasped as he dropped to his knees. Suddenly I was not so concerned with trailer rocking and the mocking that was sure to follow.

"I think you said I owed you five, right?" he asked, nibbling on the inside of my knee, pushing my legs farther apart.

"You can spread those out over time; they don't have to all be at once—mmm." I moaned as he pulled me into him. I had a brief insane image of the movie *Jaws* when the old guy goes sliding down the boat toward the awaiting shark teeth, but it was quickly thrown back out of my head at the sight of this gorgeous man kneeling between my legs.

"Brilliant," he whispered, and bent his head to me. Lips, tongue, fingers, everything and all of it, focused and pointed, swirling and twirling, he loved me as only he could. Hooking my thighs over his shoulders, he surrounded me with a constant steady pressure, knowing inherently when to slow and when to speed, when to press and when to push. When my knees were shaking and my cries were stupid and love drunk, he rose quickly and let me unbutton his jeans.

"How do you want me, Crazy?"

"I want you; that's about all I can tell you at this point, dealer's choice." I groaned, still dizzy from the three trips around the world he had already taken me on. I slipped my hands inside his jeans and grasped him, wanting and warm. I raised an eyebrow at what else I found, or rather didn't find. "Good call on the commando, George."

"I didn't want to waste any time," he insisted as I pulled him toward me with my legs, wrapping around and sliding against him.

"So this was just a booty call?" I asked in between kisses, hard and demanding.

"Hmm, lovely idea." He pulled me off the table and

spun me quickly. Placing my hands flat against the surface, he nudged my legs apart and pushed into me, hard. I hissed at the sensation, the good burn and the sweet tension.

"Christ, that's good, love," he groaned in my ear, seating himself fully inside as I arched back to meet him. Grabbing an equal handful of backside and breast, he rocked into me again, inexplicably deeper than before. I loved when he took control like this.

"You have no idea how sexy you look like this Grace, I thought about you all morning, thinking about that sweet . . . hot . . ." And that was it. I came again, hard and strong, rocking myself and very possibly the blessed trailer as I split apart, then floated back down. Back down where a very hot Brit was inside me and determined to make this last.

"Fuck, Grace," he groaned, pulling my hair back so he could kiss me. Our bodies were flush, his front pressed to my back, lined up and locked down as he slid in and out, never relenting. He chased his own release, shuddering and shaking as his fingers circled down, lower and lower until he was teasing out another orgasm from me. This one left me boneless and shivering, insides aching and legs shaking as his eyes shut tight, brow furrowed and jaw clenched.

"Garters . . . Christ, the garters are brilliant."

God*damn* we rocked that trailer.

seven

*L*ater we lay tangled on the bed, surrounded by wrappers. *Hard candy* wrappers. He lay on his back, his head propped up on my hip as I curled around him. I was moaning around a Werther's caramel in a way that sounded particularly decadent, a way Jack was noticing even though he said he was "bloody well spent." But for now, I sucked caramel only.

"Did you ever notice how if you breathe in while you're sucking on one of these, you can actually taste the burnt sugar? And feel the butter on your tongue?"

"Gimme one."

"No."

"No?"

"No. This is the first nongreen thing I've had in my mouth in weeks. Back off." I growled, feeling his scruff scratch at my thigh. I trailed a hand down, and he leaned into it, letting me rub his head. "They buzzed you again, huh?"

"Yep, keeping it pretty short. The other grunts too," he explained, again with that London accent meeting Alabama in the cutest way. He moved his head a few times, trying to get settled.

"Settle down there, squirmy."

"Grace, don't take this the wrong way, but your hip . . ."

I froze midsuck. "My hip?" I asked around my caramel.

"It's, well, it's not as comfortable as it used to be." He frowned, his hand now spanning my hip and gripping it tightly.

"You see any potted plants around here? Mama's been working out." I grinned proudly, smacking at my candy.

"Grace, come on." He laughed, switching positions so he could push me back against the pillows and get some boob time. "Thank goodness you two haven't changed," he whispered to the girls.

I swatted at his head. "You're twisted, Hamilton."

"I'm serious. Don't go overboard here, okay?"

"I'm not going overboard. It's called taking direction," I insisted as he settled against me.

He ran his hands over my tummy, flatter than it had ever been.

"Love, you look amazing, but you always look amazing. I just don't want you to get carried away with this."

He really didn't get this.

"Why did you have me cut your hair?" I asked, stilling his hand.

"What?"

"No, really, why did I cut your hair?"

"Because the part called for it," he admitted, his eyes growing serious.

"Exactly. This is the same thing. So drop it, okay?" I huffed, sitting up and shrugging into my top.

"Cutting your hair and losing a ridiculous amount of weight when you don't need to are two very different things, Grace," he insisted, trying to pull me back into bed.

"You're right. They're two very different things because there are two very different standards, aren't there?" I picked up the latest crop of magazines with him on the cover and threw them down onto the bed. As they scattered, shots of him peeked up at us. He looked drunk in most of them: leaving different clubs with the guys from his film, ball cap on, ripped T-shirt. He looked beautiful, of course, but the fact was, he was decidedly un–movie star in each shot.

"See that! Dirty shirt, half drunk, looking like you haven't slept in weeks, and what's the headline? 'Sexy Scientist Jack Hamilton Parties with Bad Boy Adam Kasen!' Can you imagine what the headline would be if I were out with you looking like that? 'Jack Hamilton and Homeless Older Woman Out on the Town.' 'Jack Hamilton and Insane Woman Go to Biker Bar.' I'd never get away with it. So think about that next time you complain about my bony hips. Bony hips are in my contract." I turned away from him, as I could feel the tears beginning to form, and focused on putting on my skirt.

Where the hell did that come from?

Head rush from the hard candy?

I could hear him getting out of the bed and coming up behind me. I let him pull me back against him, mirroring our earlier position but in much different circumstances.

"Sorry, Nuts Girl, you're totally right. It's wrong that it's like this, but you're totally right. You do what you need to do. I'm behind you one hundred percent," he whispered, slipping his hands around my middle and squeezing tight. I sighed, leaning back into him, feeling him wrap around me.

"I'm figuring this out as I go, Jack, ya know?" I whispered back.

"I know."

I spun around in his arms. "It's not like there's a manual, how to handle life in Hollywood." I sniffed back the few tears that had managed to make their way to the surface.

"Oh, I don't know. I think Holly has at least half that manual written already. She sure has plenty to say about these pictures." He nodded toward the magazines.

"Oh, I have plenty to say too, pretty boy. Don't think I haven't noticed all the partying you've been doing."

He looked a little ashamed, and once again I was reminded how young he was.

"It's under control. Don't worry," he soothed.

Not possible.

☆　☆　☆

As that week passed, it became evident that things were most certainly *not* under control. Jack stayed in town, but I was busy on set most of the week, as we raced to get as much shot as we could so the show could premiere in the summer instead of the fall. The scenes were stacking up, and while it was going by fast, I took time each day to sit and think about how far I'd come. I was really enjoying the work—the actual work that went into putting a show together like this. Working closely with the other actors, developing a shorthand with the cast and the crew, bringing this character to life, and watching as the others did as well.

And as I worked, Jack played. Sure he spent his days on the set filming, but he spent his nights out on the town. And then his days sleeping it off. He was young, and this town laid itself out for him. Clubs were packed to capacity on the nights he was in attendance, and the photographers were out in full force. After his accident, he didn't drive himself much, now employing Bryan on a much more full-time basis. Which worked out well for him: he could party even harder. Paparazzi swarmed him when he arrived and when he left, and industrious amateur photographers inside the clubs with camera phones sold shots to magazines of him sitting in VIP section after VIP section. And always with Adam right next to him.

I had to give it to the guy, Adam was smart. After his

star threatened to forever be tarnished by his past behavior, appearing with Jack so often around town had him back on the rise.

Late one night, I was awoken from a sound sleep by the sound of glass breaking and loud male laughter. Startled, I sat up straight, tingles all along the back of my neck as my hand groped for my phone, ready to call the police. But before I could even get there, the bedroom door swung open and there he was, my Brit. And he was . . . laughing?

"Grace, love, I'm so sorry. We broke your, oh man—" He doubled over with laughter.

"What the hell?" I asked, drawing the sheet closer around me as I blinked back sleep. Now that I was awake, my emotions changed to something closer to anger.

"Broke your buggery bowl. You know the one you keep our mail in? Adam tripped coming through the door and— Oh no, you're mad!"

He laughed again, sputtering as he crossed to the bed and sat down heavily next to me. The stink of whiskey was all around, and I couldn't believe what I was seeing.

"Adam? You brought Adam here?" I hissed, drawing the sheet around me even more tightly and looking around him to the hallway.

"Sorry, love, yes. He was taking me home and needed a piss. I couldn't very well let him out on the side of the road, could I?" He reached for me as I moved out of his grip.

"Where's Bryan?" I seethed.

"Night off. Besides, I told you, Adam drove me home.

Hmm . . . you're mad, aren't you?" He finally succeeded in taking my hand and pulling me toward him.

"You're kidding, right?"

He wrapped himself around me and tried to snuggle me down onto the bed. He lay back against the pillows, sighing as I unscrambled myself out of his arms.

"Jack, seriously, is he still here? Jack? Dammit." I pushed at him as he settled into the pillows, his breaths getting deeper. "Wake up, Jack." I nudged him again.

He was passed out cold. Son of a bitch. I heard the tinkle of broken pottery in the other room. I slid into my robe and made my way out to see our guest.

"Hey, Grace. Sorry about the mess. If you have a broom, I'll clean that right up."

Adam Kasen stood in the entryway, broken bowl at his feet and shit-eating grin on his handsome face.

"Thanks. I've got it," I replied, walking past him into the kitchen. He followed me.

"I'm really sorry about that. It was dark when we came in and—"

"What are you doing?" I asked quietly as I grabbed the broom.

"Trying to clean this up?"

"That's not what I meant."

He looked at me shrewdly. "You don't like me much, do you?" he asked after a beat, his head cocked to the side.

"I don't know you."

He grinned.

Hit him with the broom!

We stood across from each other, silent. The air was full.

"I'll see myself out," he finally said, backing away toward the door.

"Watch yourself," I added, nodding to the pile of broken pottery on the floor.

"I'll buy you another," he said, his hand on the door.

"Yes, you will."

He grinned once more.

Ram him with the end of the broom handle!

After he left, I cleaned up his mess and got into bed with Jack, who was still passed out.

Still think you should have whacked him upside the head with the broom . . .

☆ ☆ ☆

The next morning I had an early call, but not so early that I didn't wake up our fair Mr. Hamilton. He moaned and groaned as I pulled his covers down.

"Gracie, please, it's too early. Covers, *covers!*" he griped, inching his way down the bed and trying to burrow back under.

"I know. Sucks to be woken up so suddenly, doesn't it?" I smiled, perching at the end of the bed with a cup of coffee. He sniffed the air.

"That smells good. Bring me a cup?" he asked, still inching lower on the bed.

"Man, you're really asking for it, aren't you?" I lifted an eyebrow and the duvet farther out of his reach. He opened one eye, then the other. Confusion flooded into his face.

"What's going on?"

"I'd like to ask you the same question."

He rubbed his face, stretching. He inched again, and I held fast to the covers.

"I broke something last night, didn't I?"

"Yep."

"And you're angry, right?"

"Yep."

"Any chance we can talk about this later?"

"Jack . . ." I sighed and let the covers drop. I walked back into the bathroom, then heard him shuffling after me. He appeared in the doorway, in a duvet burrito.

"I'm sorry about the bowl, Grace. I'll buy us a new one."

"Oh no, you don't have to. Your good friend Adam already said he'd take care of it."

"Are you really this upset about a bowl?"

"Are you really so thick that you think I'd be this upset about a bowl?"

"Heh-heh, you said thick."

I whirled on him, pointing with my eyeliner. "Don't be charming. I have no patience for it right now. I'm trying to be understanding, really I am. But getting so drunk you pass out and leave that guy in our living room? Not okay with that."

"You don't like Adam. Just say it."

93

"Oh, I'll say it. I. Don't. Like. Him. At all. But what I really don't like is being woken up in the middle of the night by you, wasted out of your mind, acting like an ass!" I poked him in the chest, leaving a charcoal smudge. I started brushing my hair angrily, as he rubbed at the spot.

"Okay, so this isn't about the bowl?"

I had to hang on very tight to the hairbrush to stop me from throwing it at him. I closed my eyes, trying to calm down before the yelling began. I felt his hands on my shoulders.

"Hey, Crazy. I'm sorry. I know it's not about the bowl. I was just blowing off some steam last night. I'll make sure it doesn't happen again, okay?" he said softly, holding open his arms and the duvet. I let him fold me in.

"I just worry. I worry about you." I sighed. He smelled like a club, but underneath it all was that Hamilton s'more smell that won me over every time. "I'm allowed to worry, right?"

"Of course, if there were something to worry about. But there's not, I promise. I'm just having some fun," he soothed, his strong arms around me, enveloping me. "And Adam's a good guy. You just have to get to know him. He's a little intense, but he's cool. Maybe we'll have him over, spend some time with him. You know better than anyone that just because it's in a magazine doesn't mean it's true."

I bit my tongue. I literally bit it.

Ow . . .

"Maybe you're right. Maybe it's a good idea if I spend some time with him. I'd like to talk to him about a few things," I began, thinking this over. If Jack was going to be spending as much time with Adam on this new film as it looked like, I should know him better.

"How about we have dinner with him before Holly's party this weekend?" Jack offered, and I bit my tongue again.

Okay, seriously, stop it.

"Sure, we can do that. But no more middle-of-the-night shenanigans."

"The only one I'm shenaniganing in the middle of the night is you."

"Pfft. Right now I've got to get to the studio. I should be home early tonight. Stay in with me?"

"Sounds great, love. Just you and me." He dropped a kiss on my forehead and shuffled back to bed. He was sound asleep again within moments.

When I left the house a little later, I noticed a tan sedan following me very closely. I turned, he turned. Dammit.

☆　☆　☆

I swear I had a tan sedan tailing me all week long, but I never saw a camera, and no shots showed up in the press anywhere. I let Bryan know, and he was looking into it. Was I being paranoid? Maybe, but I was being careful.

And speaking of being careful, I was carefully remaining in my seat while I watched Adam go bananas on a poor waitress that Saturday night.

"I said medium rare. Medium rare! Does that look

medium rare to you? It's practically gray!" he sniped as she hurried his steak away, apologizing the entire time. I liked my steak cooked a certain way too, but there was a way to do this without being a—

". . . dick. She was all over my dick from the second I walked into the club," Adam drawled, settling back against the booth after the steak incident.

Jack, Adam, and I were at a very fancy restaurant, try-ing to get through dinner so we could get to Holly's party. Scratch that, I was trying to get through dinner. Jack and Adam were having the time of their life. I know couples don't always have the same friends, and that's okay, usu-ally. But for the life of me, I couldn't figure out how Jack couldn't see that this guy was a—

". . . dick! She called me a dick. Can you believe that? Guess who doesn't work for *that* production company any-more," he finished.

One more story for me to file away under my Never Have Dinner with This Dick Again heading. I watched Jack, sitting across from this guy, this recently fallen star. I real-ized I was seeing something new on Jack's face, something I hadn't really seen before. It wasn't quite envy; it wasn't quite admiration. What was it? Whatever it was, it was enough to keep him from seeing that Adam was really a dick.

"Trent! Hey, Trent!" Adam called, almost yelling across the restaurant to someone who had just walked in. I hid my face behind my bread pudding—

BREAD PUDDING?

I hid my face behind my fresh fruit cup and rolled my eyes at Adam's table manners, counting the minutes until we could escape this small quiet dinner for three.

Thankfully Adam left the table to go say hello to Trent, and I breathed a sigh of relief.

"That bad?" Jack asked, his hand sneaking under the table to take a spot slightly higher than my knee.

"How could you tell?"

"Really? You think I can't tell when you're irritated? Your lip pouts out and you get this little crinkle at the end of your nose and—"

"Five more, George. Five more."

"I said crinkle, not wrinkle. Crinkle!" He laughed, sliding his hand farther up the inside of my leg.

I patted it and sent it back toward my knee, a safer zone. "Wrinkle, crinkle, all the same thing. Besides, you want these five, believe me." I winked and saw the green begin to darken. Oh boy.

"Oh no, I want them, but just so you know, I know you're deflecting." He leaned closer to me and let his hand move north again. Damn, he was good. I picked up his hand and moved it once more, then picked up my butter knife and made a gesture toward something else below the tablecloth.

"I'm not deflecting. I just . . . I don't get it! I don't see why this person is now essential. He's an ass, Jack. A real ass," I explained, not hiding my disdain any longer.

He sighed and brought both hands up under his chin to rest. "Look, I know he can be a little direct—"

"Direct? That's a word for it."

"But he's really a good guy. I like working with him. He knows the town; he knows the business. Just lighten up, okay?"

I nodded and noticed Adam coming back to the table. This conversation needed to end. For now.

"Sorry about that. I haven't seen that guy since we wrapped *Motion Sickness*," Adam explained, snapping, actually snapping, for the waitress. She would be getting a big fat tip from me tonight. And speaking of tip, Jack was ready to go. He'd gotten antsy all of a sudden, looking around the room, slouching lower in his chair.

"Where? Who did you see?" I asked quietly, leaning back in my chair and making sure I wasn't too close to Jack.

This wasn't exactly the kind of place we normally went to, but Adam picked the restaurant. It was high-profile, frequented by industry people and hangers-on alike; it was young Hollywood, and it was risky. Jack and I drove separately, and he came in through the back entrance. It was high-profile enough that it had a private entrance in the rear for celebrities to enter and exit discreetly. Which was the opposite of what this evening was becoming.

"Four o'clock, camera phones. Those two women have been staring for the past few minutes. Plus that guy at the bar looks familiar. I've seen him recently," he muttered, deliberately not looking at the location he just gave me.

Turning nonchalantly in that direction, Adam took the opportunity to squint at the guy in question and pronounce him paparazzi.

"How do you know he's—" I started, and Adam just looked blandly at me.

"I know, okay?" he replied, grinning in the direction of the guy.

I'd had enough. "Listen, since it's clear this is about to turn into something, I'm gonna cut it short and head out. Besides, Holly's expecting me."

"You sure?" Jack asked, squeezing my knee under the table.

"Yeah, it's better this way anyway—if we don't leave at the same time."

"We'll be there soon. Don't worry." He nodded, giving me a final squeeze.

"Adam, it was great. Are you coming to Holly's?"

Please say no, please say no, please say no.

"Wouldn't miss it." He grinned.

"Great," I said through my teeth. Heading out quickly, I averted my eyes when walking by the guy in question at the bar, and I made sure to keep my head turned away from the camera phones. Now that I was gone, I had no doubt that those women would approach Jack and Adam. They were stars after all.

I piled myself into my little car and sped up into the hills. No tan sedans in sight.

☆ ☆ ☆

Holly's party was massive, much bigger than her last. Lanterns lined the driveway and laughter and music spilled out of every door and every window. Tiki torches dotted the patio, and the lights of Los Angeles spread out as the perfect backdrop. Floating candles lit up the pool, handsome waiters passed lovely noshy treats, and the bartenders rivaled those in *Cocktail*.

This was pure industry, pure Hollywood. And Jack was at the center of it. Normally shy in crowds, the months of constant attention and media appearances had thickened his skin and made him a pro. He shone now when lit from the outside. I still saw the nervous here and there, the hand in the hair, the tapping of the shoe, but as he mingled with actors, producers, directors, writers, he was a movie star. But still a secret *Golden Girls* fan.

He winked at me from across the patio as I sat in one of the comfy chairs with one of my favorite people on the planet, Nick.

"So glad to see you. I missed you!" I cried, squeezing his hand as we sipped our dirty martinis.

"I missed you too, of course, but you know I missed looking at your boy the most."

"Yes, I know this. I know my friendship with you is based solely on the ability to look at the pretty." I laughed.

"As long as we're clear, we're good!"

We sipped and gossiped. I shared stories with him

about the series, and he told me how much he was missing Los Angeles. As we chatted, I felt a pair of large, meaty hands wrap around my eyes from the back.

"Lane!" I cried, turning to find Jack's costar.

"Hey, gorgeous!" He swept me up into a tight hug. Lane was a dear, a giant teddy bear who loved nothing more than to tease Jack about my sweet rack.

"I was hoping to see you here tonight. How are things?" I asked as he set me down. Nick petted his biceps like a cat, and Lane slung an arm around his shoulders. Sighing into his dirty martini, Nick was a happy camper.

"Things are good. Where's that idiot boyfriend of yours?" Lane asked. I swiveled in my chair, tracking him through the crowd.

"He's over by the bar with Adam Kasen," a voice piped up, and Rebecca joined the group.

"Good night, nurse! It's like a Christmas special. Where are all of you coming from?" I laughed as she sat down next to me and clinked her glass to mine.

"I just snuck in, saw Jack over by the bar, and kept moving," she replied, sipping from her cocktail.

We all turned toward the bar and watched as Jack and Adam entertained the ladies who were clustered about. I knew better than to be jealous. We were solid now, and it wasn't a concern. But as I watched, that same feeling that I had when we were at the restaurant came over me. Something just didn't sit right when it came to Adam.

"What do you know about Adam? Anything?" I asked

Rebecca, leaning in. Which wasn't hard, since she'd decided to share my chair.

"That guy's a dick," she replied immediately, rolling her eyes.

Shocker.

"That's kind of what I got too."

"Worked with him on my first movie. Slept with him once and never again."

"Wait, wait, wait, what? You slept with him?" I whisper-yelled.

Lane and Nick were occupied with tales of how much Lane could bench-press.

"Sure. Have you seen him? He's gorgeous. And great in bed. But he's a dick."

"I don't like him."

"I don't like that he's hanging out with Jack." She drained the rest of her drink.

The crowd parted just enough that I caught Jack's eye, and he grinned. That panty-dropping grin. He leaned over to Adam and then, like in a music video, he started across the patio toward me. Dressed in a red vintage concert tee, leather jacket, low-slung jeans, and my favorite blessed Doc Martens, he made my heart go pitter pat.

Other parts are pittering and pattying as well . . .

As he walked, eyes followed. It was like walking porn, and all the ladies and more than a few guys turned their heads to watch his progress. And he was just walking, for pity's sake. But like a star, his gravity impacted everything around him.

"Wow," I heard Nick breathe. But I couldn't see him. All I could see was my Sweet Nuts.

Giving the guy handshake–half hug to Lane, he leaned down to press a hello kiss on Rebecca's cheek. And then to stop the huffing, he did the same for Nick. Leading me by the hand out of my chair, he walked me to the opposite seat. Sitting down, he pulled me onto his lap, wrapped his arms around my waist, and claimed me without question. Eyes were still on us from every direction, and I pondered the timing of such a public display, but sometimes, a guy needed you on his lap. Who was I to argue with that? I scratched at the back of his head as he pressed a quick kiss on the side of my neck. I could see the women from the party giving me the evil eye, but for a moment, just one moment, I didn't care.

We all continued to talk, laughing and chatting into the night. I sighed at one point, unable to keep the contentment inside.

"You seem happy," Jack whispered, pushing a piece of curly hair behind my ear.

"I am. It's nice being out and about with our friends." I leaned into his hand.

"It's nice to be able to snog my girlfriend in public for a change." He looked me straight in the eye, licking at his lips.

"Shouldn't we behave? Don't you think we've pushed it enough tonight?"

"I haven't pushed it at all."

"Where's your hand, Jack?"

"On your knee."

"In public. I'd say you've made your point. Why push it?"

He tensed underneath me. "My point? You think I'm making a point?"

"No, I think you're hanging out at a party with your friends and your very cute girlfriend. And she's sitting on your lap, looking all kinds of cozy. But the thing is, just by doing that? You're making a point. Maybe not one you're meaning to make, but a point just the same. So let's just enjoy, and not push." I slipped my hand back up and stroked the back of his neck. As I did, I casually looked around at the rest of the party. Camera phone—there it was. Did I stop? Did I continue?

He must have felt me freeze, because he looked in the same direction I was, and we both saw the flash go off.

"There, someone got it. Now can you kiss your boyfriend?" he demanded, looking back at me.

His eyes had gone dark green, but not in the way I normally liked to see them.

Swooping in like a bird of prey with the most fantastic timing ever, Holly appeared. "Grace, can you help me get some things brought out from the kitchen?" she asked, eyeing us.

Sighing heavily, Jack helped me off his lap, and he and Lane headed back to the bar. Holly asked me all kinds of questions with her eyes. We clicked across the patio, smiling and interacting with other guests. Once we made it to the kitchen, however, she rounded on me.

"Explain."

"Come on, not now. What did you need help with?"

"Please, you think I need help in the kitchen? I hired help. I got you off the lap of the Sexiest Man Alive before he got you off in public."

I started to come back at her when I remembered how far over the line we'd been that night at the club. Touché.

"Holly, look, I think you need to lay off a bit. He's really starting to feel the pressure of all this."

"I appreciate that, but you agreed at the beginning of *all of this* that for Jack, and for you for that matter, you two would keep it quiet. Off the radar. Sitting on his lap at a party that half of Hollywood is at? Not so much off the radar."

"I know! Dammit, I know that! I know I'm the one who's going to bear the brunt of this—the cracks about how old I am, the thousands of women online who will comment about how he can do so much better than me. I'm fucking aware, okay? But I am telling you, if you push him right now, not good," I snapped, tears springing to my eyes.

She backed off, poking at a crab cake on a platter.

"I know you're just doing your job. No one does it better. Truly. Jack loves you. But he's feeling it."

"He needs to quit partying so much," she said quietly, still crab poking.

"He's twenty-four, for Christ's sake! May I remind you of what we did at that age?" I smiled, trying to break the tension.

"No, you most certainly may not."

"Listen, I know he's going a little crazy lately, but it's under control, I promise. And yes, I will make sure that we keep at least five feet of distance between us the rest of the night."

"Okay, now you're just being an asshole," she replied, showing me her middle finger.

"Let's go back to your party," I encouraged, taking her hand. As we started out for the patio, Michael appeared.

"Holly, the bartender needs some more lemons. Didn't we pick some up today after the movie?"

"Yep they're on the—"

"Top shelf of the fridge, got it. Hey, Grace," he said, patting my shoulder as he went past me into the kitchen.

I looked back and forth between the two of them. "Wait a minute. Wait just a goddamn minute!"

Holly's face flushed deep red. "Let's go back to the party, asshead," she muttered, unable to contain her smile.

Did *not* see that one coming . . .

eight

I didn't have time to ponder this possible new develop-ment between Michael and Holly.

Michael and Holly?

I couldn't focus on *those two people* because things had quickly gone from strange to swagger elsewhere at the party. I circled and mingled, chatted and schmoozed, staying within an across-the-room grin of Jack, but not too close. He seemed off tonight, and while he was glued at the hip with Adam, I was steering clear. Jack tended to get handsy when drinking, and after the earlier lap powwow, I knew to make sure to keep some distance until it was time to go home.

This was new, a side to Jack I had no experience with.

It's not like you've known him all that long . . .

True, but I knew Jack. Knew his head and his good heart, and this was not like him. It was, however, like—

"Adam!" I heard my Brit bellow from across the patio. Shot glass in hand, Jack stood with Lane by the bar. Lane and he had been doing shots, but I noticed Lane had wisely switched to club soda a while ago. Lane's eyes met mine across the party, and I raised an eyebrow. He looked at his watch, then gestured for the door.

Message received. Time to go.

I picked my way through the party, finding the straightest path to the bar, trying to get there before Adam did. As I closed, I could see Jack swaying slightly, and his eyes were puffy and bloodshot. Lane had an arm draped in a friendly way across his shoulders, but as I got closer, I could see Jack was leaning heavily into his side. Lane was having to hold him up. As Jack caught sight of me, a slow grin spread across his face.

"There's my girl. Where've you been?" he slurred, eyes droopy and unfocused.

I exchanged a look with Lane and nodded.

"Hey, Sweet Nuts, you ready to go? I'm kind of tired, and things are winding down."

The party was in full swing all around us.

"Not yet, Grace. Adam and I were talking about heading over to this bar down on Sunset and checking it out. Let's all go!" he shouted, slamming his glass down on the bar. He turned toward the driveway and Lane pulled him back, shaking his head.

"Dude, not gonna happen. Let me take you home."

"No, Lane, it's okay," I said. "We drove separately. I can take him home. Come on, Jack, I want to leave. Come home with me?" I slipped my hand around him under his jacket, hugging him to me but also testing to see how steady he was. Wow, not very.

"No, I don't want to go home yet. Adam! Hey, Adam! These guys want to go home. You still want to head over to Sunset?"

"Absolutely," he said, sliding into our circle and smiling at me.

"Absolutely not. We're heading home. Can someone tell Holly we're leaving?" I asked, glaring at him. I wasn't even trying to hide how I felt about him anymore.

"I think he can decide whether he wants to go out. Lighten up, Mom." Adam chuckled.

Okay. That's it.

"We're done here. Lane, here are my keys. I'm parked not too far down the hill. Mind bringing it up for me? I don't even want to wait for valet."

He jogged off and I was left wearing a Jack jacket. Lane had really been holding him up more than I thought.

I tried to pull him over to a chair, but I couldn't get him there.

"Grace, I love you. I love you so much. You know that, right? Such a sexy girlfriend. Isn't my girlfriend sexy?" he asked some guy standing near the bar. The guy raised his glass in salute. As I struggled to keep Jack upright while he laughed and pawed at me, I saw Michael near the pool and waved him over.

"I need to get him out of here. Lane went to get my car. Can you help me get him out front without attracting a ton of attention?" I asked, turning my back on Adam. I could have asked him to help, but I'd sooner sit on an anthill.

"Sure. Of course. What the hell, Jack?" He shook his head and smiled ruefully at him. With Jack between us, we made our way to the side entrance. Several people watched, but at that point I didn't care. I wanted to get Jack home, get him sobered up, and then we were going to take this to the woodshed.

"Don't take the piss out, Mikey my man. Just having a bit of fun. That's allowed, right? This is Hollywood, after all. We're supposed to be sloshed and having a great time!" Jack yelled, planting a big kiss on my mouth at the end of his speech.

Holding him up between the two of us, I laughed in spite of myself as we guided him through the gates and toward the street.

Tan sedan.

Tan sedan.

Flashbulbs.

Yelling.

"Jack! Jack Hamilton!"

"Jack! Over here? How was the party?"

"Hey, it's the redhead! Grace, right? Hey, Grace, look over here!"

"Jack! Jack! Jack! How much did you have to drink to-night?"

"Hey, Grace, did you get him that drunk?"

"Hey, Adam? Where are you and Jack heading tonight?"

I literally couldn't see. I could make out images and silhouettes behind the cameras, I could tell the general direction they were yelling from, but I had no idea how many people were shouting at me. In between the shouts I could hear the clicking, the fast-speed lenses capturing everything. Jack piss drunk and hanging off me and Michael, and Adam somewhere behind us, probably smiling big.

I froze. I froze and stood still, gaping like a fish at the cameras. I didn't know what to do, move him forward, bring him back inside, hide him in my shoe? I panicked.

Michael luckily still had his wits about him, and he herded us to the right, holding his hand up in front of Jack's face. Now I could hear Lane calling us to where he had brought the car up, his voice rising above the loud photographers who were asking personal questions to try to get a reaction out of us. Holly had warned me before that paparazzi could and would ask rude questions to try and get a different shot. But knowing it and actually hearing it are two very different things.

"Hey, Jack, your girl's got a sweet ass!"

"Grace, Grace! Over here ,Grace! How big's his dick?"

"Grace, how's it feel to know all the women in the world want to fuck your boyfriend?"

My face flaming, I kept my head down and followed Michael as he led us in the direction of Lane and my car. Oh my God, how were we going to drive away in this? My heart beat fast, and I was legitimately in over my head.

How had they known we were here?

Once near the car, Michael and Lane put Jack into the front seat, and I managed to get around to the other side. But I couldn't drive. I was petrified. I pleaded with Michael with my eyes. I needed help. I didn't want to speak. I didn't want anything I had to say to be heard by these people. Luckily, Jack was quiet. But he had heard everything, and his eyes met mine. They looked dead.

Michael came around to my side after whispering something in Lane's ear and taking my keys. Adam stood near the car—close enough to make sure he was in the shot, I noticed. Michael opened the driver's side and ushered me into the backseat. The photographers were on my side now, so I made sure to keep my dress tucked around my legs, not wanting to flash anyone. Once inside, I looked back at the house and saw Lane walking up the sidewalk, making sure Adam came with him.

My instinct was to reach out for Jack, but that would make for a better story, so I sat back, low in the seat, my hands over my face as I was on the verge of tears.

As Michael got in and turned the ignition on, Jack spoke into the back of his hand. "I fucking hate this."

The *redhead* Plays Her Hand

Two hours later, and I mean two *solid* hours later, the three of us made it home. Jack sat in the backyard, slouched into the love seat under a thick cashmere blanket, coffee in hand. I kept sneaking a peek at him from the window off the kitchen. He hadn't moved or spoken since we got home.

We called Bryan after we left, because we didn't know where to go or what to do. I didn't want to lead them back to the house, even though at this point I was pretty sure the press knew where we lived. Michael didn't want to keep driving around up in the hills. The hairpin turns at night were sharp enough without a legion of tan sedans keeping pace. Finally, after speaking with Bryan, we arranged a switch. We drove to a parking garage over by the Beverly Center, where he was waiting with his Suburban, the dark-tinted windows making it difficult to see inside. The ride had sobered Jack somewhat, and we were hurried into the SUV and back on the road within moments, leaving my car behind to pick up the next day. We had managed to lose the photographers just long enough to get our cars switched. As we were pulling out I saw tan sedan after tan sedan drive in, looking for my car.

They were good.

Now Bryan had gone, Jack was bundled on the patio, and Michael and I were nursing cups of coffee, which had been nicely complemented by a heavy splash of Jameson. A very heavy splash—essentially it was Jameson with a shot of coffee and not the other way around. As the Irish whiskey hit my tummy, I warmed considerably, beginning to unwind a bit and let my body process everything that had just happened. My hands finally stopped shaking when it became almost impossible to get the cup to my mouth without spilling. My hands knew never to waste Irish whiskey, so they behaved.

I leaned against the counter, sipping and staring but not really seeing anything in front of me. All I could see were those flashbulbs, hear those terrible things they were shouting, and then Jack's words as we pulled away.

"How're you doing?" Michael asked, raising the bottle once more and adding another substantial splash to my cup and his own.

"I don't know. I honestly don't know." I sighed, holding my head in my hand.

This was Jack's life, my life, and how we chose to deal with this now would dictate how we handled things in the future. It was so easy to think this kind of thing would be something you could easily get past, that the money we were making and the spoils this kind of industry provided made up for it. But no amount of money, no amount of special VIP treatment and swag-bag goodies justified the treatment we had just received. Jack had already been in one accident. So was I being dramatic when my brain went to the worse possible scenario? No.

I loved this life, however. I loved the work and the opportunity, the high that I got performing again. And the paycheck was nothing to sneeze at. Jack was right: we could take what he had already made and the money I had in savings, plus my new income, and we could disappear. Seychelles? Sure. East end of London? Of course. Farm in Iowa where I could grow my own salads and put up jars of jam and beans for us to survive the hard, lean winter?

Okay, you're not Laura Ingalls . . .

Regardless, Iowa had its own appeal, and there's no question Jack would look fantastic in overalls with a pitchfork.

But realistically we wouldn't do any of those things. Because I had fought to get back here, and I wasn't letting some slimeball with a telephoto lens run me out of anywhere. So we would deal. But how?

"I was not prepared for that. Next time I will be," I muttered, looking past Michael's concerned eyes to my bundle on the patio, who still hadn't moved.

☆ ☆ ☆

Michael called a cab and left a little while later, promising to check in tomorrow. I didn't ask him about what might or might not be going on with Holly. I would let her squirm for a bit before I put on the real pressure. It was rare I had something juicy like this that I could press out of her, and I was going to enjoy getting her to tell me.

For now, I headed outside and poked Jack with my toe. He was still wrapped up. Wordlessly, he unfolded his arms and let me sit on his lap, sharing his blanket with me. He held me tight, cradling me into his chest and letting our breathing sync. In. Out. In. Out.

We sat in the quiet night, interrupted only occasionally by a coyote howl. Laurel Canyon was magical, especially at night. I could understand why so many musicians and artists set up shop here so many years ago. It was inspiring at every turn.

He sighed heavily, his arms tightening, bringing me as close as he could. I let him, his entire body was craving contact, and I wanted to be that for him, his contact. I threaded my hand through his, breathing in his scent, which was concentrated thickly at my favorite spot on his neck, just below his ear. Every limb intertwined, the blanket covering us from the world, I sat with my sweet boy, listening to his heartbeat.

"Can we talk about this tomorrow?" he asked quietly, his body tense.

"Yes, but we *will* talk about it," I replied, squeezing his hand.

"I love you."

"I love you more."

"Not bloody likely."

Every time I closed my eyes I saw those damn flashbulbs.

nine

Time heartthrob Jack Hamilton and rumored girlfriend Grace Sheridan were partying hard in the Hollywood Hills last night! The couple was photographed leaving the party, with Jack intoxicated to the point of being held up by his girlfriend and another party guest. Sources from inside the party last night tell us, "He was drinking a lot, spending most of his time at the bar with Adam Kasen."

Jack Hamilton skipped the fender and went right for the bender, getting so drunk last night at a party hosted by his manager, Holly Newman, he had to be helped out to a waiting car! Grace Sheridan, older actress, and Michael O'Connell, writer and creator of Grace's new show on Venue, held up the Sexy Scientist Guy as they left the party last night. Sources inside the party confirm that while Jack and Grace refuse to confirm their relationship, the two got very chummy there. "She was totally sitting on his lap. They were kissing and ignoring everyone else they were sitting with. She knew there were people watching too, and she made sure everyone saw she was with him." The actress hid in the backseat as they sped away; Jack appeared to be passed out cold in the front seat.

In the hills of Beverly last night, photographers caught Jack Hamilton sneaking out of a party hosted by his manager, so drunk he was barely able to walk to his car! By his side was rumored girlfriend Grace Sheridan, nine years his senior and star of the upcoming show on Venue, *Mabel's Unstable?* The pair struggled to their car, helped by fellow actors Lane Robbins and Adam Kasen, Hollywood bad boy. Kasen, a castmate of Jack's in the still-in-production soldier flick *Soldier Boy*, has been spotted out on the town with Jack. The two actors have been seen partying at various nightclubs and bars in Los Angeles lately. Sources close to the unconfirmed couple say that Grace is "furious at Jack for spending so much time out at night." Grace sat in the backseat of the car last night as the couple sped away from photographers, both trying to hide their faces from cameras. Dr. Richard Pearson, psychiatrist and expert on substance abuse, speculates on Jack's condition. "He's displayed the classic signs of someone who is having difficulty dealing with the pressure this industry can place on young stars. He is in real trouble. He's clearly not handling the fame well."

☆   ☆   ☆

I closed my laptop and thought of Jack, still in bed and sound asleep. Sawing logs but still gloriously cute. I made coffee and didn't think about it. I sliced peaches and nectarines for a fruit salad and didn't think about it. I perched on the end of my kitchen island, the granite cool underneath me as I hyperventilated, not thinking about it.

Why was it necessary that every time they referred to me, they made sure to comment on the nine-year age difference? I knew it; he knew it; anyone could see it, but really? Every time?

I snot-sobbed, letting everything out in a way I hadn't for a long time. Everything that had happened lately, everything we were going through would once have ended up in the Drawer, where all bad things went. In the past, when I couldn't deal with something, I literally didn't deal with it. Instead, I walled all things unpleasant into a tight little box, which eventually exploded. And landed on everyone around me. This had happened spectacularly at Jack's *Time* premiere the previous year.

Now I vowed to deal with things as they happened, in the moment and in the present. This resulted in a lot more tears but a much less confused head. And now I needed to talk to Jack. Armed with a breakfast tray loaded down with treats, I headed into our bedroom. Sprawled across his side with one hand on my pillow, searching out missing boobies more than likely, was the Sexiest Man Alive. Still snoring, he wore the sheets low on his hips, revealing that happy trail that made me more than happy. I set down the tray and curled into his side, pressing kisses across his shoulder and chest as he stirred. Green sleepy eyes opened to mine, and a sweet smile crept across his face.

"Hey."

"Hey, yourself," I whispered, dipping down to kiss on that sweet smile. His hands tangled into my hair, and he tried to pull me down to him, coaxing me with promises of what he'd do to me if I let him.

I almost let him. It would be a wonderful way to get lost and avoid what had happened, even if just for the morning. But I had nectarines. And a Brit to take to the woodshed, although in a kinder way than I'd originally thought I'd be taking him.

"No, no, Sweet Nuts, I made breakfast. Come on, let's eat."

"Oh, I'll eat all right."

"That's crass, love."

"Never heard any complaints," he sassed, licking his lips and beginning to flip me over. I knew I had to take control. Once he was south of my belly button he would own me, and I wouldn't even be able to spell "woodshed."

It's an easy word to spell. Come on, let him do it.

"I have nectarines," I protested.

"So do I," he responded immediately, leading my hand south on his body as well. I copped a quick feel—I wasn't made of steel—then wisely sat up, removing his hands from my body before I could get too distracted. I scooted away from him on the bed, pouring some coffee as he protested.

"Killing me, Grace." He sighed as he sank back onto his pillow, draping his arm across his eyes and adjusting himself with his other hand.

I forced my eyes back to the breakfast and away from the accidental erotica that was playing out on the other side of the bed. I brought over the tray, sitting cross-legged opposite him, keeping the tray between us. I knew him. If I were next to him, the tray would go flying.

He sat up, running his hands through his hair as though he still had it and grimacing as he did so. Tongue thick, he gestured for the bottle of water I had brought. I handed it to him. He drained it. I sugared his coffee and passed it to him. He accepted it gratefully. His eyes were bright green this morning, made even more striking by the redness and circles underneath. He looked young and old at the same time, and as I ate my fruit, I contemplated how to proceed.

"You're pissed again," he offered, making my decision for me.

"I'm pissed again," I admitted, nibbling on a muffin.

He was sticking to coffee, turning his nose up at any food, actually paling a little when I offered him some bacon. He was hungover. Good. He needed to feel this.

"Grace, I didn't know there were photographers out there. How could I have known that?"

"Oh, I'm not pissed about that. I'm pissed about the fact that you were so drunk off your ass that now *that's* the story on every gossip site this morning: your inability to deal with your fame in any other way than drinking."

"Oh, now I'm an alcoholic?"

"I didn't say that, but the press isn't that far off from it."

"That's ridiculous. I'm not an alcoholic."

"No shit. What you are is partying way too much and making an ass of yourself. And how shocking, Adam Kasen is there every time this happens."

"You think he's behind this?"

"I don't really care who's behind this. I don't care who made sure the press knew exactly where we were last night. I don't care who's quoted as a source in every article online right now. What I care about is you and how you're handling yourself in public."

"Oh, great. Now I've got another woman telling me what to do. Between you and Holly managing every single aspect of my career, I've about had it," he snapped, stepping out of the bed and onto the floor, remembering afterward that he was naked.

He stood there, his anger dissipating in the cool air, along with anything else that might have been worked up.

"I'm not wearing any pants."

"I can see that."

"Where are my pants?"

"In the bathroom on the floor, where you left them last night after you threw up."

"I threw up?"

"You don't remember that?"

"No. I remember being out back with you, and then . . . bollocks, that's the last thing I remember." He sighed, hands on his hips as he surveyed the room.

"I'm still naked," he said after a moment.

"I'm aware of this," I replied, trying to keep my stern face on. He knew me better, however.

"If I apologize naked, will that hold any more weight than a clothed apology?"

"I don't want you to apologize, Jack. I just want you to think next time, think about what you're doing."

"So then a naked apology would be wasted?" He bumped his hips back and forth a bit as I struggled not to laugh.

"I'd rather the apology be wasted than my boyfriend."

"That was pretty good, Crazy."

"Still not kidding."

"Still not wearing pants," he said, now turning himself toward the bathroom. "Did you say they were this way?" He pointed in a rather unconventional way.

He had recovered quickly. I was going to lose control of this conversation very soon. I could tell where this was headed. I crawled across the bed to him, sitting on my knees in front of him, bringing him close and hugging him. Pressing my face into his tummy, I kissed him quickly then turned my face up to his, which I found gazing down at me. He pushed a curl behind my ear, then brought his hand to my mouth, where I kissed his knuckles.

"I know I've been saying this a lot lately, but it's not sinking in. Just be careful, okay?"

"I will, Grace. I will. Now, about sinking in?" He pressed his body against me in a way that could not be misinterpreted.

"Would you quit being so charming? I'm still pissed at you," I warned as he pushed me back against the bed and had me out of my yoga pants in two seconds flat.

"I know," he answered, pressing into my body exquisitely.

Turns out I was able to orbit the earth a few times and still be pissed off.

☆ ☆ ☆

"Put him on the phone."

"Holly, I told you. He's in the shower."

"Get him out."

"No. But I promise he'll call you as soon as he's done."

"Bring the phone into the bathroom. You can tell him everything I'm saying."

"Do you have this kind of access to everyone you represent or just the ones fucking your best friend?"

"Cute, asshead. Real cute."

She chuckled, and I could tell she was backing down a bit. I breathed out. This being in between the two of them was beginning to wear a bit thin. I curled my legs underneath me, settling into the comfy sofa with another cup of coffee. After making sure I wasn't too pissed to come—repeatedly because he's thorough like that—Jack had disappeared into the shower to clear his head, and I finished breakfast. It was a rare day lately that we were both at home with nowhere to go and nowhere we needed to be, so I was planning on circling the wagons a bit and spending a quiet day with my boy.

"I assume you've already seen the pictures?" Holly asked.

"I have. Did you notice no deer-in-headlights this time?"

"Yep, you're learning. Few more of those and you'll be a pro."

I bit my tongue. She called me out on my silence.

"I know you're not quiet over there because you're surprised by this, are you?"

"I just didn't expect it last night is all. How did they know we were there?"

"You're kidding, right?"

"Adam?"

"Adam," she replied.

"You're sure?"

"Not completely, but it makes the most sense. Although honestly, it could have been anyone. There's no real rhyme or reason. You two could go parade down Sunset in front of Grauman's Chinese right now and no one would notice, but you buy one box of condoms at the grocery store, and it'll be front-page news. Don't buy your own condoms, by the way. I'll get someone to get you some when you need them."

"Oh, please, we haven't used condoms since we first were together."

"You're being careful, though, right? Although Hollywood babies are a great accessory . . ."

I laughed. "Ha! And yes, we're being careful. Would your rule also apply to purchasing multiple containers of whipped cream at a time?"

"Yeah, don't do that. Oatmeal is safe, though. No one cares if you're buying oatmeal."

"Does Michael like oatmeal?"

"Nah, he's a Cheerios guy. He— Dammit. Well played."

"Spill it!" I screamed into the phone, thrilled that she had given up the dirt so easily.

"There's nothing to spill, actually."

"Bullshit, spill it." I giggled, pushing her. It was nice to be the pushy one.

"There's nothing really to tell. It just, sort of, happened."

"Exactly what happened?"

"It's just, it's good. Really good, okay?" she replied, a smile evident in her voice.

"What about Lane?"

"I adore Lane. He's a great guy, but that was never going to be anything beyond what it was."

"Amazing sex?"

"Amazing sex, yes."

"How's the sex with Michael?" I asked, knowing full well how good it was from our one-night stand back in college. This wasn't weird for me, and I hoped it wasn't going to be weird for them.

"Um, well, the thing is . . ."

"You haven't fucked him yet?" I shrieked.

Jack padded down the hall from the bedroom, towel around his waist, still dripping. "What are you yelling about?" he asked.

"Tell you later," I mouthed, and he went back into the bedroom.

"Weren't you the one who told me you couldn't believe it when I said Jack and I hadn't had sex yet?"

"Grace, let me just—"

"*Get on that stick* I think were the actual words you yelled at me in front of a shocked Starbucks, in fact," I teased, loving every second of this.

"Oh, suck it, asshead." I could tell she was still smiling.

"But you like him?" I asked, thinking back on how long we had all been friends. I never would have put those two together, but in my mind, he was always in *my* past, not hers as much. Yet there was something to be said for being friends as long as they had.

"I really think I do."

We both sighed.

"If you haven't slept with him, how do you know he takes Cheerios?"

"He fell asleep here one night a few weeks ago when we

were watching a movie. That's all. I may have slept on the couch next to him."

"How cute! Anything else happen?"

"Not really. We've kissed, but that's about all."

Holly never took this long to pounce on anyone. This was different.

"So are you officially an item?" I asked, trying to get more juice. She wasn't having it.

"Okay, back to business. Just have Jack call me as soon as he's out of the shower?"

"Yes, ma'am," I fibbed. I'd let him at least put pants on before he had to face another firing squad.

"And heads-up, I've got a call with the producers tomorrow about your paparazzi session last night. I'm sure they've got some thoughts."

"Great."

"That's my job. You let me worry about it."

After we hung up, I sat on the couch for a bit, coffee now cold.

What would the producers want to talk about with Holly?

That your personal life is exploding all over the Internet?

Oh yeah . . .

☆ ☆ ☆

That day started tense and ended lovely. Jack and I lazed around the house all day, watching TV, drinking coffee, doing laundry, just having a day where we didn't have to do a thing. It was nice. Toward the end, we talked about going out for dinner but realized that eating somewhere in public was not the kind of thing we were up for, not after last night. We ordered in Chinese, ate it at the dining room table off my new dishes (a splurge after I saw what Holly had negotiated for me), and then decided to take a drive. Bryan had already brought my car back from the parking garage.

It was risky, heading out in a car we knew was easily recognized, but I didn't want to be trapped in the house, and I could tell Jack was getting antsy. At night, it wouldn't be as obvious who was in the car, and if we kept the top up during most of the trip, we decided it was worth that very risk.

Jack drove our favorite drive, Topanga Canyon all the way to PCH, pulling over at a little canyon store for hot chocolates and to drop the top. With the tunes on, the night breeze in my hair, and Jack's hand on my knee, I could finally relax in my favorite city in the world. As we turned right onto the coastal highway, the ocean scented the air. The moon hung low in the sky, and while the stars twinkled over the water, my star relaxed as well. He squeezed my knee as the music switched to an old favorite, "Into the Mystic." I smiled to myself as I thought of the first time we'd taken a drive like this, this song and this man next to me making for a very sweet memory. I chuckled, letting my hand drift out of the car and into the night, rolling it along imaginary hills and valleys. I sang softly along with Van Morrison, Jack's voice joining in on the chorus. My left hand dropped down to his on my knee, and I nestled my fingers in his.

In this moment, in this car, on this stretch of highway, we were a couple in love. We were not an older woman and a younger man, Jack wasn't the Sexiest Man Alive, but he *was* the sexiest man in my world. I wasn't an up-and-coming actress who'd been asked about the size of her boyfriend's dick the night before by a total stranger, I was a girl in a convertible in my pajamas, holding hands with the man I was in love with.

And for the record, it was perfectly sized.

Word.

"What are you smiling at over there, Crazy?"

"How can you see me smiling? It's almost pitch-black out here!" I laughed, this part of PCH was all curves and cliffs.

"I can tell when you're smiling. I don't need to see it to know it's there. What are you thinking about?"

"You. Us. The first time we went for a drive. I was totally falling for you by then."

"I was falling for you the moment you pushed your boobies in my face, even with the sparkle." He laughed, untangling his hand from mine as he turned off into a scenic overlook.

"Parking? How *Beach Blanket Bingo*!" I laughed as he turned off the engine.

Now I could hear the surf, not too far below us. Van Morrison, waves, and my Sweet Nuts. We sank back into our seats, faces turned up to the Milky Way. We talked and laughed, held hands and sighed into the night. We really were so far removed from anything Hollywood, only the barest hint of light from Santa Monica Pier was noticeable in the distance as the highway curved back in on itself.

I leaned in and stole a kiss. Soft, gentle, lips and mouths caressing and pressing each other in quiet affection.

Another car pulled into the overlook, headlights breaking our bubble and reminding us where we were and what we were doing. Another couple had the same idea we did. Checking them out, we backed away, leaving them to their passionate necking.

"Home, or drive on?"

"Take me home, Jack," I answered, stealing just one more kiss.

☆   ☆   ☆

He held my arms above my head, teasing my body with his tongue. I arched up underneath him, writhing to bring me closer to his mouth, to him. Naked, under the man I loved more than anything else in the world, I whispered to him, telling him how much I adored him, how much I needed him.

"Soon, Crazy, soon," he chided, letting his mouth envelope my right nipple as my hands strained to touch him.

131

My skin was on fire. His good weight pressed down on me as I longed to wrap myself around him, in every way possible. As his teeth nipped, his lips spoke to my skin, told me I was beautiful, I was sexy, I was his. I could feel him, heavy and wanting between my twisting legs. I tried to bring him inside, inside me, where I needed to reach him the most.

He released my hands but slid down my body, head nestled between my legs, prodding me open with his hands, nudging me with his nose, laughing into my warmth, and biting down hard on my Hamilton Brand, making it stronger, indelibly marking me once more. He licked and sucked patiently, persistently at me, and I came hard on his tongue, sent above and beyond by his sweet smile once more. The scruff on his head roughed more than pleasantly at the inside of my thighs, making me so sensitive to his every touch. His strong hands held me still, pushing my hips down into the mattress, meeting my thrusts with gentle but intense pressure, covering my sex with his face and his mouth, nibbling and humming through me, causing a chain of orgasms that made me call out his name over and over again.

Crashing up my body to join me again, his mouth now assaulted my own, my taste and his tongue joining with mine. He flipped me quickly, positioning me to straddle his hips as I rose above him.

"Brilliant," he chanted in the moonlight, watching me as I sank down onto him, taking him deep inside me, nothing between us, nothing else existing in the world except for the exquisite feel of him. His hands spanned my waist, thumbs dipping down to circle just above where we were joined, applying pressure as we spun out of control together. I rode him hard, like he loved me to, squeezing him inside and out, touching my own breasts the way I knew he wanted to, bouncing and letting my head tip back, my hair tickling his thighs as I felt him growing impossibly harder inside me.

"Grace. Jesus, Grace." He groaned, guttural and explosive below me as I came all around him, his hips thrusting up into me, driving us together over and over again, primal and gentle all at the same time. He came hard, and loud, prayerlike obscenities spilling from his mouth. His head tilted back against the pillow, brow furrowed and jaw clenched, in the way I loved him most.

I collapsed onto his chest, both of us breathing heavily, sweat slick and warm between us. I lay on top, his arms wrapped around my back, drawing images on my body that I couldn't see but knew were there.

"I wish I could stay here forever, just like this, inside," he whispered in my ear.

He went back to the desert the following morning.

ten

Variety Magazine

Production continues on the new Venue show *Mabel's Unstable?* Billed as a musical comedy with strong adult themes, this marks the first of its kind on the new network as well as the television debut of Grace Sheridan. The show is a look at Los Angeles through the eyes of a former beauty queen struggling to find her place in a town where youth is valued above anything else. Set against the backdrop of Beverly Hills, the main character Mabel (Sheridan) is pitted against her ex-husband's new wife, Bianca (Leslie Franklin). Although Sheridan is new to the scene, early reports are that she's exceptionally strong in this role and is winning over any naysayers opposed to the casting of an unknown in such a high-profile role. Originally set as a stage musical written by Michael O'Connell, Sheridan originated the role of Mabel in the workshop production late last year. The network accelerated production of *Mabel's Unstable?* for a summer debut when producers axed *Pickpocket*, a series that debuted to low ratings last fall.

Twitter

From @Jackinmybox 9:37 p.m. OMG! Jack Hamilton just walked into the restaurant I am in! Holy shit, I'm dying! 9th Street Tavern in Las Vegas. Get here now!

From @Jackinmybox 10:17 p.m. Hamilton is sitting 20 ft from me at 9th Street Tavern. Kasen is here. I want to be his beer bottle so badly . . .

From @Jackinmybox 10:55 p.m. Jack Hamilton is leaving the bar, heading out with other guys he's with. Going to follow in my car!

From @Jackinmybox 11:42 p.m. Damn! Outside Ghostbar at Palms, trying to get in! Hamilton is inside! Need to get inside!!

People

Out on the town and in your face, Adam Kasen was overheard yelling at a bartender and seen throwing a beer bottle at the popular watering hole Tease in Las Vegas last night. On location nearby shooting the gritty war drama *Soldier Boy*, Kasen was there with several members of the cast, including Jack Hamilton. Looking somewhat embarrassed by his costar's behavior, Hamilton nevertheless coaxed Kasen back into the VIP section of the club, where the group partied well into the night. Kasen, a longtime party boy, is said to be one of the reasons Hamilton has been photographed out on the town so much in recent weeks. Meanwhile, rumored girlfriend and older actress Grace Sheridan is back in Los Angeles, working on her new series, *Mable's Unstable?*, for cable channel Venue. While the two have never commented on their alleged relationship, Sheridan is said to be unhappy with Hamilton's recent behavior and blaming Kasen for the new party-boy persona. Kasen's rep made this statement following the incident: "Adam was in attendance at that club that evening, but the incident reported never took place. Adam would never behave that way."

InStyle

Who wore it better? Photographed at a promotional event for her new movie, Jennifer Aniston sported a black tank dress by Michael Kors, the same dress worn by curvy newcomer Grace Sheridan. Sheridan, the rumored girlfriend of Jack Hamilton, wore the dress to a Kate Spade event in Los Angeles. Curvy hourglass or athletic build—who wore it better? What say you, InStylers?

Twitter

From @Jack'sFavoriteGal 11:17 p.m. OMG waiting for Jack Hamilton to come outside. I want to ask him to sign my arm! Or something else . . .

From @Jack'sFavoriteGal 11:23 p.m. Holy shit! Just saw Adam Kasen look outside! I think I can see Jack's head! I'm going to vomit!

From @Jack'sFavoriteGal 11:42 p.m. I'm so pissed! I waited here for 3 hrs when I heard he was here, and he wouldn't even sign my-cont.

From @Jack'sFavoriteGal 11:43 p.m. cont.-arm! I had a Sharpie and everything! He wouldn't sign anything, just cussed and Bryan made us all move! He-cont.

From@Jack'sFavoriteGal 11:44 p.m. cont.-didn't even look at us! There were about 30 of us. He owes us something! SO PISSED

Us Weekly

Jack Hamilton snaps at fans! Surrounded by autograph seekers while leaving a nightclub on the Las Vegas strip, the normally quiet and reserved star snapped at fans as they asked for pictures and autographs. "He seemed really out of it. I got his autograph last year when he was on *Good Day LA*, and he was much nicer! He barely spoke to any of us and when he did, he told us to move out of the way." Reports also note that Hamilton was staggering out of the club after an evening of partying and losing a bundle earlier that night at the Palms Casino Resort. Sexy Scientist Guy is a jerk? Say it ain't so, Hamilton!

Twitter

From @LAXforHamiltonSEX 2:31p.m. I swear to God I just saw Jack Hamilton pull into the parking lot at Top of the Glen in Bel Air. I think it's him and that redhead!

From @LAXforHamiltonSEX 2:37 p.m. Fucking right it's him! OMG Jack Hamilton is going into the pharmacy. I'm totally going in to see what they're getting . . .

Access Hollywood

Still wondering about whether Jack Hamilton is single? Let's break this down. New pictures have emerged from what looks to be a date night for the *Time* heartthrob and rumored gal pal Grace Sheridan, herself an actress and starring in a new series for Venue, set to premiere this summer. Dressed casually in T-shirt and jeans, the young star was snapped walking closely with Sheridan outside Top of the Glen. The two appeared to be laughing and sharing an ice cream, until they noticed photographers and quickly separated.

While no recent pictures have been taken of the pair, they were photographed repeatedly last year, when they were decidedly less guarded. What follows is what we know:

Sources close to the couple have confirmed that the two met at a party last summer hosted by manager Holly Newman (both are now represented by Newman). The first picture of the two of them together was snapped at Malibu eatery Gladstones. Additional photos were circulated later that week of the two at Japanese restaurant Yamashiro. The following week they were spotted shopping at Whole Foods, grabbing lunch at Fatburger, and while there are no pictures to confirm, hotel staff have reported the two spent a weekend at a luxury hotel in Santa Barbara.

Flash forward several weeks to pictures that surfaced of the two holding hands in New York's Central Park, where we now know Grace was living while working on her new musical/now TV series *Mabel's Unstable?*

The next time we saw the couple in the same place at the same time was at the premiere of *Time*, Hamilton's breakout role. Walking the red carpet, a smart photographer recognized Sheridan, who until this time had been known only as the unidentified redhead. She gave her name to one of the photographers, and the entire press line was abuzz that she was the redhead Hamilton had been seen with so many times.

Since then, mum's the word. The camera-shy couple

has refused to speak about their relationship, and no incriminating photos have surfaced since the pictures in New York City. When asked to comment, their shared rep Holly Newman has only said, "They're great friends. They met at a party I hosted for several of my clients months ago. They're thrown together a lot. They're not a couple."

Others have a different opinion.

"They have to keep it quiet; Jack's fans would flip if they knew he was unavailable," says a source close to the couple. Fan sites of the actor have been musing for months about whether the two are a real life couple.

"Of course they aren't. It's all publicity! Think about it: Grace has the same manager as Jack does. She's behind it all. Press for Jack means press for Grace. It's all about raising her profile. If you ask me, he can do a lot better," says Molly Hunter, who runs the *Southern Girls for Jack Hamilton* blog, whose readers are in the they're-not-dating camp.

Recently Hamilton's behavior has raised some red flags. While appearing in the past to be a quiet and reserved actor, he's been hitting the party and nightclub circuit heavily, photographed at all hours of the night, often appearing heavily intoxicated. No word on how Sheridan is handling the time apart or Hamilton's new life as the party persona.

The question is, now that Grace's star is on the rise, will they or won't they reveal their true relationship?

E! Online

Production closed for the new series *Mabel's Unstable?*, and actress Grace Sheridan celebrated with close friends at a restaurant in the trendy neighborhood of Los Feliz. Cast members, writers, and director David Lancaster gathered together to toast to the new show's success. But that's not the big story . . . Originally slated for a fall release, rumor has it that while production and subsequent ordering of a full season before an episode had even aired was based partly on the originality of the show, the quick pickup may also be linked to the star's alleged relationship with Jack Hamilton. Was the show picked up because of the obvious connection between Sheridan, a previously unknown actress with no credits to her name, and her high-profile relationship with Hamilton? Was the channel counting on her name staying linked to Hamilton? Stay tuned for more on that . . .

Press were camped outside the private party to see if Hamilton would show up to support his girlfriend. The pair has never commented publicly on the status of their relationship, and the pictures most indicative of a close relationship were captured before *Time* was released and before Sheridan was cast in the upcoming series. Since then they have been careful to avoid any pictures that could confirm the nature of their relationship, although several shots have been captured, most recently at a party at Holly Newman's home (manager for both Hamilton and Sheridan) in late March. At the time, Hamilton was obviously intoxicated and being helped to a waiting car by both Sheridan and Michael O'Connell (writer and creator of *Mabel's Unstable?*). Since then Hamilton has been seen partying many nights, usually in the company of his castmate from *Soldier Boy* Adam Kasen in either L.A. or Las Vegas. Hamilton was not seen entering the private party, but tweets from inside the restaurant confirmed he was in attendance. Sources inside the party report that Hamilton was quiet and reserved, sitting close to Sheridan or at her table and mingling with other party guests. While no pictures of the two have emerged, reports from inside confirm that they were holding hands and acting as though they were a couple. The two actors left in separate cars from the party.

Hamiltoned.com

Grace Sheridan and Jack Hamilton! Caught! Well, kind of . . . you be the judge. Hamiltoned.com has obtained exclusive pictures of the perhaps couple snuggling in a corner booth at a private wrap party for Sheridan's series *Mabel's Unstable?* in Los Feliz last night. While grainy at best, we have enhanced the upper-left corner of the shot, which clearly shows Jack's hand on Grace's shoulder! Whether you like them as a couple, we here at *Hamiltoned* thinks it's great that he's found someone he is clearly so comfortable with. Here's hoping being the older one in the relationship she can keep a tighter leash on him! Good luck, Grace! Now who here is kind of excited about this new series she is in?

JackedOff.com

Jack Hamilton breaks it off with Grace Sheridon't! In this exclusive shot from her stupid wrap party for her stupid new series about a washed-up beauty queen (beauty is questionable), the two were caught sitting in a corner booth. You totally can't see it, but if you blow it up (like we did here) you can see he is clearly pushing her away when she tries to sit too close to him. We have long suspected that she's totally in love with him (how can we blame her?) and using their mutual manager to try and get to him. Puhlease! Girl (Woman!), he was only there to help drum up publicity for your stupid new series! Which will tank. You heard it here first. Remember that! Even though we don't want him dating *anyone*, can he at least date someone his own age? And not spend any more nights with this old redheaded hag? Was that bitchy??? Leave your comments here . . .

ENT

Reshoots have been ordered for scenes from the new show *Mabel's Unstable?*, premiering this summer on cable channel Venue. Sources close to the show have reported that the reshoots are allegedly due to weight gain by the lead actress, Grace Sheridan. The thirty-three-year-old actress has struggled with her weight in the past, as shown in these pictures obtained exclusively by TMZ. Taken several years ago before she moved back to Los Angeles, Sheridan appears at least fifty pounds heavier and as a very different-looking woman than the one who's been spotted out and about with the hottest actor of his generation. Does Jack know his girlfriend is a former fatty?

While much slimmer now, Sheridan is at the top end size-wise for an actress. Her curves are well noted in these pictures from the *Time* premiere last fall. Sources from the studio have confirmed that Grace was asked to drop weight before shooting began on *Mabel's Unstable?*, and while she complied at the time, by the end of shooting her weight began to creep back up.

"She is significantly larger than the other actresses on the series, and she really worked hard to get her weight down. But it's noticeable now. The producers noticed, and now we're in reshoots. You figure it out," said an unnamed source from the studio.

CurvyGirlGuide.com

Responding to a story from *ENT* on May 25, we at CGG posted an article about Grace Sheridan and her "curvy girl" status. Grace Sheridan is five five, and as close as we can project, she is probably a size 6, maybe a size 8. With an athletically naturally curvy build, Sheridan *is* larger than most Hollywood actresses. Most the ladies in the fall TV lineup wear a size 2, if not a size 0. Most are petite, many barely over five two. Suddenly Grace Sheridan is a giant!

We asked our readers what they thought about the story *ENT* put out there, along with the pictures of an admittedly plus-size Sheridan taken several years ago. You responded *well.* We received more e-mails and more comments on this than any other story this year, *combined.*

We barely knew who Grace Sheridan was a few months ago. Now we know. And we like. And we will watch. And we will cheer. Thank *God* there's a woman on TV that's a size 8. Still a few sizes smaller than the average American woman, but we're not too picky. Unlike Hollywood. Go, Sheridan, go!

And while normally we would refrain from commenting on a celebrity's love life, if reports are in fact true and she is dating Super Sexy Scientist Guy? We. Are. Officially. A. Fan. Of them both.

StarTrackers

A heated exchange took place between director David Lancaster and actress Grace Sheridan on the set of the Venue show where the cast and crew were filming reshoots. The director reportedly brought everyone back to restage some scenes after producers were said to be "concerned about the look of the show" once Sheridan put back on the weight she was asked to lose. Arguing outside of her trailer about a wardrobe choice, Sheridan seemed angry and frustrated with the director's request that she "cover up" for one of the steamier scenes set to be redone. As a new actress to this industry, standing up to a director of Lancaster's caliber is almost unheard of. A wardrobe consultant on the series, Amber Bigalow, has stated, "I love Grace. I love working with her. It's great to dress a real woman for a change, instead of the impossibly thin actresses I normally work with. Nothing against other actresses, but she's a great change of pace from the bodies I normally see. She looks like me, at least she would if I worked my ass off!"

Since this story was first reported, opinions have run rampant on the Internet, both scorning and praising the new actress. Sheridan has not commented, but her manager, Holly Newman, did confirm that while the actress was frustrated that the story was being reported, she was pleased to see that it had opened up a dialogue.

The series is set to debut in two weeks, so let's hope the scenes are completed by then . . .

eleven

*U*nexpected. That was a word, a word that defined everything that had happened to my life in the last few months. Unexpected.

Unexpected: the idea that my age would continue to be reported whenever Jack and I were mentioned.

Unexpected: the notion that our relationship was routinely the lead story on most entertainment blogs and entertainment TV shows when it was a slow news day, and sometimes when it wasn't.

Unexpected: that a weight gain of sixteen pounds, only seven pounds more than when I was cast in this role, would yield the media coverage that it had and a possible endorsement deal from California Weight Loss Systems.

Unexpected: that my career as an actress, which I had dreamed of since I was a child, was now being overshadowed by a size 8 pair of jeans and my unconfirmed relationship with the Sexiest Man Alive.

Unexpected: Jack's behavior and constant partying, particularly when he was on location.

Unexpected: the small but increasingly vocal contingent of fans who had begun to support me, even though my show had yet to premiere and I had yet to comment on the recent reports of my fighting with my director.

Unexpected: the reports were true.

Unexpected: Grace fans?

Unexpected: the fact that I had yet to appear on television but was almost famous—almost famous for nothing other than who I was dating and what I weighed.

Expected: most of Jack's fans continued to hate me, writing post after post online about how thoroughly they despised me for getting to "fuck our Brit."

☆ ☆ ☆

I sat in Holly's office after debriefing the latest online diatribes and the best way to handle the press junket I had scheduled the next day. This time tomorrow I'd be in front of every reporter and online entertainment bunny, all of them knowing they were not allowed to ask me about Jack but still trying as many creative ways to trip me up and get me to make their interview stand out from the other one hundred I would sit through.

I'd gone from just wanting to come back to Los Angeles

and try to get a job singing a toothpaste jingle or watching a toddler dance around in the newest kind of diapers with a really big baby load to this: a series that was going to debut to high ratings even if the show was shit, which it was not, and a press junket where I would have to sit and watch as reporters showed pictures of me at my heaviest and tried to get me to comment on why weight was such an issue in Hollywood.

As Jim Morrison said, this is the strangest life I've ever known.

Holly had done her best to offer me different ways to answer certain questions, strategies to steer the conversation back to the work, the series, and away from my personal life. We knew there wouldn't be a way to completely avoid everything, but there were ways to try to keep some control.

"So, do you have a boyfriend?"

"I'm so busy, I barely even have time to get a pedicure!"

"Are you dating anyone?"

"I've been so focused on this exciting new chapter in my life, in my career, that I'm really just excited about the work right now, and what might happen next."

"So have you been to Santa Barbara recently?"

"It's beautiful, isn't it? One of my favorite places in Southern California."

"What does Jack Hamilton think about the pictures that have surfaced recently of you considerably heavier than you are now?"

Silence.

"You have to be faster than that, Grace. You were doing really well," Holly prodded gently.

"Can we take a break?" I sat back in my chair and leaned my head on my hand.

"Sure, but you ask for a break during this junket and you'll be a diva who is combative and unresponsive during interviews." She tossed me a bottle of water. I sipped and thought while she pecked on her laptop.

"Sixteen pounds! Sixteen pounds and they're ready to get a crane to lift me out of the house! I'm underweight for my height, for God's sake. It's ridiculous!" I snapped, flipping through the most recent pictures of me in another tabloid magazine. The weight I had lost came back on as soon as I stopped the cucumber-and-air diet. I kept up the additional workouts, trying like hell to get back to at least my starting point, but my body knew where it was healthiest, and it was where I was now. Me + 16. "I can't believe this is the story; this is how this new series is being framed. I feel terrible for the other actors."

"Don't. It's press. Not the kind of press I would have liked, but it's press. And it's starting to turn in our favor, so buck up, asshead."

"Were you always this tough?" I snorted into my water.

"Yep."

"Does Michael like it when you're tough?"

"Not answering that." She smiled, a blush creeping into her cheeks.

Michael and Holly had officially been an item for some time now. They went into it slow, starting with a few dates here and there, spending time together when they could, and it had developed into a relationship. I had never seen her happier. She'd always been someone who dished everything—and I mean everything—about the guys she was dating. This one she was keeping pretty close to the vest, which showed me how much she was truly in love. I still saw Michael on set all the time, and it was now clear to me (and everyone else who spent any time with him) that Michael thought the sun rose and set on Holly. Still, it was nice having my friend with me as I went through this. Both my friends, actually.

"While we're breaking, can we talk about Jack?" Holly asked.

"He's your client. You talk to him." I sighed, knowing where this was going.

Jack's behavior had gone from questionable to really questionable in the last few weeks. He'd been on location longer than initially planned, mostly due to constant script rewrites and weather delays. Which made for plenty of playtime in Las Vegas, only an hour away. We talked every day, e-mailed, texted, and he came home as often as he could. But there was beginning to be a breach between Home Jack and On-Location Jack. Guess which one I preferred?

At the beginning, even though I didn't like Adam, I brushed most of it off. Jack was young and having a good time, and as hard as he worked, he deserved to blow off a little steam. But we were getting into a gray area now, beyond steam blowing and into just plain blowing it. He was due back in town tonight, and I planned on seducing him, then trying, once again, to talk some sense into him.

Adam Kasen continued to be at the center of the trouble. I knew I didn't like him, didn't trust him, and my instincts had proven to be true. The earlier reports of his having cleaned up his act were bollocks, to use a phrase from Jack, and he was just as much of a party boy as he always was. Getting cast in the same movie as Jack was the best thing he could have done for his career, as he was all over the tabloids again and constantly linked with my boyfriend. My sweet, young, beautiful boyfriend who was smart but not infallible. Who was smart but impressionable.

And Adam was impressioning him right off a cliff and within reach of Dr. Drew, who was already commenting to anyone who would listen that Jack would be the next celebrity involved in a Lindsay Lohan–size scandal.

Not on my watch. I wasn't going to let it happen.

The problem was he'd grown increasingly belligerent whenever Holly tried to talk to him about his public persona—the way he was behaving with his fans and the choices he was making. He didn't want to hear it from her, and he barely wanted to hear it from me.

"He's coming home tonight. I'll talk to him," I told her. "But you're his manager. There's only so much I can do." I hoped I'd closed the subject before it really opened.

Jack felt terrible for what was being said about me in the press. He felt it was his fault—he felt directly responsible for the snipes and barbs being thrown at me by his fans.

"But if you weren't with me, this wouldn't be happening! Of course it's my fault!" he shouted on the phone one night after a particularly nasty blog post had surfaced. I tried not to look anymore, but someone had shown it to him on set, and he exploded when he saw the expletives used to describe my ass . . . in a pair of shorts I wore one day to the gym. They were on the short side.

"I don't see it that way, Jack. There's not much anyone could say about me that would make me rethink being with you. Unless Joey McIntyre got involved. I'd have to really think hard about that one," I joked, trying to sooth him.

"Who's that?" he asked, his voice still tense and angry.

"Duh, he's the youngest New Kid on the Block, and my personal favorite. I covet him."

"You covet him?"

"Yes. This would be a good time for us to make our lists. You know, celebrities we are allowed to run away with if the opportunity arises? However, in your case, you actually have access to any celebrity you want, so I may have to be the only one in our relationship to have this privilege."

"Now, now, wait a minute. I demand my list be in consideration," he challenged, his voice relaxing now into the Jack I knew, the one I loved.

"Wait, wait, you already have a list?"

"Of course! Catherine Zeta-Jones is on that list."

"Uh-oh, anyone else I need to know about?"

"Hmm, I have always had a soft spot for Jennifer Lopez. I'd be down with Jenny from the block."

"This list is fascinating. Anyone else?" I laughed, sinking back into my bed. We were catching up after playing phone tag for two days. I was exhausted after a long day of reshoots but wanting to connect with my Sweet Nuts.

"I think the only other one on the list might be Norah Jones: great voice, decent tits, lovely face."

"Okay, enough. Enough. No redheads on your list?"

"There's only one redhead for me, Crazy, you know that. You're my one and only ginger."

"Oh, that's sweet, love!" I sighed, pointing my toes as his words washed over me. I liked being his one and only.

"Who's on your list? Come on, give it up!"

"Well, Joey Joe you know about. That goes without saying. And I suppose Johnny Depp is always on the list, now and forever."

"He could be on my list, actually. He is quite dashing."

"And there's this new actor—he's been around only for a little while. Someone introduced me to his work last year. He's pretty dreamy."

"Last year. Is that so?"

"Yeah, he's an up-and-comer, one to watch for sure. I think his name's Jack Hammond or Hamfield. Something like that."

"I'll give you a hamfield!" We both laughed.

"Are you going out tonight?" I asked after we had quieted down.

"No, I'm too tired."

"I wish you were here, George."

"Me too, Gracie, me too."

"You still with me, asshead?" Holly's voice brought me back from my daydreams.

"What's that? Oh, yeah. What are we talking about?"

"What does Jack Hamilton think about the pictures that have surfaced recently of you considerably heavier than you are now?"

"I imagine he feels the same way any other actor would feel if pictures of him were sold to a tabloid to make a quick buck, to profit off of someone else's personal struggle. Was I heavier than I am now at one point? Yep, and while for me personally I made a choice to live a healthier lifestyle, it doesn't take away from the fact that women in this industry—and in society for that matter—are held to a standard that men are not. So show that picture as often as you need to. That was me then, and this is me now. And I'm okay with it," I finished, my voice growing stronger at the end. I realized I wasn't just shoveling bullshit to a reporter. I believed everything I'd just said. And I was going to tell anyone who asked me what I really thought. I glanced at Holly, waiting for her reaction.

"Okay, fruitcake, I think we're done here. Let's go talk Michael into making us dirty martinis and bringing them to us in my hot tub." She snapped her planner closed and winked at me. Press junket, here we come.

Later that night, I was home waiting for Jack. He was actually driving himself back from the desert for a change. He liked the drive. He said he liked the peacefulness he derived from speeding through the desert at night. But he was more than two hours late, and as I cleaned the sink for the tenth time, I considered calling him again. Then I saw his headlights pull into the driveway.

We both had new cars, my little convertible I traded in on a large Escalade that I felt safer in when driving. And Jack now had his own convertible safely tucked away in a private garage in the Valley. He now drove a much less conspicuous but still tricked-out Tahoe when he was out and about without Bryan.

I smoothed my shirt as I walked to the front door, nervous energy charging through me. I hadn't seen him since the wrap party for my show, and I was anxious to see him, hold him.

I opened the door, and there he was. Hair starting to grow out a bit and looking messy, even though it couldn't be more than a half inch long. Circles, huge bruised-looking circles under his eyes. He looked exhausted, and even the way he was walking seemed tired, plodding across the pavement with his duffel bag and guitar. I was glad to see he still had it with him. He seemed to have lost some interest in playing over the last few months. His smile, though, that still belonged to me, and it greeted me twenty feet from our front door. He was home.

"Hey."

"Hey, yourself," he replied, walking past me inside the door, dropping his belongings and catching me into a close embrace. I wrapped my arms around him, sighing as I breathed in his scent, accented by sun and sage from the desert he'd been living in. His body was lean and hard against my own. He had lost some weight while he was shooting, and he seemed to be all angles and limbs, hugging me tight.

We held each other in front of the front door, kissing and connecting, holding and remembering. I pulled back to look at him, resting my forehead against his as he leaned down.

"I'm so glad you're home."

"Me too, love."

"Are you hungry?"

"I'm too tired to know." He laughed ruefully, looking down the hall toward our bedroom.

"How about you take a nice, hot shower, and I'll heat something up for you. How does that sound?"

"Can you bring it to me in that red silky thing you wear for me sometimes?" he asked, one eyebrow raising.

"I thought you were tired?" I pushed back against his chest as he nuzzled into my hair.

"I'm never too tired for that, Crazy." He pulled me close again and lifted me a few inches off the ground, swinging my legs around in a circle.

"Okay, you go shower. I'll make you something to eat,

then I'll play dress up for you. How does that sound?" I
teased, removing myself from his arms and starting for
the kitchen. I turned to see him watching me walk away.
Grinning big was his only answer as he headed the opposite
way. I heard the shower turn on, and I smiled to myself as I
fixed him a snack.

A little of this, a little of that, and then I slipped into his
favorite red negligee, lacy and see-through in all the right
places. I waited a few moments after I heard the shower
turn off, then headed into the bedroom with a tray piled
high with all of his favorites.

There, in our bed, Jack lay sideways, still in his towel,
sound asleep. I set the tray down and sat next to him on the
bed, trying to rouse him enough to have him turn the other
way. He sighed in his sleep, turning on his side, reaching
out for me and placing his head in my lap. With a small sigh
escaping, he was back to sleep almost immediately.

I sat in my lace and peekaboo, running my fingertips
across his face and down along his neck, through the
closely cropped hair and across his eyelids.

My star needed some sleep.

☆ ☆ ☆

A pair of solid hands pulled me backward, sliding me
against a warm body. I shuddered a bit, sleep pushing from
my eyes as I realized I was in our bed, with my Jack. My
star was no longer sleeping. My star was on the prowl.

"Jack, you should sleep," I protested, rolling over and raising up on one elbow, peering down at him. He ran his arm from my knee to my thigh, up and over my backside, plucking at the red lace he loved so. His hand was warm, and so was his smile.

"I slept," he whispered,

"You still look tired." I caught his roving hand and brought it to my lips for a kiss.

"What a nice thing to say. Do I get five orgasms now?"

"Funny." I chuckled, relaxing into his side and tucking in, resting my head on his shoulder. I sighed, still sleepy but craving his skin.

"I could probably handle at least one, then a snack?" He pressed his lips against my forehead. I threw one leg over, sat up above him, and smiled.

"I can handle that." I went to work.

☆ ☆ ☆

A while later, I lay in our bed, snuggled on Jack. I wrapped around him like a blanket, still perched on top of him, legs and arms around him, my head tucked into his shoulder. His hands traced a path from my thigh to my backside, up to my shoulders, then pressed into each dent in my spine. They were hands no longer frantic and frenzied, now quiet and soothing.

"I missed you, Crazy," he breathed into my hair, and I sighed, content with his hands on me.

"You have no idea," I answered, kissing his ear, tickling with my lips until he laughed.

"How are things here going?" he asked, bringing his hands up to move my hair away from my face, his green eyes piercing even in the moonlight.

"Good. Busy, but good."

"No, I mean, how are you doing with everything? You ready for tomorrow?"

"The junket?"

"The junket. You ready for that?" He sat up underneath me, my legs automatically going around his waist. He sat cross-legged with me on his lap, his strong hands dipping down to my backside and pulling me closer.

"I think so. I mean, Holly and I prepped and went over the likely questions, when to dodge and when to answer." I nodded, feeling my tummy clench a little at the thought of facing the firing squad in less than twelve hours.

"I hear what you're saying, but how are you really feeling?" he prodded, his hands moving under the red lace to be closer to me.

"I'm scared to death," I admitted, throwing my arms around his neck and clutching him close. He chuckled into my hair, holding me tight.

"I know, sweet girl." He got it.

"It just makes no sense. I haven't even done anything yet, and they all want to know how I feel about being a fat actress in Hollywood, and how you're dealing with my weight gain. How absurd! This makes no sense!" I spilled my secrets to the back of his head.

"None of it makes any sense. The sooner you get that, the easier it'll be," he said, pulling back just enough to kiss me soundly on the forehead.

"How are you dealing with Grace's recent weight gain, Mr. Hamilton?" I asked, thrusting my thumb microphone into his face.

"Yes, well, it's pretty tough to take. I suppose really the only thing to do is just grab a handful and go to town," he answered deadpan, followed quickly by him actually grabbing a handful.

We wrestled on the bed, slapping and tickling. We finally came to rest somewhere near the headboard, Jack pinning me down and playing with my lace once more.

"You're going to be great. You know that, right?" he said, breathing hard from our playful fighting. "Just be yourself. That's who I love. They'll love her too."

"And when they ask me about dating you?"

"Tell them yes, tell them no, tell them to bugger off. I'm not the story. You're the story. So tell it your own way, Nuts Girl." He gave my bottom a slap. "Now where's that snack? I'm starving."

After a few minutes, I perched cross-legged in our bed and watched Jack slurp leftover sesame noodles and crunch through the egg rolls I had reheated for him. Naked, sheet tucked around his middle, he ate everything with gusto, telling me about the rest of the shoot and how much he'd enjoyed working on this project.

"I mean, what other job in the world would I, some wanker from London, get to fire off rounds from big giant guns and drive a tank—a sodding tank! Are there any more egg rolls?"

I chuckled as I went to the kitchen. It always made me laugh how the more excited he was about something, the thicker the accent got.

I set about heating up the rest of the egg rolls, toying with the idea of slicing up some fruit for him as well, when I heard his phone go off. It was on the counter. And he was in the other room. It was Adam calling. I debated whether I should take it to him or throw it out the window, but then I remembered that the windows were closed, and I didn't want to replace anything right now, and that the mature thing to do would be to take the phone to Jack.

You wanted to talk to him about this tonight anyway. Now's your chance . . .

I realize that, but things were going so well.

Give him the phone, heat up his egg rolls, and then have your Come to Jesus conversation.

Yeah, yeah, yeah.

I took him the phone, throwing it maybe a little harder than I would have normally. He was still in bed, sheet pulled down low on his hips as he reclined against the headboard.

"Phone call," I said, leaving the bedroom as he answered it. I finished the reheating, then headed back in, just as he was finishing up his call.

"Right then, tomorrow. Sure thing. Yep, 'bye." He hung up and looked hungrily at the plate I brought him. He reached for it, but I held it just out of his reach.

"What's up, love?" he asked, a puzzled grin making its way across his face.

"We're going to talk, and then you will get your egg rolls. Fair enough?" I sat at the end of the bed, curling my legs underneath me.

I was still in my red negligee, and I realized this conversation was entirely too serious for the amount of peekaboo I was still in. A look of frustration crossed his face, one I'd seen lately when he was confronted with photographers but rarely directed toward me. He sighed, but sat back against the headboard.

"Okay, so I'm not really sure how to say this, since you've been doing this longer than I have, certainly, and you're an adult and all, and really you're—"

"Say what you want to say, Grace," he said quietly.

"I don't like the path you're on. It worries me, it worries your friends, and it's worrying Holly."

"Is this coming from you or from her?"

"Me. Both. Me. Jack, I know I've said this a lot lately, but I'm worried about you. I've never seen you like this with your fans. You've been downright rude a few times. That's not like you. And you know how I feel about Adam."

"That's what this is about, isn't it?"

"It's part of it, yes. He's just . . . he's not good for you. You're a different person when he's around."

"Grace, I can't go anywhere in public without either a bodyguard or a driver hardly at all anymore. My girlfriend is attacked for dating me, even though the question of whether we're really dating can't even be answered because some focus group somewhere says it would be bad for my career to be seen as unavailable right now. I can't go to a restaurant without someone tweeting it and fifty people showing up within twenty minutes, and if I don't feel like signing autographs one night because I'm tired as fuck, then I'm an asshole who doesn't care about his fans. I blow off a little steam, and everyone is concerned. To use one of your American phrases, everyone needs to just chill out a bit. Everything is fine. Are we done?" He got out of bed and headed over to the chair where his clothes were.

"Wait a minute. Where are you going?"

"For a drive. I need to get out of here for a bit."

"But you just got home! Jack, I need to be able to talk to you about this stuff, okay? I need to know that when you're gone, when you're on location, that you're okay. You can't blame me for being concerned." I stood in front of him as he stuffed his legs into his jeans and pulled on his shirt.

"You talked; I listened. I hope you heard what I said too. There's nothing to be worried about, okay?" He planted a kiss on my forehead absently on his way out of the bedroom. I followed him, my mind whirling at how quickly this conversation had turned.

"Wait, Jack, what's happening here? Are you really leaving?"

"Just for a bit. I'll be back soon. It's fine, Grace. We're fine. I know what you're saying, and I appreciate your concern. I really do."

His eyes were hidden from me as he pulled on a jacket and headed out into the night. I stood in the doorway, still in my red lace, shivering in the night air.

"Tell Holly the next time she goes through you to get to me, we're going to have a real problem," he said, sliding into his car.

I watched him go, then went back inside. I turned out all the lights, except for the one in the entryway, then padded back to our room. I left the red lace on the floor of the bathroom, slipped into one of his T-shirts, and got into bed. Stunned, I lay on my pillow, more worried than I'd been in a long time.

☆　☆　☆

Sometime in the early-morning light, Jack came home. He came in, I heard him undress, and I felt him climb into bed.

Come over here. Please, come over here, I silently begged, needing to feel his arms around me. After what felt like an eternity smashed into twenty seconds, he wriggled over to my side of the bed, slipping his arms around and under me, hands surrounding my breasts and laying his head on my pillow. I breathed out, letting him hold me.

"I love you so much, Jack," I said quietly.

"I know," he whispered back, kissing the side of my neck and going to sleep.

My alarm, set to wake me up for my first day of press interviews, went off thirty-seven minutes later. I looked like hell.

twelve

*T*he press junket was tough. I'll admit, I didn't expect it to be so hard. Was I digging ditches? Nope. Answering phones in a call center somewhere for ten hours in a row? Uh-uh. Was this a hard job? Not in the traditional sense, nope. No way. Was that press junket hard? Hard as a motherfucker.

I'll never watch a celebrity interview the same way. Even though I had prepared for this—I knew what to expect, I felt ready to go—it was hard. You sit in a hotel room, with the windows blocked out behind you, publicity posters sitting all around, and every ten minutes another journalist comes in and asks you essentially the same questions the last thirteen did. And you try to answer them differently but not stray too far from the "script." You smile and nod and thank them when they tell you they loved what they've seen of the series so far, and you wonder if they are really being truthful.

And when they get clever, when they start asking questions and you know exactly where they're trying to lead you to (Hamiltontown) you smile and nod again, and then evade. Because as much as they would like you to believe they're in charge of this interview, it's up to you to keep it on the material that you feel comfortable with.

I'd done well. I was pretty impressed at how I'd handled things. Holly was there. She had conversations with each producer ahead of time, and then again with each interviewer before we began to make sure they stayed on topic and only on preapproved subjects: the series, my costars, my recent rise to fame, adjusting to life in the limelight. They were each allowed to ask one question about my weight—something I had initially been against but was warming up to.

Was my body a little out of control right now? I couldn't honestly say yes, because while I had abandoned the cucumber-and-air idiocy, I was eating and exercising with the same zeal I had been for the last few years.

I shook my head to clear it, getting ready for the last interview. A beautiful blonde from *ENT* breezed into the room, shaking hands with me and smiling her perfect teeth at the camera as they miked her. Holly reminded her once more what she could and couldn't ask, and she smiled again. The camera light went on, and we made nice for a few moments—about the series, my costars, the usual. I stifled a yawn as I went through the motions, thinking about getting a dirty martini as soon as this was all over, wondering if I could talk Holly into joining me. I snorted a little at the thought of her turning down a cocktail, losing my focus, and that's when the deer-in-headlights happened.

"I'm sorry, what?"

"I said, what do you think about the pictures that we released just this afternoon?"

"Pictures? Sorry, I've been inside all day. What pictures are you talking about?" I asked, my eyes fluttering to Holly, who shrugged her shoulders, clearly not knowing what was going on either.

"Oh, of course. You probably haven't seen them yet, have you? Here, I have some copies with me," she purred, handing me a stack of prints. Before they were even in my hand, I could see they were of Jack. And a girl. A girl wearing not a lot of clothing. And by *not a lot* I mean panties and that was it. They were kissing, his hands in her hair and her hands on his chest. Passionate. Intense. Shot after shot of his mouth on hers, on her neck, on her—

I thrust them back at her, my hands shaking. Holly was about ready to climb out of her skin, pacing in a room that was too small for pacing.

"How do these pictures make you feel, Grace? I mean, come on, isn't it about time you two admit your relationship? Or is it not cheating if you've never really said you were an item?"

I stared at her. I was rattled, totally rattled.

"Is this because of the weight gain? Men can be so funny about that, can't they?" she asked, her face painted with fake concern.

"My weight gain?"

"Oh, well sure. It can't be a coincidence that just as you began to put on weight, sorry, *put back on*, that's when Jack started stepping out all over town? Care to comment?"

Holly stepped between us. "That's it. This interview is over," she snapped, shielding me from the camera. "You knew what was off-limits."

"Oh, please, Holly, it's what we all want to know, but no one had the guts to ask. This is news. I have an obligation to my audience to—"

"Get over yourself, Barbie. We're through. Grace, let's go."

She turned to me, pulling me out of the chair and walking me from the room, keeping herself between me and the camera the entire time. I was still frozen, shocked but furious with myself for not being able to respond. How had this happened? And what were those pictures? I turned back into the room, looking again at the stack of pictures on the table, the camera following me as I was ushered away, the simpering look on the interviewer's face as she knew she'd gotten me.

Damn . . . this town was vicious.

The *redhead* Plays Her Hand

☆ ☆ ☆

Once Holly got me into the other room, she went back in. I could hear her yelling. She was on a tear, and I was very glad to not be on the receiving end of it. That reporter wouldn't get another interview for years with me, or Jack, or any of Holly's clientele. I rubbed my eyes and kicked off my heels, trying to center and breathe and come to terms with what I had just seen.

Check yourself here. We don't know what we just saw.

We saw Jack with his hands on another woman. That's what we saw.

I'd like another look at those . . .

Just as I was thinking about heading back in to get the pictures, Holly burst through the door, cheeks flushed red and her don't-fuck-with-me face on. She had the pictures in her hand, and she was slapping on her reading glasses, which she didn't officially have.

"Barbie is gone. You might see her doing the weather in some little town in Oregon, but she's not working here again." Holly placed the pictures on the table in front of us. "I wanted another look at these."

"Oh, Christ, I want to look, but I don't want to look. Does that make sense?"

"Of course it does, fruitcake. Let's not drop our teeth here. Let me just take a look . . . Mmm-hmm," she said under her breath, holding one up to the light. There he was: Jack, in all his glory. The shaggy curls were gone, re-placed by his buzz cut. Whatever this was, it was recent. I gasped as I took in the images again, his hands all over this woman. Whoever she was, they were passionate. I felt my heart drop, could he have really . . . Jesus, could he?

"Wait a minute! Christ on a crutch, this is from his movie! Oh, I could *throttle* that Barbie!" Holly cried, thrusting the pictures back to me. "This is from his new movie. That's the girl they've been shooting with. She's an actress. You can even see the crew off to the side if you squint. What a bitch!"

I examined the pictures, my heart still pounding but beginning to regulate a bit.

"Grace, she did this just to throw you." Holly scrolled through her phone. "Damn those vultures. They've had this up all day too, claiming he's having a fling with a costar."

She handed me the phone. I snatched it to look for myself. With a headline made to make people stop and read, the article had zero facts and tons of hot pics, which made it the most clicked-on story of the day. And, of course, there was me at my heaviest, meant to draw a contrast between who I was and who Jack should be dating now.

"Son of a bitch," I seethed, scrambling for my own phone. Texts had been pouring in from Jack all day.

Crazy—call me before you open any emails today . . .

Hey, make sure you call me when you get a break, ok?

Right then. You've either seen them and are laughing at how low these prats will sink, or you've seen them and

are pissed, which I can't blame you for. Please call me
as soon as you can . . .

As I was reading the last of the texts, he called. I answered.

"Grace?"

"Yep."

"You saw them."

"Yep."

"Fucking ridiculous. Is Holly with you?"

"Yep."

"You tell her next time she needs to be out in front of
something like this. I'm bloody well tired of this."

"Yep." I sighed tiredly, the weight of the day beginning
to weigh on me.

"Is that all you're going say?"

"I'll be home soon, Jack," I replied, hanging up.

This wasn't his fault, not by a long shot. But the
roller-coaster of emotions had just bottomed out, and I was
exhausted. I looked at Holly, who was furiously typing on
her phone.

"We're done for the day, right?"

"Yep," she answered with a rueful grin. I hugged her,
grabbed my bag, and headed out to my car. Where I turned
the music up as loud as it would go and took the long way
home.

This is the life you chose . . .

Yep.

I pulled into my drive and noticed Jack's car was home. I sat in my front seat for a moment, collecting myself. This day had been a mix of extreme highs and lows. Highs being holding my own throughout a press junket that could have pulled me under a wave of bullshit. Once you got past the questions you knew they had to ask, some of the reporters actually gave me some great feedback about the show. Not only had they watched it, they enjoyed it. It was a heady thing, knowing that people were seeing your work and getting something out of it. Lows being obvious, and something I wanted to forget about. But I couldn't, that was the old Grace. The sweep everything under the carpet, lock-it-up-in-the-Drawer Grace. That's where I was tempted to send this entire debacle with Jack and the pictures. But nope. I was an adult now, or at least I was playing one on TV. The truth was, I wasn't mad about the pictures—at least not mad at Jack. How could I be? He was just as much a target here as I was. As I engaged in my front-seat contemplation, I saw the curtains flutter a bit in the front window, the dining room. Squinting, I could make out the shape of Jack moving around, lighting candles.

Interesting. What was he up to? With a smile, I got out of the car and let myself in the front door, just catching sight of him heading back into the kitchen. Kicking off my heels and setting down my bag, I glanced into the dining room. The table was set, candles were lit, flowers were arranged. Rounding the corner, I spied him in front of the stove, every burner going, every pot and pan in California either full of something or burned in the sink. Pasta crunched underfoot, alerting him to my presence. As he spun around, I laughed out loud when I saw the state of his shirt, which was covered in sauce.

"What are you doing?" I laughed as he slammed the lid back down on something that spittered and sputtered on the burner.

"Dammit, I wanted to have everything done when you got home." He grabbed a spoon and flicked tomato something or other all over the backsplash. Which is what a backsplash is for, I suppose . . .

"What's all this, George?" I asked, coming to rest on a high stool out of the line of fire.

"I just wanted to make you dinner, something nice. Turns out cooking is really bloody hard!" He struggled with a colander. The colander was winning. "I'd kiss you but I'm dirty."

"I like you dirty. I'll risk it."

He smiled, but kept his eyes on the colander and the pasta that was now escaping. "I felt terrible about today. I just wanted, I wanted to do something that could— Oh, damn this linguine," he mumbled.

"Can I help you? Please?" I slipped down off the stool and walked to him. Quietly I finished draining the pasta, leaving it in the colander.

He stood next to me, leaning over the sink, face troubled. "I just hate that this happened, that they would use me to go after you in this way." He sighed.

"I know," I answered, leaning into his side. He smelled like garlic. He smelled wonderful.

"I wish I could tell you this kind of thing won't happen again, but it will, Grace."

"I know."

"It's gonna get worse."

"I know." I sighed into his shoulder. "But the good outweighs the bad."

"Does it?"

"Of course it does. Now feed me this wonderful dinner."

I went back to my perch as he finished. I could have helped more, but I wanted to let him do this for me. Over dinner we talked about some of the better parts of the day, and we went about the business of getting past this. Past the bullshit. Past the part where someone, several someones actually, went out of their way to try to hurt both of us. We both sighed into our linguine several times.

thirteen

$\mathcal{I}$ loved spending quality time with my new trainer, Megan.

"As far as I can tell, you were doing great, Grace, and then you crashed your system with that stupid diet. You worked out too much, you weren't eating enough, and your body responded by holding on to everything once you started eating again. It'll take some time, but we can get a little of this off, although you're pretty much where your body wants you to be."

"My body wants me to be high in the sky, twisted like a pretzel?"

"In the meantime, we work on your inner strength." She laughed, ignoring my feeble joke, as she downward dogged me on the balcony. Megan was an actual exercise physiologist, with a degree and zero interest in being an actor.

She had her own workout facility high above the city in the Wilshire corridor. She was organic, honest, and a breath of fresh air. Literally, up this high, you could smell the ocean above the smog. I looked forward to these workouts.

"I just want to get back to where I was, that's all." I sighed through my legs as she had me switch poses.

"I'd like you to be even better than you were before." She winked. "What does your boyfriend think about everything?"

"Please. He thinks the more for him to love, the better." I snorted, her hands on my hips as she coaxed me into another shape. And it was true. Jack loved me for who I was, hips and all. Just wish the press did. After Holly put out a statement ridiculing the website that posted the pictures of Jack and his costar, the press pounced on me. And again, every time they showed Jack with this younger actress, they did a side by side of me. Always at a weird angle; always with me looking bigger than I was. For God's sake, I was a size 8! But that was a tank in Hollywood, apparently, and no one was going to let me forget it.

But in the other camp, a smaller but quite vocal group of women online were expressing their support. More than one blogger had written about the fuss being made about my weight, increasing the dialogue about women on film and TV and the thin-thin-thin image we were all supposed to mold ourselves into. Not gonna lie, those bloggers made it easier for me to grin and bear this idiocy.

Speaking of grinning and bearing it . . .

"Okay, uncle! Uncle, I give!" I collapsed to the mat and breathed heavily after the last set of crunches were finished. Megan laughed and threw me a bottle of water, which I took gratefully. Drinking it down, I stared out at Los Angeles. From this high up, the palm trees swayed in the breeze, the glitter from a hundred Bentleys making the street below sparkle. What a town. Absently I rubbed my necklace from Jack.

His public.

His public continued to rage about me, online at least. The pictures of him and his new costar had brought another round of sniping from his biggest online fan clubs. He was never really dating me—I was a cougar who was fame hungry—it was exhausting. What was I to do? Did I admit that I hated what the press was saying about me? Did I comment? Did I shy away? Did I cower in the corner, or did I come out swinging, teeth bared and claws out like a *cougar*?

And in addition to all this bullshit going on about the size of my ass and whether I was sleeping with Sexy Scientist Guy, I had the biggest thing ever in my professional career going on. Which, by the way, was being overshadowed by this inane chatter. Would be nice if that could be the focus.

Glad to see we are getting back on track here . . .

My new show was set to premiere next week, and there were more interviews to go to, radio shows to call in to, hoops to jump through, and talk show hosts to charm. And

I was supposed to be focusing on potted plants and their place in my natural world?

Pick your path. You don't get to decide how the public reacts. You only get to decide how you react.

True, very true.

Victim? Warrior? Pick. Your. Path.

As I was contemplating, I saw a woman walk nervously into the gym, peering through the window. Pretty. Plump. Her eyes darting everywhere, she tensed when she saw me watching her. Her hands tugged at her T-shirt, pulling it down a bit, trying to cover up probably without even knowing it. I smiled at her, and she seemed to relax, but only a bit. Megan spied her through the window and waved her out.

"Hey, Chelsea, I've gotta take a quick call," Megan told her. "Go ahead and start stretching out for a few, and then we'll get started, okay?" She grabbed her phone and ducked back inside. Chelsea looked at me, then did a double take.

"Um, are you Grace Sheridan?"

"Have we met before?" I asked, walking over after picking up my bag.

She smiled shyly at me, again picking at her shirt and tugging it down a bit. "Well, um, I'm a big fan of Jack Hamilton." She blushed furiously. "And, well, you know, you're kind of all over the Internet lately." She blushed even more.

"Ah, well, yes. That's true." I chuckled. "And you're correct. I'm Grace." I extended my hand to her.

She shook it with a grin. "I'm Chelsea. Oh my God, I can't believe it! I've been seeing commercials for your new show. I can't wait!"

"Really? Wow, that's great. You'll have to let me know what you think after next week."

"I gotta tell you, at first I only knew who you were because of, well, your pictures with Jack. And you know, at first, of course, I was jealous because, well, my God, he's gorgeous!"

She giggled, becoming more animated as she talked. I laughed with her, nodding my head. He *was* gorgeous.

"But then, when the press started picking on you? Dammit, that pissed me off! And I thought, well, shit, if anyone is gonna be with that beautiful man, I like the idea that it's someone like you. Does that make sense? Sorry, I know I'm babbling, but I have to know, are you two dating? Please tell me yes," she finally ended, breathing heavily. Her eyes were dancing, her cheeks still pink.

I took a breath on my own. "If I say yes, are you going straight to TMZ?" I winked.

"Fuck no!" she exclaimed, then slapped her hand over her mouth. "I mean . . . actually, I do mean fuck no!"

"Then fuck yes, we're dating," I answered, and she squealed.

I threw my head back and laughed, louder than I had in a while. As we laughed, Megan came sauntering back outside, looking like a very pretty drill sergeant.

"Grace? You still here? Usually my clients can't wait to get out of here when I'm done with them. Chelsea, get your ass over on that mat and strike a mean warrior pose!"

Warrior?

Fuck yes. I spun toward Megan.

"Megan, what if I told you I never wanted to weigh myself again. How would you feel about that?"

"Awesome."

"And if I said I didn't care what I weighed, as long as I was strong?"

"Awesome."

"Fantastic. Thanks, Megan. Nice to meet you!" I called over to Chelsea, who was indeed striking a mean-ass warrior pose.

"You too, Grace! And tell Jack I said hi!" She giggled, her warrior becoming a little unbalanced as Megan pushed me to the door.

"Go away now, Grace. Can't have you distracting my clients." She shook her head.

"I'm going, I'm going. But seriously, I'm not weighing myself anymore," I told her.

"Good girl." She winked.

I left feeling lighter than I had in weeks.

fourteen

LateNightRecap.com

Grace Sheridan was the toast of late-night this week, with appearances on Jay Leno, David Letterman, and Jimmy Fallon. While all three hosts tried to get her to comment on the status of her relationship with alleged boyfriend Jack Hamilton, Grace deftly kept the conversation focused on her career and her new show, *Mable Unstable?*, set to premiere in just two days. But the other hot topic that has dogged her lately, her weight, was not off-limits at all. In fact, Grace spoke candidly to Jimmy Fallon when he asked about her weight and what being asked to lose weight for this role had done to her:

"Well, Jimmy. Can I call you Jimmy?"

"It is my name."

"Can I just tell you—before we talk about my giant ass—how big of a crush I have on you? Seriously, big crush, Jimmy."

"Well. Now I'm blushing."

"Then this would be a good time to talk about my giant ass, right? Since you're already blushing?"

"It seems like a good time. But really, how in the world did this story get started? And I gotta tell you, for all the fellas in the audience, I'm just gonna say, it's not giant, but you do have one sweet ass."

(Audience applauding)

"Thanks, boys! I guess it started when I was cast in *Mable Unstable?* I'm new to this industry. Let's not pretend, okay? And I know it's just part of it, losing weight or gaining weight for a role. Makes sense, right? But then my body figured out it was exactly where it was supposed to be! And I realized I was not willing to risk my health, especially when in the real world outside of Hollywood, no one would ever call me fat! So this is me, curves and all."

"Thank God for curves. That's all I can say."

"Aw, thanks, Jimmy."

"And now I'm blushing again . . ."

Grace told similar stories on *Late Show* and *The Tonight Show*, responding to her critics with an honest assessment of her body and choice words about what Hollywood expects from women. Looks like Grace Sheridan isn't playing . . .

CelebTracker.com

Grace Sheridan continues to dominate the headlines this week as she's crossed the country twice to promote her new show premiering tomorrow on Venue. Appearing with the ladies on *The View*, she took on her critics once more, answering questions about the pictures that have surfaced of her prior to her return to acting, when she was substantially heavier.

"That was me. Would I have preferred that those pictures of me when I was not in a great place in my life never surfaced? Of course. But I have to own that part of my life too. I was out of control, unhappy, and feeling buried by a situation that was my own creation. I struggled with my weight the way so many women in this country do, and I still struggle with it. But for me, being healthy was a choice I made for myself, to be strong and to be aware of the decisions I made on a daily basis, so I could be the kind of person I wanted to be."

When asked about whether she is dating Jack Hamilton, Sheridan once again dodged the question, stating only, "He's pretty cute, isn't he?"

TMZ

A private screening for *Mabel's Unstable?* was arranged tonight at Sam's, a restaurant in Hollywood, with the entire cast in attendance, including Grace Sheridan and

Jack Hamilton. For a couple who isn't dating, they sure show up at the same place an awful lot, don't they? They arrived separately. Grace showed up with her manager, Holly Newman, and the creator of the new show, Michael O'Connell. Jack arrived much later with bad boy Adam Kasen in tow. Adam stopped outside to sign autographs for a few minutes, rolling his eyes when asked about whether he was causing friction between Jack and Grace. "Are they dating?" he asked the crowd, then smirked and disappeared inside.

I settled back in my chair, tummy fluttering in anticipation. All night I had moved from table to table, cluster to cluster of people, chatting, talking—I suppose you could even say schmoozing. The cast and crew, their families and friends and plus ones, everyone was here to watch the first episode of *Mabel's Unstable?* and get their first glimpse at the new show. Michael and I worked the room together for a bit, explaining how we'd known each other since college and talking about the development of the characters as they took life in New York last year. He was so very proud, and he even strutted a bit as the early praise was heaped on about the world he'd created. Holly worked the room as well, all business hidden behind a perfect smile.

I'd watched as Michael's eyes sought hers across the crowd, her wink making him stutter a bit while he talked to a film producer who had bankrolled most of the movies made in the nineties and now looking for a new project to sink his dough into. I'd left Michael's side to grab a quick drink and take another look for the Brit.

He was late. And not just a little late. We'd lost touch around lunchtime. He'd had a meeting, and I was occupied with radio interviews all day. We'd agreed to arrive separately, but now that I was sitting in my seat, the show, *my* show, about to start, I wanted him there. I was nervous, more nervous than I ever thought I'd be, and I needed his hand to hold. In the dark, I could hold his hand and not worry about cameras or roving eyes or gossiping mouths. I could watch myself on-screen, and even though I'd flinch and blush as I watched, my hand would be in his, and I'd enjoy the moment.

But now, with the lights flashing to let everyone know to take their seats, he was still not here. Holly and Michael slid into their seats, leaving the space next to me open. Holly raised her eyebrows in question, and I shrugged. I checked my phone again, still nothing. David Lancaster stood up to make a quick speech, thanking everyone for coming, and then with light applause, the lights went out. As the opening credits began to roll, I closed my eyes and took a breath. As I exhaled, I felt someone slide into the seat next to me, and I opened my eyes. Jack.

Jack. Smelling like alcohol and slouching down into his chair. Grabbing at my hand he leaned in and whispered "Sorry I'm late, Crazy. Traffic was hell. We got stuck on the 405."

"Who is we?" I whispered back as his whiskey breath fanned over me. A few seats down I could see Holly staring over, and I waved her away.

"Adam. He wanted to come along and support my girl. He still feels really bad about everything."

"He feels bad? I can't believe—"

"Shh, let's talk about it later. It's starting."

He clutched my hand close as images began to appear on the screen. Suddenly there I was, thirty feet tall with a potted plant. People began to cheer all around me.

"Well, look at you." He grinned, and just like that, I forgot all about Adam. Having never worked in television before, I'd never been a part of taping something you wouldn't see for weeks and weeks, and then you still never know what you'll end up with. Sure, I'd seen the dailies. But you never know which cut they'll use, how they'll edit it together, and how much music can shape a scene. And now, watching the finished project, I was in awe of the work that had gone into it. I was nervous, sure, but I enjoyed the shit out of it. I laughed. I hid my face in Jack's shoulder during the sex scene. I rolled my eyes every time I saw myself carrying a book . . . but I was proud.

There was a moment, sitting there in the dark and watching myself on-screen, where I realized I had come full circle. I had truly changed my life, fulfilled a dream I'd had since as early as I could remember, and I was now making a living as an actress. I was getting paid to sing and act and pretend to be someone else, and it was something

I don't think I will ever be able to adequately describe. I'd sat in a theater similar to this one not very long ago, watching actors onstage and sobbing because I was no longer a part of that world. And here I was, inside a moment with a dramatically different outcome.

A tear trickled down my cheek at the closing credits, and I was so full of happiness I could burst. As the lights came up, Jack beamed at me as he stood. All around, people stood and applauded as I smiled. I clapped my hands off when Michael was pushed forward for his standing ovation and watched as Holly planted a big, giant, sloppy kiss on his mouth in front of everyone. As the crowd began to disperse, I looked at Jack, who was watching Michael and Holly.

His eyes met mine, and they were a bit sad. They were also bloodshot. I saw Adam coming down the aisle toward us, and I turned back to Jack.

"Why were you late, Jack?"

"I told you, traffic," he said, eyes now on the floor.

Adam made his way over, slapping Jack on the back and grinning at me. "Grace! Show was great. I really enjoyed what you did up there," he exclaimed, turning toward the crowd and nodding a little. As I watched, he positioned himself between Jack and me just as a woman with a camera phone snapped a shot: Adam smiling, Jack sullen, and me ready to spit nails.

"Can I talk to you, please?" I pulled on Jack's sleeves as soon as I knew the camera was put away.

"Oooh, here we go." Adam laughed, holding up his hands in mock surrender as I led Jack to a quiet corner.

"What the hell, Jack? I can't believe you brought him here. What were you thinking?"

"I'm sorry. I was trying to get away, and he insisted on coming. He wanted to be here. I told you he feels really bad about the way things have been with you two and—"

"He should feel bad, but that's not why—"

"When I realized how late it had gotten, it was just easier to bring him along. Christ, I didn't mean to be so late, but if he didn't come with me, then I—"

"You would bring him here, knowing how much tonight meant to me? How—"

"—would have been even more late and . . . wait a minute, this is ridiculous." He finally stopped. We'd been talking over each other. "Say what you want to say, Grace."

"I already said it. I can't believe you brought him here." I crossed my arms and stared hard at him. He was a mess. Torn T-shirt under a dirty blazer, jeans that were always a bit tattered but now looked positively uninhabitable. Taking a closer look, his eyes *were* bloodshot, but they were wild too—spacey and not at all Jack. He ran his hand over his shorn hair, and I could see he knew I had noticed the change. As he looked anywhere but at me, I saw him catch sight of someone.

"Oh, bloody hell. Here it comes."

Holly barreled over, standing next to us and effectively blocking us from the rest of the crowd. "Guys, what's going on? And what the hell, Jack? You get jumped on your way over here?" She fixed the collar on his blazer. Wrong move.

"Jesus, enough!" he snapped, jerking away from her hands.

"Whoa, what's the problem?" she asked, narrowing her eyes.

"How much time do you have?" he muttered, eyes scanning the crowd. Nodding to someone, he took my hand and squeezed it. "Come on, Crazy. Let's go get a drink."

He started to pull me after him when Holly placed her hand on ours. We looked like a football team in a huddle deciding on a play.

"No hand-holding," she instructed, her voice all business.

"Oh, fucking give it a rest, why don't you?" Jack growled, continuing to tug on my hand.

I saw Adam near the bar, watching the entire thing, and I dug in my designer heels. "Jack, I don't think—"

"You're not actually going to listen to her, are you?" he asked quietly.

I could see some of the crowd had begun to take an interest in our corner. Camera phones. The last thing I needed at my premiere was a scene.

Like the one you almost caused at his *premiere?*

Ouch.

But still, coming late, coming drunk, bringing Adam? Who was currently smirking at me from across the room. I looked at Jack again, his eyes were fuzzy.

193

"Come on, Jack. Let's go get some coffee." I squeezed his hand but let go of it before Holly could say anything else. When the hell had I become the adult in this relationship? I waved over a waiter and as Jack fumed next to me, I asked for black coffee.

Holly started to say something else, but I shook my head at her. With a warning glance in his direction, she turned back into the crowd, distracting the camera phones by asking loudly if she had really just seen Zac Efron by the bar.

I put a cup of coffee in Jack's hand. He ignored it.

"Jack, what's going on?" I asked quietly. He sighed.

"Nothing, Crazy. Everything's fine," he answered as a few members of the cast came over to say hello.

The conversation that needed to happen would have to wait, so I introduced Jack and put on my game face. Our eyes met, and he winked.

Winking wasn't enough this time.

☆ ☆ ☆

Hours later I was back at home, tired and confused. As I changed and got ready for bed, I thought back over the evening. Since we'd arrived separately, we also left separately, Jack had Bryan come to pick him up after I left so we weren't photographed together. Tonight had been a huge night for me professionally, and I was pleased, but I was at a loss as to what I needed to do with Jack. I had alarm bells going off everywhere, but for goodness sake, what was I supposed to do about it? He was young; he was rich; he could do whatever he wanted whenever the mood struck.

But that wasn't Jack—at least not the Jack I knew. And I'd like to think he was a strong enough person that he wouldn't let someone like Adam influence him so completely to have changed overnight. No, this behavior was only partly Adam. The rest was Jack.

And Jack had hurt me tonight. Coming late, clearly under the influence, and bringing Adam? I was pissed. Concerned, but also pissed. I knew we weren't a couple who would embrace in front of a crowd—no public groping—but I still very much wanted him there by my side tonight. I'd been nervous, and I wanted his support.

Were you supportive on his big night?

No, no, I was a total asshole. But do two idiots make a right?

As I was thinking, I heard the front door open and close. Slipping into my white polo, I pushed my hair back with a headband and washed my face. As I applied my moisturizer, I noticed that the lines around my eyes looked a bit more pronounced that normal tonight. It's amazing how fast a few drinks dehydrated my skin. After adding a bit of extra eye cream, I was brushing my teeth when Jack finally made an appearance in the mirror behind me. I nodded to him, then spit.

Pressing a quick kiss into the space between my neck and shoulder, he started for the bedroom, taking off his clothes as he went. I sighed, knowing his silence meant he didn't want to talk about it.

I stood in the doorway to the bedroom, our bedroom, and watched him as he shuffled out of his T-shirt and jeans, tossing them into the hamper. I watched as he went about the business of getting ready for bed, plugging in his phone, sipping on the glass of water I had already placed on his nightstand, walking without his normal grace but with the gait of a much older and tired man.

He was exhausted, that much was obvious. As well he should be—the partying was beginning to take its toll. But he still was stunning. Long and lean, still tanned from working in the desert, he was beautiful. He stood with his back to me, stretching his arms over his head and running his hands through his hair, which was just beginning to grow out again.

"You going to say something or are you just going to ogle me?" He smirked, looking over his shoulder at me, his eyes going a much darker shade of green. The body might be tired, but there was no doubt this man was still very much only twenty-four.

"What do you want me to say?" I asked, wisely staying in the doorway. I knew us, and if I got too close, the only talking tonight would be of the dirty variety.

"You're pissed again?"

"Pissed, yes, but I'm hurt, Jack," I replied, getting a roll of his eyes in return.

The lust that had come up in his face was quickly re-placed by irritation.

"Because I brought Adam?"

"If you have to ask that question, then—"

"Listen, okay? He really felt bad about the last few times he's been around. He knew how important tonight was, I've been going on and on about how proud I am of you. He wanted to come along and show his support. How is that such a bad thing? Bloody hell, Grace, the guy can't win with you!"

He walked past me and into the bathroom. As he splashed water on his face, I counted to ten. I didn't want this to escalate further, but now I was getting more than pissed, I was getting mad.

"You're kidding, right?"

"What?" he asked from under the towel.

"You don't get to be pissed at me, okay?"

"I'm sorry I was late, I really am. I can't believe you're getting so upset about this." He turned off the water and looked at me in the mirror.

Pie-eyed, I stared back, incredulous that he still didn't get it. "This was my night. The only one here that gets to be pissed is me!"

"Oh, that's rich. You complaining about a big night get-ting ruined? What about the fucking meltdown you had on me last year?" he yelled, turning and throwing his towel into the corner.

"Jack! Look, we can all agree I was a jerk that night, but it's like you went out of your way to be an ass tonight!"

Eyes blazing, we stared each other down. Tension radiated off him in waves. Every muscle was drawn tight and ready to snap. He looked as though he was going to say something else, but then a shadow passed over his face. Resigned, he moved past me into the bedroom.

"Grace, look, I'm tired. I don't want to talk about this anymore. I'm going to bed." He yanked the sheets down and got in. Shutting down and getting in.

"Wait. Wait a minute. We're not done talking about this," I insisted, following him and tugging on the covers.

He tugged them out of my hands and pulled them up, slumping down against the pillows. He rubbed his eyes, his hands dragging down across his face. "Christ, does everything have to be such a big fucking deal? I'm sorry I was late. I'm sorry I brought Adam. It will never happen again. Now I'm going to bed." He sighed and turned off the light.

I stood there for a moment in the dark.

"Not kidding, Grace. I'm done talking about this." His voice floated across to me.

Shaking, I walked away.

I grabbed a bottle of red wine and a glass, then headed out to the back porch and curled into the love seat. I filled the glass almost to the rim, covered up with a throw, and let the tears flow.

What was happening?

☆ ☆ ☆

I sat in the quiet, looking up at the stars for at least an hour. Even though my mind was whirling, I felt almost numb. Things were so very off right now between us. I didn't even know where to turn, what to think, whether to be upset or just concerned. Was I blowing this up out of proportion? There was no primer for this, no checklist of knowing when your celebrity boyfriend was going off the rails or just being a normal twenty-four-year-old guy.

A normal twenty-four-year-old guy who was chased by paparazzi on a regular basis and screamed at by adoring fans whenever he went out in public. A guy who couldn't get ice cream with his girlfriend without it showing up on Twitter, and a guy who couldn't have a bad night without TMZ questioning whether he was in the middle of a breakdown.

I sighed.

"I hate when you sigh," a voice said from the porch. I looked over and could make out his silhouette, leaning in the doorway.

I smiled into the darkness. "It's just deep breathing, really."

He crossed the patio to sit next to me, taking my glass of wine and draining the rest. "I hate when I make you sigh. How about that?"

"Good thing you weren't here when I was crying then," I responded softly.

Now he was the one sighing. He moved his hands under the blanket, pulling my feet into his lap and kneading at my toes, rubbing my skin. I leaned down and flung the other half over him. He was in his skivvies after all, and it was chilly. With his hands anchoring me, I stretched out a bit, leaning back into the pillows and watching him thoughtfully.

"Can I apologize for real now?" he asked, looking at me.

I had my Jack back. I nodded.

"I'm so sorry for being an ass tonight. You were right to be pissed. And may I tell you again, for the record, you were amazing."

"Thanks."

"Seriously, Grace, I'm so proud of you. You killed it. It's gonna be a huge success."

"Well, we'll see about that. Right now I'm not so worried about whether my show does well. I'm a little more focused on how well a certain Brit is doing." I shifted a bit toward him to sweep my hand across his brow. He squeezed my foot.

"See, that's the exact opposite of the thing I want you to be focused on right now. You should be enjoying this, focusing on you and everything you have going right now. Don't worry about a prat like me. I'm fine." He pulled me across the love seat and into his lap.

"I wish I could believe you, George." I breathed into his neck as he clutched me close.

"I wish you could too," he answered, lifting me and carrying me into the house.

He pressed countless kisses into my skin, shifting me in his arms so I could wrap my legs around his waist as he walked, feeling his strong body underneath and all around me. In between the thousand kisses, his lips told me how beautiful I looked tonight, how lovely, how he couldn't believe I was his, how he didn't deserve me. I tried to argue with him, but each time I tried to speak he planted another searing kiss on me, stopping my thoughts right in their track and funneling them into an entirely different thought process—one where we existed alone, just mouths and lips and arms and legs and tongues and all the time in the world.

His arms were tight around me, hands roaming, then settling on my bottom, pushing me where he wanted me most. I chuckled in spite of myself and didn't let go of him when he placed me on the bed, my legs bringing him down to me.

"Something funny?" he asked, his fingers hurrying to unbutton my shirt. I answered with my mouth to his, kissing him deeply and letting my body tell him how much I needed him, wanted him, loved him.

"You're the beautiful one, Jack." I sighed, this time in a very different way than before. He stretched above me, all long limbs and bronzed skin. His eyes flashed green, even through the darkness. His fingers blazed a trail toward where my panties would be, if I were wearing any . . .

Finding me bare beneath brought forth a deep groan from him, and he ripped the last of my buttons through the buttonholes as he grew impatient.

"Dammit, you tore my shirt."

"I'll buy you another." He grinned as my feet alone managed to push his boxers down and entirely off his legs. "Impressive."

"You got that right," I managed as he nudged against me with the part of him that never failed to intoxicate. Seconds later, he was inside.

"Christ, that feels good," he breathed into my ear, then leaned back to rise up on his knees, digging his hands deep into my hips. I arched my back, throwing my head into the pillow, arms opened wide. He slowed his thrusts, tilting my hips up higher as he circled his own. Now he let one hand creep higher on my body, fingers teasing at my nipples, then pressing into my mouth as I kissed his hand.

"So beautiful," he whispered as his hand now drifted lower, sweeping across my abdomen, dipping into my belly button, fluttering below. Kissing his own fingers, he returned them to me, where we were joined, where he now pushed into me agonizingly slowly. My entire body was taut, my hands tangled in my hair as he pressed into me. His fingers sought me, where I needed him, circling and twirling, rubbing slick and hot. I panted, bowing off the bed as he touched me, bringing me closer to the edge.

"Love to watch you come. Love to watch you come apart for me, for me," he whispered as I writhed before him. He seated himself fully inside again, now speeding up his thrusts. "God, you should see yourself." He groaned as

I brought one of my hands down to tangle with his, guiding him as he rode me harder.

Tiny specks of light began to dance at the corners of my vision, and my body contracted, pulling him deeper, so deep into me as he held me open wide. I chanted his name over and over again as my orgasm raced through me.

"Mmm . . . that's my girl." He moaned, his eyes closing as I burst around him. He fell forward onto me, sweat slippery between us as he shook in my arms. "Love you, love you so much, Grace. I'm so sorry." He murmured into my neck, his arms now tight as a band around me as he exploded. I scratched at his scalp and soothed him, hugging my legs around his back and keeping him inside as long as I could.

"I know, Jack. I know," I whispered, kissing everywhere I could reach. Slipping out of me with a loss I desperately felt, he turned me onto my side so he could wrap his arms around me, tucking me into him, back to front, with his hands full of me.

I realized as he slipped toward sleep that we had avoided once again discussing what had happened tonight, and that at some point we were going to take this to the woodshed. But it wasn't tonight.

fifteen

When I opened my eyes the next morning, I was staring into green. Jack was awake, turned sideways on his pillow and watching me. I grinned back at him, snuggling deeper into the covers and into him, breathing in the scent of his warm skin all over me. Kissing the exact center of his chest, I rested my head over his heart, the tiny hairs tickling my nose.

"How long have you been up?" I asked, my voice thick with sleep.

"Awhile."

"You should have woken me up."

"I wanted to let you sleep. I know it's been a busy week."

"It's been a busy everything." I groaned and stretched a

bit, which resulted in the sheets pulling down just enough that the boobies made their first appearance of the day.

Just as Jack waggled his eyebrows enough to communicate his intent and make the girls go on point, his phone buzzed on his nightstand. Huffing, he rolled away to get it as I pulled myself together a bit. I sat up to lean against the headboard and could see over his shoulder just enough to note the call was from Adam, although Jack at least had the good sense to not answer it. Rolling back over with a mischievous gleam in his eye, he looked right where he'd left the girls, grumbling audibly when he saw they had been put away.

"But, wait, where did they—"

"Shut it, George. We're talking."

"We're already talking, Grace."

"If the boobies are out, no talking will happen."

He snorted and tried to sneak a peek. "Just because you're incapable of paying attention doesn't mean I can't."

"No way. Uh-uh. No boobies till we talk." I tucked the sheets under each armpit and clenched my hands at my sides.

"How about one booby? One booby while we talk, and if I can contain myself, then I get them both before breakfast," he offered, throwing his hands up in the air in supplication.

"How old are you?" I asked, raising one eyebrow.

"You know ruddy well how old I am. Recovery time,

remember? Now drop the sheet on the left one and talk, woman." He poked me in the left shoulder.

Sighing, I adjusted the sheet so that the . . . good lord . . . so that the "left one" was out.

"Okay, what are we talking about?" he asked it.

"Eyes up here, George. It's out, but you still have to make eye contact." I grabbed his chin and twisted him to look straight ahead.

He blinked, shook his head, and then looked me in the eye finally.

"Okay, let's talk about last night, just for a minute. I don't want to rehash everything, I promise."

He sighed heavily, then nodded for me to go on.

"I mainly just want to talk about Adam, but in a calm, rational way. I want you to understand more about why I don't like him. I probably shouldn't even say I don't like him. I barely know the guy and—"

"Grace?"

"Yeah?"

"You don't like him. It's okay. You can say it."

"Okay, yeah. I don't like him. But more than that, I don't trust him. But hear me out. Haven't you noticed that whenever we're out, whenever you're out—if he's there, the cameras are there? I mean, yeah, they're there some-times even when he isn't around, but have you ever been somewhere with him when they *aren't* there?" I nudged his chin once again. His eyes had started to drift south.

With a cheeky grin, he met my eyes once more. "Off the top of my head? No, no, I can't. So you think he's calling them, orchestrating all of this? For what purpose, Grace?"

"His career," I answered quickly. "It makes sense. He was over; he was being cast in all kinds of crap, and then once he was cast in a film with you—the new heir apparent to his golden-boy status—now he's getting exposure again, right? Maybe he's ensuring that doesn't go away. He's making sure people are talking about him again."

"Seems a stretch to me. He's always complaining about the paparazzi. He can't stand them when they're around," he said, but I could finally see the wheels beginning to turn just the tiniest bit.

I didn't want to lose any ground, so as much as I wanted to smack him upside the naive, I kept quiet, let him think on it for another moment. He chewed on his lower lip, looking pensive, and I let the sheet drop on the right one. He looked back up at me in surprise.

"You've earned it." I smiled.

"Are we done talking? Already?"

"I said what I needed to say. You listened. I appreciate that," I answered softly as he reached out to cup an exposed breast. His fingers were tender as he stroked me, not sexual this time, but deeply sensual. Comforting. Warm. Coaxing me onto my back, he snuggled into me, head on my breast, fingers now pressing into each tiny dent between my ribs. We breathed together, watching as the sun crawled across the ceiling.

"When are you leaving to go back to the desert?" I asked the top of his head. I hated that he had to leave again, but they still had a few scenes left to shoot.

"Two days."

"I'll be glad when you're done. It'll be nice to have you at home for a while." I kissed his forehead.

He was quiet for a minute, then started to get out of bed. He leaned back down over me and gave me a small smile. "Let's get some breakfast, Crazy."

☆　☆　☆

Once I had him full of toast and marmalade, we relaxed over coffee, which is what we were doing when Holly called. Kissing me on the head, he took off for the shower before I could even answer, mouthing the words *in the shower* to me. I rolled my eyes as I answered the phone. I wasn't sure what was going on there.

"Hey, dillweed."

"Hey, asshead. What are your plans this afternoon?"

"Um, I didn't really have any. Was going to go for a run maybe?"

"Nope, you're shopping with me."

"I am?"

"Yep, let's meet at Monica's at one. I need to get some new dresses—something beachy and cute."

"Ah. You and Michael going somewhere fun?"

"Perhaps, can you go?"

209

"Sure, I'll see you there."

"By the way, do you still want us all to come over tomorrow night to watch?" she asked. We'd talked about getting together to watch the night the show premiered on TV.

"Yes, definitely. I need everyone here to make sure I don't go looking for the bad reviews."

"Can we bring anything?"

"Yes. Vodka. Lots. Not sure what you guys will all drink, but the vodka's for me." My heart stuttered a bit when I thought about the fact that my TV show would be debuting tomorrow night for all the world to see. Well, the American world. "Okay, see you in a bit," I said, starting to hang up.

"Wait, wait, is Jack there with you?"

"He's in the shower. Why?"

"But he's been home with you all morning?"

"Yeah, why? What's up?"

"I'm going to wring that limey's neck! Never mind. Not your problem. Tell him to check his fucking messages, okay?"

"Okay," I answered, not wanting to get involved.

"Okay, see you in a bit, fruitcake." She hung up.

Thoughtful, I sat there for a bit, tossing my phone back and forth. I didn't want to get involved, but I had to admit I was curious what was going on.

Not your problem. Don't get involved.

Yeah, yeah, yeah.

I headed back toward the bathroom, smiling when I

heard him humming in the shower. Opening the door, I reached out for him through the steam.

"Hey, get that sweet ass in here." He grinned, shampoo suds turning his head into a cotton ball.

"Nope, no time. I'm meeting Holly for some retail therapy," I answered, dodging his soapy hands. He responded by sticking his tongue out at me. "Speaking of Holly, she told me to tell you to check your messages?" I tried, raising my eyebrows but keeping my tone light. He nodded at me but submerged under the spray. "I'm also going to pick up some things while I'm out today for tomorrow night. I was thinking we'd just make little nibbly things and everyone can nosh while we watch. Sound good to you?"

"Wait, what? We're having people over tomorrow night?" He emerged from under the spray.

"Yes, Jack, for the show, remember? It's on TV?"

He stood there, blank-faced, as the shampoo washed down the drain.

"Right, sure, of course. Who's coming?"

"Holly, Michael, Nick, Lane is going to try, and I think Rebecca too."

He grimaced. I waited for him to say something, but he was quiet.

"So, nibbly things? Okay?" I prompted.

"Sure, sounds good, Grace." He nodded again, then returned to the spray, ending the conversation.

"I'll see you later this afternoon then?" I asked, backing

out of the bathroom. He nodded once more, then turned toward the water.

☆ ☆ ☆

"And then he just went right back under the spray! It's like he totally forgot about everyone coming over tomorrow night!" I exclaimed into the mirror as I waited for Holly to come out in yet another dress. We'd been at the boutique for only fifteen minutes, but she'd already found several she just had to have.

"Are you sure you told him to call me?" she asked over the dressing room door.

"I did. I told him to check his messages, as directed."

"Did he?" Her head popped up over the door.

"That I don't know. I told you, I just deliver the messages. I'm not getting involved." I sipped the champagne the boutique had so thoughtfully provided. "What's going on anyway?"

"Thought you weren't getting involved." She chuckled, coming out in a strapless dress that was sex on legs.

"I'm not; I'm not. Forget I asked."

"He's just really hard to get ahold of right now, and we're in the middle of negotiating the *Time* sequel. Not a great time to go incommunicado." She poofed her cleavage. "What do you think?"

"Hot. Way hot. What are all these dresses for anyway?"

"Michael's taking me somewhere tropical. Not sure where. He just said bring frilly dresses."

"Frilly?"

"I figured out that frilly translates to skimpy in Michael language."

"Not even close."

"Yeah, frilly means flouncy, which means blowy, which means barely there. That took about five minutes and some show-and-tell to figure out what he meant." She laughed, a blush creeping into her cheeks.

"I'm so glad you two are together," I said suddenly. I watched her smile into the mirror.

"You are?"

"Are you kidding? Of course! Things worked out perfectly."

"Not gonna lie, I wasn't sure you'd be okay with it," she said as she turned toward me.

"Why wouldn't I be okay with it?" I asked her, looking everywhere else.

She huffed as she headed back into the dressing room. After a moment the dress came up over her head. "Grace, shut up. Obviously there's history between you."

"Okay, sure, but it's just that: history. Honestly, I couldn't be happier for you two."

She poked her head back up over the door. "I'm pretty happy too. Now we just need to get Jack figured out and my world will be all roses and fucking fairy tales."

"I'm getting worried, Holly, like, really worried." I met her eyes.

She nodded. "Me too, fruitcake."

☆ ☆ ☆

The next day started out like all Shit Days: totally normal. Sex with Jack—awesome. Breakfast after sex with Jack—delicious. Call-in radio interviews all afternoon—stellar. That night? Oh boy.

Jack was out and about most of the afternoon, which was better for me. Talking about myself was weird, and talking on the radio—selling myself and my show—was hard to do when you have a hot Brit making faces at you and trying all manner of naughty to get you to screw up. Once the interviews were over, I went for a run in Griffith Park to unwind and calm my nerves. No such luck. I was wired. I ran my normal circuit almost ten minutes faster than I usually did, and I could've gone another round without thinking twice. I was nervous, I could admit that. Tonight was the real test. Up until now only industry people had seen the show, now it was up to the public to say if it was any good.

I kept busy all afternoon: cutting up fruit for a salad, setting out plates and bowls and silverware for everyone, mixing up a batch of margaritas to go with the guacamole I made with avocados from my trees in back, and I was just putting the finishing touches on a cheese platter when Jack blew in.

"Crazy, you ready for tonight? I'm ready. You ready?"

he shouted from the front door. I caught sight of a black Suburban as it left the driveway. Was it Bryan? Or was it Adam? They both drove the same car . . .

Before I could think on it too long, Jack swept me up in his arms and swung me around. "Mmm, I missed my girl!" he murmured, pressing wet kisses all along my neck and into the top of my dress. "Christ, Grace, you know what it does to me when you wear that apron."

I pulled away from him for a moment, laughing as I smoothed my dress. I did know what it did to him when I wore this apron.

That's why you put it on.

Also to protect my dress from the avocados. That green stain is hard to remove.

Who are you fooling?

No one. I totally wore the apron to drive him crazy.

Speaking of crazy, Jack was looking all around the house, taking in the spread I'd laid out for our friends.

"Everything looks great, looks great. When are they all getting here?"

"Um, any minute now. I think Holly and Michael were going to—"

"Do I have time for a shower? I'm just gonna take a quick shower before everyone gets here, okay? Okay, Grace?" He started for the bedroom.

I caught his arm before he could get away. Turning him toward me, I took him in. His face was flushed, and his eyes were almost black as he looked down at me.

"You okay?" I asked, smoothing his hair back from his face.

"Of course. Why?"

"I dunno," I replied as his arms came around me.

He tapped out a drumbeat on my bum, his hands moving fast.

"Totally fine, Grace. Excited for tonight?"

"Um, yeah, I think so. A little nervous but—"

"I'm gonna hit the shower before everyone gets here, okay?" He kissed me soundly on the forehead before peeling away and heading off down the hallway.

I looked around, wondering what the hell just happened. Out of the corner of my eye I saw Holly's Mercedes pulling into the drive. I shook my head to clear it, then untied the apron and threw it into the kitchen as I went out to greet my friends. This was Michael's big night as much as it was mine, and I wanted to enjoy it with him. Besides, I had all night to worry over this latest development.

Twenty minutes later I had Michael and Holly slicing up French bread to make little crostini when I heard Nick's voice at the front door.

"Grace! There's a big ol' hunk of man out here on your porch. Let him in!" he called. When I came around the corner, I burst out laughing. Nick was grinning ear to ear at Lane, who stood sheepish with his hands full: literally with bottles of wine and figuratively with Nick and his waggling eyebrows.

"There's two big ol' hunks of man out here! I love it! Get in here, you two." I laughed again as Nick gestured for Lane to go in first, ever the gentleman.

Lane leaned down to give me a kiss on the cheek. "Where's that idiot boyfriend of yours?"

"He's in the shower. He'll be out in a bit." I swatted him on the butt as he passed.

"The shower, you say? I'll go get him, let him know everyone's here," Nick insisted, nudging past me on the way to the bedroom.

"Hold it, mister. No ogling my man." I grabbed his arm and swung him around. He pouted a bit.

"You're no fun now that you have your own TV show," he huffed on his way to the kitchen, where he immediately began antagonizing Michael. He really was in heaven around our boys. And speaking of boys, where *was* mine?

I headed to the bedroom, where I could still hear water running. Which is why I was so surprised to find Jack on the bed, sound asleep in his clothes. What the hell?

"Jack," I called as I moved into the bathroom to turn off the shower. "Jack, wake up!"

His snores confirmed that he was out good.

"Hey, wake up!" I prodded, annoyed.

"Hey, Crazy, what's going on?" He smiled through his sleepy eyes.

"I could ask you the same question," I said, and his eyes opened wide.

"Just closing my eyes for a minute before I shower. Can you turn the water on for me?" he asked, rolling over, away from me.

"You already turned on the water. It's been running for thirty minutes! There's probably no hot water left, not to mention that we have a houseful of people now. No time to take a shower."

He rolled back over and looked at the clock, then rubbed his eyes. "Fuck. Okay, just give me five minutes and I'll be right there."

I watched him as he rubbed at his face, and he met my gaze through confused eyes.

"I'll be right there, okay?" he snapped.

"Yeah, sure. Whatever, Jack." I sighed, leaving the bedroom and feeling the sting of tears.

Once in the hallway, I hovered for a moment, listening as he got up. I wiped away a tear that got away, then took a breath before heading back out to the kitchen. Holly took one look at me and headed me off at the back door.

"Just going to light the candles," I said before she could say anything. I grabbed the lighter and went to work on the tiki torches.

"Sure, Grace," she answered, watching me. I kept my back to her as I moved from torch to torch. As I looked at the bedroom, I could see him standing in the window, watching me too. I turned my back to him as well.

He'd better watch it. You've got a torch.

That's for goddamn sure.

☆　☆　☆

Dinner was . . . tense. Jack finally made an appearance, disheveled and tired-looking. Which made no sense at all, since he'd gone to bed with me early the night before and slept in this morning. But he could barely keep his eyes open. Also might have had something to do with the double whiskey he poured himself to go with the dinner, which he barely ate.

As usual, he sparred with Nick, who made a joke about his bedroom eyes. Other than that, however, Jack sat at his end of the dining room table, avoiding my eyes and any topic of conversation that had to do with partying, drinking, clubbing, or being an asshole in general. Holly wisely kept silent about the missed calls. She knew better than to mix business with pleasure. But you could tell it was killing her not to say anything directly to him. Lane was curiously quiet as well. Initially I thought perhaps it was tension about Holly and Michael, but in fact, Michael and Lane got along extremely well. They even made plans to go mountain biking the following weekend.

Then after we'd eaten and were getting assembled in the living room to watch the show, Nick cornered me in the kitchen as I finished cleaning up.

"You know I think you're pretty, right?"

"Oh boy, what are you working up to?" I smiled into the cupboard, turning around with an armful of coffee cups. He took them from me and set them out for everyone as

I got the cream from the fridge. On second thought, I also pulled out a bottle of Kahlúa from under the counter. I poured a hefty dash into my coffee cup, and he nodded when I offered him some as well.

"What's going on?" he asked.

I scooted around him to grab the sugar bowl, grabbed the carafe of coffee, and gestured for him to help me into the other room. "With what?" I asked.

"Grace, come on. What the hell is up with my pretty boy?" He placed a hand on my arm as I tried to balance everything.

"I don't know what you mean," I insisted, not wanting to get into this now.

"Grace, you know I only—"

But he was cut off by raised voices coming from the backyard. I stole a quick glance at the clock. The show was starting in less than ten minutes.

"Unbelievable. What now?" I rushed toward the French doors. Through the glass I could see Jack and Lane, inches apart and looking critical. Pushing open the doors, I moved outside to hear the end of their argument.

"Seriously, dude, get your shit together. This affects other people too, you know!" Lane's voice was full of anger.

"Oh, come on. How does this affect you?" Jack sneered.

"You think these jobs just roll in? You not signing means my ass could be out of a job. You ever think about that?"

"No way. You can't put that on me." Jack walked away, grabbing his glass off the patio table.

Lane followed, talking to his back as Jack drained his whiskey. "I *can* put that on you, and I *will* put that on you if you're the reason this movie doesn't get made. If you think you can walk away from a franchise like this without it impacting everyone else, you're insane!"

By now Holly and Michael were perched on the back of the couch in the living room, listening through the other set of French doors as Jack and Lane continued to go at it in the backyard. I wanted to stop this, I should stop this, but I had no idea things had gotten so bad with the *Time* sequel that Lane even knew. Why didn't I know about this? Why wasn't Jack talking to me?

I didn't have time to follow that train of thought any further because the next thing I knew, Jack turned around to face Lane and saw all of us watching.

"Enough!" he shouted. The whiskey glass he'd been holding now flew across the backyard and hit the side of the house, shattering into a thousand pieces across the patio. I gasped, and then . . .

Quiet.

The quiet pressed in on all sides, the pressure building in my ears and behind my eyes. I was vaguely aware that Michael started to get up from the couch, but Holly held him in place. Later on I could remember seeing Lane back away from Jack, shaking his head. I could still feel Nick's hand on my arm, his grip tight.

What I was completely and totally focused on at the time was the sight of Jack, barely standing and pale, with splotches of red anger across his cheeks. Shaking. His eyes searched for mine, and when he found me they looked haunted and vacant. Then, punching through the quiet came the strains of the theme song for *Mabel*— upbeat and bouncy and completely inappropriate for the moment. A glaring reminder of what this night was about, was supposed to be about.

"Out," I breathed, so quietly that I could barely hear it. "All of you, out please." I did not take my eyes off Jack. "You, stay right there."

Nick squeezed my elbow before moving away. I heard Holly and Michael discussing quietly whether one of them should stay, but they wisely left as well. Lane was long gone by now. My eyes never left Jack. I could hear my own voice coming from the living room, as my TV show was now airing across the entire West Coast. The West Coast would have to wait. I had someone to take to the woodshed.

sixteen

So here's the thing, Jack. I've tried to be understanding. I've tried to back off. I've tried to ignore what's going on, tried to not be a nagging girlfriend."

I walked in a circle around him, keeping my anger in check as best I could. To his credit, he let me circle.

"I've been up at night worrying about where you were and what you were doing. I've let you change the subject. I've pretended things were fine and dandy. I've even fucked you when I should have been talking to you." I stopped in front of him and looked him square in the eye. "But no more, Jack. You know I love you more than anything on this entire planet, but this shit ends now. You either talk to me, tell me what the hell is going on—"

"Or what?" he challenged, speaking for the first time.

And I raged.

"Why are you making this so difficult? Why can't you talk to me? And what the hell, Jack? Not signing on for the *Time* sequel? Why didn't you talk to me? I had no idea that—"

"Why does everything have to be such a big deal? Christ, Grace, I know you're pissed. I know you're disappointed. You think I don't know everyone's talking about me right now? That you and Holly are doing nothing but trying to figure out how to get me back in line, back in step, back to doing what a movie star is supposed to do? Well, fuck that. I'm not a puppet everyone can just play with!" Finally some spark came back in his eyes, which were now spitting fire.

"Is that what you think we're doing? We're worried! All your friends are worried—"

"Oh, sure. They're worried. Let me tell you what they're worried about. Lane's worried about his next job, Holly's worried about losing her paycheck, and you're too busy worrying about me to notice that being connected to me is just—"

"Wait a minute. Wait a goddamned minute! You think Holly is only worried about a paycheck? She has never done anything but help you and think about your career. She's making sure you have one and don't blow the whole thing like that idiot Adam Kasen! And where do you get off telling me what I should be worried about?" I yelled, the anger and frustration and concern that had been percolating for months now bubbling over and landing all over the patio.

Jack seethed, his entire body tense, his jaw clenched. "If you could see this clearly you would see that—"

"Don't you dare tell me what I see. I can't believe you would—"

"Stop. Fucking. Interrupting. Me," he managed, his voice quietly dangerous. "I can't go anywhere without being recognized. I can't go to the grocery store without a clerk telling *The National Enquirer* what kind of frozen pizza I like. I'm scared to death to put the top down and drive around town because I might get fucking run off the road by vultures who care more about getting a picture of me with my *is she or isn't she my girlfriend* than they do about safety, and I can't have a fucking drink after a long day of dealing with all of that bullshit without everyone telling me they're worried about how I'm handling things! This is it, Grace. This is my reality, and this is how I'm deal-ing with it, okay?" He was well and truly yelling now too.

"Jack, love, if that was it, I could understand." I crossed the distance between us and put my hands on his shoul-ders, but he shrugged me off. "But you *aren't* dealing with this. That's why I'm so concerned."

"You have no idea," he spat, his eyes going black again, reminding me of when he'd come in earlier.

"Drinks at the end of the day, my ass. What the hell were you on today?" I saw the shame cross his features for just a moment, and I had my answer. "I won't watch you do this," I whispered, my voice shaking, and I watched as his eyes hardened, even to me.

"You don't have to," he replied, leaving me on the patio. I watched in stunned silence through the window as he

threw his things into his duffel bag, then came back outside. My show continued to play this entire time, providing
a surreal soundtrack to some very real drama.

"I'm heading back to the desert." He stood in the doorway with his bag over his shoulder, looking impossibly
young. "I'll call you when I can."

When he can? Wait, what's happening here?

"What do you mean? Wait, Jack. Don't go. Let's talk
about this."

"This is clearly not a place I can be right now. Besides, I
gotta go make a movie."

The anger in his voice was so thick it broke my heart.
I flashed back to a night not so long ago, a different backyard, but still Jack and me. And a great space between us.
But this wasn't something I could help him with. He was
making it clear he didn't want me right now. He didn't
need anyone. My throat lumped. "I love you, Jack."

He nodded and smiled a small smile. "I'll call you."

And then he left. And I had to let him go.

As I sat in my love seat, with my ever-loving show still
playing in the background, I realized that was the first time
he didn't say he loved me back.

☆ ☆ ☆

Reviews came in all night, and by the time I woke up
the next morning, the show was literally an overnight success. And when I say woke up the next morning, I mean

I crawled out of bed after not sleeping a damn wink. I sobbed, I cried, I threw some things, I punched my pillow, and then I sobbed some more. But then I focused on me.

My phone was filled with texts from everyone I knew, with the exception of the Brit I very much wanted to hear from. Holly let me know in no less than fourteen texts that every reviewer she was worried about was raving, and that I was the talk of the town today. She also let me know if I didn't call her soon, she was coming over.

Michael let me know in only four texts that he had already heard from the network, which was asking about ideas he had for the next season—the next season? Hadn't been officially picked up, but the fact that the executives were already wondering what he might have up his North Face sleeve was very encouraging.

Lane texted me to tell me he was sorry he picked a fight with my idiot boyfriend on my big night, but that he'd recorded it, watched it later, and loved it. And to tell Jack to call him whenever but that the next time he threw a glass he'd lay him out.

My Google alerts were off the charts. The blogs that liked me now *really* liked me. The blogs that hated me for my connection to Jack were rabid in their continued hatred. But the headline that most caught my eye was from CelebWatch.com, an online site known for their topical discussions about Hollywood and the standard of beauty.

If Grace Sheridan Is Plus-size, Hollywood Needs a New Scale

The article went on to not only praise the show and the entire cast but also call out every other website that had insinuated themselves right into my pants and what size they might be. Printing a picture of Marilyn Monroe, they reminded their readers that by today's standards, Marilyn would be plus-size. A side-by-side comparison showed how I was significantly smaller than she was and yet still billed as a curvy actress. I laughed when I saw the side-by-side shot. She was and always will be a bombshell.

And in that moment, I realized how out of control everything had become. Big, small, curvy, or bony, beauty was beauty. I was healthy. I was exactly the size I was supposed to be, and that was it.

The most wonderful thing about the article? There was no mention of Jack and whether we were dating. It was solely about me, my show, and my abilities as an actress—for once not that man I might be sleeping with.

The man I was still very much worried about. But also the man who left last night, left me with a patio full of glass rather than stay and fight with me about what was really going on with him. I lay back in bed, biting my nails as our conversation played back over for the thousandth time. My brain was pudding at this point. I had analyzed it forward and backward and spent just as much time cursing his name for leaving as I did contemplating how I could have pushed him so far that I let him leave.

Drugs. Dammit, he was turning into a Hollywood cliché. My experience with drugs was limited. Holly and I had partied in college plenty, but only with pot. And we never bought it. There were always guys who would share. In fact, the first time I ever smoked pot was with Holly and Michael, on the floor of his sister's living room. Cypress Hill, a rose-colored bong, and about eighteen boxes of Snackwell's later, I had successfully inhaled.

But that was it for me. Never did anything else. I'm sure harder drugs were around, but I was never aware of it—certainly not clued in enough to recognize it in anyone else. However, I *was* aware enough to know that occasional use didn't lead automatically to a pretty place in Malibu with a curfew and required wristbands for visitors.

So what *had* Jack been on yesterday? And was it the first time?

Hi, naive? I think someone's on the phone . . . something about a bridge for sale?

This explained a lot. But I was more concerned that there was a side to Jack I had no clue about, and no clue how to help.

The phone rang as I was locked inside my own *After School Special.* "He's taking drugs, Holly," I said as my greeting.

"Did I call a hotline?"

I smiled in spite of myself. "Jack. He's taking drugs."

She swore into the phone. "I'm on my way over there. I'm gonna kick his ass."

"You'll have to drive a little farther than Laurel Canyon. He left for the desert last night." I sighed.

"What? After we left?"

"About fifteen minutes after you left, yes. The fucking *Mabel* theme song was playing during our Come to Jesus meeting."

"Ah, shit. I'm on my way. How many bagels do you want?"

"No bagels, but I wouldn't say no to egg rolls later."

"Done. And can we also talk about how fucking huge your show was last night?"

"I love you."

"I love you too, fruitcake. I'm on my way."

I got out of bed, made it, and headed for the shower. By the time Holly arrived, I had on a dress, had curled my hair, and had my lips glossed. In the past, egg rolls would have been the beginning of a spiral, the way to cope with anything tough that came my way. Egg rolls would have morphed into pans of fried noodles, fried wontons, fried anything. Couple that with my couch, a sloppy ponytail that hadn't seen shampoo in days, and a marathon of *My So-Called Life*, and I could turn any crisis into an excuse to cocoon.

Drugs? *Pfft.* Egg rolls were my gateway. But now I could have my egg rolls with a side of yoga and solve my problems with a clear head. And a hit TV show . . .

The *redhead* Plays Her Hand

☆ ☆ ☆

Holly stayed for the better part of the afternoon, during which I told her everything that happened the night before. She kicked herself as well. Working in Hollywood as long as she had, she was convinced she should have seen this coming. It was so ridiculously clear, it was like missing the forest for the cocaine. Addict? Probably not. That couldn't have gotten past me for too long. But the partying had certainly progressed. But while we, of course, spent time talking about the Brit, we also talked about the redhead.

We planned another round of interviews—lots of women's magazines had contacted Holly about doing photo shoots and feature stories on me, something that boggled my mind but pleased me to no end. I'd not planned this, couldn't have planned this, but I wasn't going to say no to a dialogue that was so important and needed to happen. So photo shoot? Hells yes.

I was still riding high, enjoying this ray of sunshine when I finally heard from the person I'd been waiting to hear from. But no call. I got a text.

Saw the headlines today, looks like you're a hit.

Now, there was nothing mean-spirited about this text, not at all. And there was nothing about it that should have antagonized me so. But when I read it, it pissed me off.

It would appear so, yes.

I pressed SEND, then waited to see his response. I'm sure this was his way of testing the waters, seeing what kind of a mood I was in after leaving me the night before. The waters were decidedly cool. He responded right away.

Is this how it's going to be now?

Good question. I wondered if I was right to push him this way. There was no right answer here. I just knew how I felt, and how I felt was sad but also a little betrayed. We'd come so far this past year, shared so much, and gone through it all together. Did I really miss all those signs?

The truth was no. I saw them all and talked to him about everything I was worried about. But should I have pushed harder? Sooner? I wanted to help him. Christ, I wanted to help him. But he not only didn't want my help, he didn't even want to be around me right now. Aaaand back to pissed.

It's this way because you wanted it this way, Jack. You left. So go, live it up, go bananas. But like I told you last night, I'm not gonna watch.

He didn't respond. And I didn't text him again. And even though no one ever plans it, that was the beginning of the end.

seventeen

ENT

On a break from shooting *Soldier Boy*, Jack Hamilton and company spilled into the lobby of the Palms Casino Resort in Las Vegas late Friday night after reportedly losing more than $50,000 at the poker tables. Hamilton was in good spirits, however, something you'd think losing all that money would dampen. But he seemed to be flying high, disappearing into a black Suburban with several other actors from the set, including Adam Kasen. Kasen, who has been a fixture on the Hollywood party scene for a few years now, has been inseparable from his castmate Hamilton since the two met in preproduction. Hamilton stopped to sign a few autographs, laughing and chatting with fans, although he beat a hasty retreat when our reporter asked him about the latest details of his never-confirmed and often-denied relationship with actress Grace Sheridan. Just before Kasen got into the car, our reporter asked him the same question, to which he replied, "Grace who?"

Grace who indeed, if the number of ladies who followed Kasen into the car have anything to say about it.

TVRatings.com

Mabel's Unstable?, written and created by Michael O'Connell, directed by David Lancaster, and starring the actress everyone is talking about these days, Grace Sheridan, premiered recently to rave reviews and huge ratings! The preshow gossip focused on who was dating who and which actress wasn't getting along with her director, but *Mabel's Unstable?* has proved to everyone that sex + singing + Beverly Hills is a mix that can't miss. Who knew? Well, Venue knew, and the cable channel is reportedly in talks with the creative team behind *Mabel's Unstable?* to order a full season.

Hamiltoned.com

Thanks to all of you who have been out watching for our guy, we can now report that yes, it's true. Jack Hamilton was thrown out of Chuckles comedy club by security when he became disruptive to the comedians onstage. We'd heard reports from several eyewitnesses, but the incident was finally confirmed this morning by a representative from the club. Jack! Shame on you.

Entertainment Tonight

Grace Sheridan is mad as hell, and she's not gonna take it anymore! When pictures appeared of the actress in a recent photo spread for *Southern California Style*, a fashion magazine about exactly that, the curvy actress was decidedly uncurvy, something that was immediately noticeable. Sheridan has been very vocal about her past struggles with her weight and the difficulties she had losing a few pounds for her role on *Mabel's Unstable?* In fact, it was these very struggles that brought attention to her beyond her alleged relationship with Jack Hamilton. When the magazine was published, her manager Holly Newman responded to criticism that her pictures were more than retouched. "Like any actress, Grace understands that with photo shoots comes retouching, but not reconstruction. Grace is proud of her body, she's worked hard for it, and she has asked the magazine to publish the photos as they were taken. For God's sake, people, she's got a butt. Get over it."

We at *ET* have obtained the original photos, and you can see that extensive work was done to reduce the size of not only her hips but also her thighs, arms, and stomach. Once it was clear that the photos had been doctored, a swell of support, which started online, flooded the office of *Southern California Style* with letters, e-mails, and phone calls speaking out in favor of Sheridan. Whether the magazine will reprint the pictures is not clear, but what is clear is that this actress has kick-started a conversation that will continue.

JackedOff.com

Don't you worry, Jacky boy. We've got your back. How dare they throw him out of a club? Don't they know that having someone as famous and fabulous as Jack Hamilton in their stupid comedy club is the best thing that could happen to them??

And anyone who thinks that cow Grace Sheridon't will be around this time next year is full of it! They were never dating, people. Come on! She used him for some press, and now she's making sure its all about her. *Please!* She sucks, her show sucks, her fans suck, and the only thing good we can say about her is that . . . actually we can't say anything good about her. We're just glad our boy has decided to stay in Vegas awhile longer. No one can pretend they're dating anymore if they're not even in the same city. We love you, Jack!

CurvyGirlGuide.com

We love Grace Sheridan! Her new show *Mabel's Unstable?* debuted a few weeks ago, and she is our new guilty pleasure. We love her for her voice; for h̶e̶r̶ ̶d̶a̶u̶g̶h̶t̶e̶r, Mabel; for her curves; and for her willingness to speak up when it comes to what's beautiful. Recently photographed in lingerie for an upcoming spread in *People*, Grace gave us at CGG a sneak peek at her in her barely-theres, and she's *gorgeous*!

While she seemed cool before, her new stance of refusing any and all retouching on her photos is the coolest thing ever! Making sure they'll be printed with every single curve and dimple, she is a real woman who real women can identify with. It's actually ridiculous that this conversation is centered around someone that is *not plus-size, for the love of all that is holy*, but we're just glad it's happening. She knows which side her bread is buttered on. We're on your side, Grace, because we know you're on ours!

CelebTracker.com

Shooting wrapped on the film *Soldier Boy* starring Jack Hamilton this week after an extended location shoot that went weeks beyond the initial schedule. Stories from the set have reported more recent trouble with the cast showing up late to work, not having lines memorized, and arguing with the crew. What remains to be seen is whether the film itself will have as large of a draw as the shooting did.

Fans of the actors, in large part fans of Jack Hamilton, showed up in droves when filming locations were leaked to the press. Barricades and fleets of black Suburbans were required to shuttle the cast back and forth, and security was out in full force as fans jostled to get a glimpse of their favorite Sexy Scientist Guy. Although in the past Hamilton has usually been willing to pose for pictures and sign autographs, reports from those working inside the closed set say that having the fans around this time really seemed to cause a problem. He's reported to have said they were breaking his concentration, and once even went as far as to demand that the fans be removed from a location before he would come out of his trailer. But trouble on set or not, the film has wrapped, and the studio is hoping for a quick turnaround and release, likely to capitalize on the continued success and interest in Jack Hamilton and the renewed interest in Adam Kasen, former golden boy and confirmed Hollywood bad boy.

TMZ

Redhead out on the town, but where's her Scientist Guy? Last night our photographers caught up with Grace Sheridan as she left a restaurant in West Hollywood. Reports inside said she met with her manager, Holly Newman, and the writer for her hit show, *Mabel's Unstable?*, Michael O'Connell, before leaving alone. She didn't answer any questions, but when asked about her are-they-or-aren't-they boyfriend, Jack Hamilton, she was visibly upset. Reports that he has plans to stay in the Nevada desert indefinitely, even though filming has ended on his new movie, *Soldier Boy*, certainly has set tongues wagging about the future for this couple, the worst-kept secret in Tinseltown. With Sheridan's new solo success and her outspoken views on beauty standards, does she need the Scientist Guy?

The same night Sheridan dined with friends in Los Angeles, Hamilton was spotted in the VIP section of Lush, which seems to have become the actor's nightly habit. Seen out almost every night on the town, the formerly private actor seems hell-bent on embracing the Hollywood culture of live fast and hard.

☆ ☆ ☆

Are they or aren't they? Wasn't that the question everyone wanted the answer to, including yours truly.

I sat back in my seat, closed out of the window on my phone, and promised once more to never ever, ever, ever google myself again. Or Jack. Neither. Both. Never. I pulled out of the parking garage on Wilshire after a grueling session with Megan, looking everywhere for tan sedans. All clear. Never googling again.

Who are you kidding?

Okay, I won't until tomorrow.

Again, who are you kidding?

I knew I would do it again later today, so this was just a

little lie I told myself—a lie that made it easier to rational-ize inside where the crazy hides that I somehow now had a life where I could google myself. Myself!

Flights of fancy aside, let's go back to the question on deck.

Are they or aren't they?

Sadly, all evidence would point to *aren't they*.

Since the night Jack left for the desert we had not spoken, something that I could scarcely believe. But that's how it happens. A day becomes two, two becomes five, a freaking week goes by, then two? And then the ludicrous becomes real. At that point, it's just semantics. Who's gonna be the one to reach out? Who's gonna be the bigger person or the weakest weenie? Apparently, we were both semantic.

If someone had told me six months ago that Jack and I would break up without even a phone call, I'd have said no way. Never happen. Not to us. But were we broken up? See, that's the thing of it. When shit goes bad, sometimes you can get bogged down in it, wrap yourself in it, but still not know. I'd analyzed the *he saids* and the *she should haves*, but in the end, I still didn't know. But if I stepped back from it, then yes, we were probably broken up.

I winced even as I thought it, so I rolled down the win-dows and breathed deep, getting a little hit of smog to clear my head.

A boy and a girl meet, fall in love, and hide their romance because of boy's fan club. Girl breaks his heart because she's an idiot. Boy and girl get back together. Boy and girl have sex, have sex, have more of the sex. Girl gets TV show; boy drinks. Girl gets famous over sixteen pounds. Boy drinks more; girl lets boy leave one night knowing this can't possibly be the end. Girl sweeps up glass. Boy doesn't come back.

And in the interim, girl kicks ass. Is girl enjoying it? She's trying to.

The show was a hit. It continued to gain momentum, and by the middle of the shortened summer season, a full season had been ordered. Same writer. Same cast. New director. Hee-hee.

We went into production on the new season almost immediately, and I threw myself into the work—creating, owning, listening, and responding. Michael's writing had hit new strides, taking Mabel and the entire cast into places as an actress I was terrified of, which made it all the more exhilarating when I *did* go there and *didn't* shy away.

Professionally, I was killing it. Personally, I was a ghost town.

Jack had texted me—twice, in fact, since the first time. First to tell me congratulations on the show getting picked up, that he hadn't missed an episode, and that he was proud of me. The second time, weeks later, he texted me a picture of a television. On the screen? *The Golden Girls*.

I responded both times, but he never texted back. What could I glean from these texts? He was keeping tabs on what I was up to and that he was as happy as I was about the Golden Gs being back on TV Land.

He called one night too, late. After 3:00 a.m. When I answered, he said nothing. But I could hear him breathing.

"Jack? Hey, you there?"

Breathing.

"Jack, you okay?"

Heavy breathing.

"Seriously? That's what you called me for?"

Groan.

Yeah, I may have let him finish. I mean, come on. And I did only a few things on my end, just a few. But we never spoke. He never said a word. I cried afterward.

So are we or aren't we? Seriously, someone please clue me in.

I kept tabs on him as much as I could through the Google stalking and the little bits Holly knew. He'd finally responded to her, signed on to do the next *Time* movie, and then went back to not answering his phone when she called. She eventually got him on the line, told him she wasn't going to work with him this way and that if he wanted another manager he could find one. He relented but let her know in no uncertain terms that he was on a break until the *Time* sequel started shooting this fall. He didn't want to do any interviews, he wasn't doing any TV appearances, and he essentially wanted to be left alone until he had to do promotion for *Soldier Boy*, to which he'd already agreed to do.

He wanted to be left alone, wanted to do his thing and not apologize for it, and that was it. He was like Howard Hughes meets Charlie Sheen, with a side of Dylan McKay.

So Holly did what he asked and didn't point out that his behavior was beginning to garner him a reputation, that it could cost him future jobs. She knew if he fired her, there would be a huge line of people interested in representing him—he was still a very much in demand movie star. And in her way, even if they weren't speaking, as long as she worked with him she could still keep the tiniest of eyes on him. And in the tiniest of ways, it made me feel better.

And through the tiniest of hints, I believed he was also letting me know he didn't want me to contact him. He knew Holly well enough to know that she'd tell me everything, let me know he was okay but she'd also relay that he didn't want anyone contacting him. So I didn't.

And it was killing me. Because in the middle of all of this—this drama surrounding Jack and how he was choosing to deal with the pressure—I got left out in the cold. I lost my boyfriend. I was pissed, sure, but I was hurt, and more than that, I was lonely.

Seriously lonely. I missed the fuck out of Jack. My house felt too big, my bed felt too wide, and every time I saw a bag of Chex Mix, my heart broke a little more. Like the melba toasts at the bottom of the bag, I was broken into pieces. And kind of tossed aside like the pretzels no one wanted.

I longed to be able to share with him what was going on with me, how I had my own pressures and problems to deal with, not to mention needing someone to celebrate these successes as they happened. I'd lost my biggest cheerleader, my shower partner, and the guy who made me laugh louder and moan deeper than anyone else ever could, all at the same time. And oh my God, it hurt.

The street blurred in front of me as tears made their way from the pit of my stomach and out through my eyeballs. I pulled over as soon as I could, wracked with sobs as I let it wash over me: the overwhelming sadness mixed with my very real fear that it was over and my George would not be holding my boobies up in the shower ever again. I cried until I was hoarse, until my eyes were puffy and swollen, until I looked like I'd been hit in the face with a shovel and then backhoed with mascara goo.

But even in this moment, my radar was up, and when I saw a tan sedan turning around on the side street, I gulped my emotion down and pulled back out into traffic. I wiped my nose on my sleeve like a kid would do and hoped like hell it was just a tan sedan filled with normal people and not vultures and their cameras . . . who would sell a story with a title like "The Redhead Breaks Down."

Are they or aren't they? Could you be broken up and not know it? Could you be broken up even if you were still in love with him and you were pretty sure he was still in love with you too? I had no answers.

I lost the sedan in traffic and made my way back up into the canyons. I'd google Jack as soon as I got home to make sure nothing new was going on. Ironic that the same tan sedans I hated were also the only way I knew what he was doing, how he was doing. I was buying into the system that contributed to the very issues he was having so much trouble dealing with. And watching him deteriorate, watching him make an ass of himself? It was really hard.

☆　☆　☆

Michael came over for dinner that night. He wanted to run through some ideas about making changes for a few of the later episodes. Now that we had a full season of thirteen episodes to work with, he was able to really delve into some of the other characters, making it a true ensemble piece.

Did any other lead actress have such a close relationship with the creator and head writer of the show? Probably not, but they probably also didn't have the history Michael and I had. Since Jack left, Michael had stepped even more into the role of big brother. He checked in with me sometimes even more often than Holly, who was going to try to stop by after work as well. These two. They were keeping me busy, keeping me occupied. It was sweet, really.

As he tore lettuce for a salad, Michael told me about an incident during their vacation in Fiji, the "someplace tropical" he had hinted at.

"So this poor girl, who had just spilled an entire tray of mai tais all over the place, was just trying to clean up—clean up the table, clean up the floor, and clean up, well, my lap."

"Your lap?" I laughed, reaching over him to grab the tongs.

"Yeah, it kind of went, well, all over my pants." He grinned, turning red.

"And let me guess, when she went in to clean, Holly had something to say about it?"

"She really did. She was not having it." He laughed and grabbed an avocado to slice for the salad. I watched him for a moment, his smile continuing as he thought about it and about the girl he was in love with. God, I missed that look. For the second time today, tears sprang to my eyes, and I turned away, not wanting Michael to see me upset. The timer went off on the oven and, wiping my eyes a bit, I grabbed the oven mitts to take out the chicken I was roasting.

"You need help with that?" he asked.

"Nope I got it," I said, keeping my face turned away. I pulled out the dish, but eyes blurred, I caught the edge of the oven, my hand slipped, and down went the chicken. I tried to catch it, but missed, and the casserole dish shattered on the floor.

"Son of a bitch!" I stared at the mess at my feet. Throwing the mitts aside, I kicked the chicken, stomping my feet. "Son of a *bitch*!" I slammed the oven door and turned in a circle, repeating the same curse over and over again. Tears streamed down my face, and the chicken was now chicken hash under my shoes as I vented and raged. That poor chicken—it had no idea. "I just feel . . . so goddamned . . . *helpless*! It's like he's driving toward a cliff, and I can't do a thing about it," I sputtered, sinking to the floor and looking up at Michael, who was holding the salad and watching me unravel.

He put down the salad. "Aw, Grace, I know." He pulled me up from the floor and wrapped his arms around me. I literally cried on his shoulder, ankle-deep in chicken and temporary insanity and scared to death. Through my sobs I heard the clicking of heels across the floor and looked up to see Holly. She looked at us, looked at the mess, and smiled ruefully.

"Well, fruitcake, looks like we're ordering in tonight."

I might have cried on her shoulder as well.

☆ ☆ ☆

When I packed the two of them off that night, the kitchen had been cleaned. Michael had taken the broken dish out to the garbage while Holly and I mopped the floor. After my meltdown we ended up ordering pizza and ate it on the floor in the family room while watching mindless television and laughing, keeping things light.

I'd let it all out tonight, my frustrations and my fear, and now I was exhausted. Turning out the lights, I headed back to the bedroom, my gaze automatically going to his side of the bed. I washed my face, brushed my teeth, and crawled under the covers. I tossed and turned for a few moments, finally slipping across to his side, to his pillow. The sheets had been washed numerous times since he'd left, but if I closed my eyes and breathed deeply enough, I swore I could still get a hit of my Brit.

Tucked in and cried out, I sunk into sleep. I was not at all prepared for the call that would come in at 2:37 a.m.

"Grace?"

"Hmm . . ." I mumbled, running my hands through my hair, trying to wake up. Holly was on the phone. At 2:37 in the morning. Why the hell was Holly calling me at 2:37 in the morning? I sat up in bed.

"Why the hell are you calling me at 2:37 in the morning? What's wrong?"

"Grace, take it easy."

"Why would you tell me to take it easy? What's going on?" Panic gripped me as I got out of bed and began to pace.

"Shit. I didn't even know if I should call you or not. To be honest, I don't know what's going on."

"Holly! Tell me what you know or—"

"Jack got himself into a fight at some club. He's pretty messed up."

I covered my face with my hand. Oh no.

"It's a mess, Grace. Cops are there, photographers are there, there are already people who were in the club posting pictures of it. It looks like fucking chaos. That's about all I know. One of the guys he was with called me when they took him in."

"Wait, took him in? Took him in where?"

"I think your boy got himself arrested." She sighed. "I honestly don't even know what to do at this point."

I closed my eyes tightly and breathed deep.

"I do." I reached for my pants. "I'm going to Vegas."

eighteen

I stopped for gas just outside of Las Vegas. I put the nozzle into the tank and leaned back against my car, looking at the dawn beginning to creep over the desert.

I had flown out of the house approximately seven minutes after hanging up the phone with Holly. I threw some clothes in a bag, grabbed my purse, and got in the car. Got back out of the car, went back inside for my shoes, and was on the highway in moments.

I didn't have a clue what I would find when I got there, or what kind of reception I would get, but I was barreling down on the city of sin with determination. Something Jack had said to me when he came to see me in New York kept zinging around in my head: "I'm in this thing *with* you, a willing participant, and you can't decide for both of us."

Smart guy. He was totally right, though, and I *had* shut him out and shut him down last year when I went through my own meltdown. Granted, I hadn't been in a bar fight, but I had been just as out of my mind as he seemed to be. I scrolled through my phone, checking the newsfeeds on all the gossip sites. Ugh, it was everywhere.

As breakfast came to the East Coast, people tuning in to their morning talk shows were getting their first taste of the events of the night before and how their Super Sexy Scientist Guy was a barroom brawler. Holly managed it as best she could, but she said only that there would be a statement later in the day. While I drove across the desert, she blew up the phones at the LVPD, finding out anything she could.

She called to tell me Jack hadn't been charged. Yet. He was at the local hospital, being treated for injuries she'd been able to confirm were "non–life-threatening," but that was it. I had no idea what shape he'd be in when I got there.

My phone beeped. I had a new text from Holly.

Talked to communications director at the hospital. You're good to go. She said drive around and go thru the ambulance bay. No press back there. Call me later, fruitcake. Xo

I finished filling up the tank and got back on the road.

☆ ☆ ☆

My navigation system took me straight to the hospital, and as I drove to the back entrance, I could see a gaggle of photographers outside the main doors. Keeping that in mind, I parked as close as I could to where the ambulances were housed, then used them for cover as I made my way to the back door. The fact that I was using anything for cover, rather than just entering the hospital the regular way, brought home to me one more time how far outside the *regular way* things were.

I was recognized by a hospital security guard immediately, and he ushered me to the elevator. "Your boy's up on the fifth floor. Just tell them at the desk who you are," he said, nodding as the door opened.

"Okay, thanks. Thanks so much." I stepped into the elevator and smiled at him, my tummy suddenly very nervous at the thought that Jack was only five floors away from me.

"Oh, and Ms. Sheridan?" he said just as I pressed the button.

"Yes?"

"I'm a— I'm a big fan," he stuttered, his neck and ears going the color of a kidney bean.

The door closed, and I was left with an embarrassed smile of my own. Surreal.

Before I could blink, the door opened again and I was faced with a desk full of nurses who looked at me suspiciously. I imagine once word got out who was on the fifth floor, there were lots of people who seemed to have business up there.

I walked to the desk and gave someone my name. By now my throat was dry, but my palms were not. I just wanted to see him, to make sure he was okay.

I walked to the end of the hall, turned the knob, and went into his room.

Lying on the bed, his face turned toward the window, was Jack. His arm in a sling, looking bruised and pale, his left eye a starburst of gray and purple, it was Jack. I gasped as I saw him—I couldn't help it. He looked so beautiful and so terrible at the same time, and my eyes filled with tears.

Hearing my noise, he turned to the door with an impatient groan, but his eyes widened as he took me in. The smile that threatened to break over his face was luminous, and my heart caught in my throat. But then shame crept in, and he looked down at the bed.

"What are *you* doing here?" he asked quietly, wincing.

I closed the door behind me and walked toward the bed. I stood next to him until he looked up at me. I smoothed his hair back from his face, the entire world stopping as I touched his skin.

"Where else would I be, you stupid jerk?" I grinned down at him, scratching at his scalp lightly.

Relief broke across his face, crowding out the shame.

He closed his eyes, a small smile at the edge of his mouth, and leaned in to my hand.

"Grace, I'm so—"

"Shhh . . . not now. Let's just get you fixed up and get you out of here. There'll be time for that." I sat down on the edge of the bed. With my fingers, I traced the face I knew so well, running a path from his forehead to his cheekbones, along his strong jaw, now colored with bruises, to his mouth, which was split in two places. When I looked back up, his eyes were on mine.

"I'm glad you're here," he murmured.

☆　☆　☆

The doctor who had treated Jack came in a little while later to let us know he was being released. He had no injuries other than a badly sprained shoulder, a black eye, a few stitches in his forehead, and a split lip. With prescriptions for pain medication and instructions on aftercare for the stitches and shoulder in hand, we began filling out paperwork for his release. The doctor wanted Jack to remain until after lunch, which would also give us time to make some plans.

The lawyer Holly had hired arrived, and while he took Jack's statement, I stepped out to call her. She answered on the first ring.

"How bad is he?"

"Not too bad. Sprained shoulder, black eye—he looks worse than he really is."

"He got lucky. Doesn't sound like the police are going to press charges. But you can bet there'll be a lawsuit."

"I was afraid of that. They're letting him out after lunch. How's the press?" I looked through the window into his room.

"Stories are all over the place. His fans love him, though. They just want to know he's okay. He needs to release a statement."

"No, he doesn't. You put out a statement for him. He's fine, he's resting. Just a few scrapes, but he's okay. That's it."

"Sure, sure. I can work with that. You'll be so pleased to know that I've heard through the grapevine—the grapevine being his sleazy publicist—that Adam is in the same hospital."

"Great! There'll be a doctor close by when I slap that face right off his head," I snapped. "Not kidding, Holly. I better not see that guy."

"Easy, trigger. He's too busy tweeting to worry about you. This kind of press is great for him. Furthers his bad-boy image, you know?"

I seethed.

"Anyway, I've got Bryan flying out there now. He should be there soon. He can get you guys out, but where are you going to go?"

I peeked back into his room. He looked exhausted.

"We'll go back to his hotel. He needs to get some sleep.

That'll give the lawyer time to figure out everything and determine whether Jack can leave town. This is quite a mess." I sighed, leaning against the wall and yawning. The night and the drive were taking their toll.

"Yep, but we'll figure it out. I talked to the hospital administrator, and they're gonna play ball. They've had VIPs there before, so they know how to handle this kind of thing. I'll handle the press on this end."

"You got it. And, hey, Holly?"

"Yeah?"

"Thanks for calling me last night."

"Of course. Besides, you would've killed me if I let you wake up to this, right?"

"Dead. Would have killed you dead." I laughed.

We said our good-byes just as I saw Bryan coming down the hall. He and I went into Jack's room and began to plan exactly how to get him out of there with the least amount of fuss and muss.

In the end, it was Adam who created a perfect diversion. That asshole held a press conference right in front of the hospital while we slipped out the back in a laundry truck. Honestly, sometimes it was like being in a movie . . .

☆   ☆   ☆

"Wow," I breathed, setting down my bag. Spread out in front of me was a bird's-eye view of Las Vegas as seen through the impossibly tall, floor-to-ceiling windows of the Brit's suite. This place was mac daddy and tricked out: dining room, living room, two bedrooms—sweet mother-of-pearl, it was a palace! "Wow," I said again, earning a sheepish smile from Jack as he moved past me and farther inside.

He had said not a word since we left the hospital, other than a slipped curse when he bumped his shoulder while moving from the laundry truck into Bryan's Suburban. Now he moved around the giant suite, first sitting on the couch, then moving to the dining room table, standing by the balcony but not going out. He fretted and fidgeted, not able to stand still but clearly dead on his feet. Nervous. He was nervous. His eyes met mine, then glanced away, then came right back just as fast, full of questions.

Not ready for that, I said briskly, "Okay, let's get you comfortable and into bed. You need to get some sleep." I crossed to him, tugging on his good arm. "Come on, baller, which giant bedroom is yours?"

He rolled his eyes but began to move toward one of the rooms. Once inside, he let me help him out of his jacket, which was a little difficult with the sling on his arm. Pulling down the covers, I patted the pillow.

He finally broke the silence. "You think a nap is gonna make this better?"

"I think it's a start, yes. And then we'll see."

"We?" he asked.

"Yeah." I nodded. "We. Now get in bed."

He looked like he wanted to say more, but he wisely got in. As I smoothed the covers down I caught a glimpse of tomcat on his face. "Would be nicer if you got in with me . . ."

"Sleep, Jack," I warned as he snorted, settling back.

I went into the bathroom to splash some water on my face, and by the time I was finished, he was sound asleep. I went back out to the living room, tucked my legs underneath me on the couch, and began to decide what to do next.

In a town built on playing the odds, I hoped like hell I hadn't bet everything on a long shot . . .

Seriously? Gambling metaphors?

Quiet.

nineteen

*J*ack slept all day, through the night, and well into the following afternoon. Calls came in almost constantly—everyone wanted updates, everyone wanted to know what was going on. With the exception of the lawyer, who gave us the all clear to go back to L.A. when Jack was ready, I stopped answering the phone, needing the quiet.

Holly put out a statement acknowledging that indeed there had been an incident involving Jack Hamilton but that he was fine and in good health, and there was no further information to be shared with the media at this time.

Adam, on the other hand, took full advantage of the interest, using the press to tell his own story. He spun a tale that furthered his bad-boy image: that it was just him and his friends out on the town for a night of drunken excess. Confirming an earlier eyewitness account, Adam let the press infer that it was Jack who had started the fight, had escalated the argument that ended in punches thrown, and that Adam had just jumped into the fray to "help out my boys."

Yeah. He'd called too. I picked up, then promptly hung up the phone, then called down to the front desk to make sure no more calls got through, and that they knew Adam Kasen was not to be allowed upstairs under any circumstances. Jack could argue with me about it later, but that guy wasn't getting anywhere near me.

I slept too, on the couch. Thinly. Not much more than dozing, really, so when Jack finally came out of the bedroom, rubbing his eyes, I sat right up. Wide-awake.

"Hi," he said.

"Hi, yourself," I replied.

He looked around the room, looked at the light outside. "I'm starving."

"I'll bet. You've been asleep for a thousand years."

"That would explain why I feel a thousand years old." He smiled, wincing as his face wrinkled a bit and stretched his stitches.

"You need to eat, then take some of your pain medicine. You slept through the first round." I started for the table where I'd left everything from the hospital. "Come on Jack, you really must be starving, and then we should probably—"

He stopped me with a hand on my arm as I walked past him. "Then we talk, Grace," he said, his fingertips brushing over my skin as he held me in place. "Then we talk."

I stopped breathing.

He licked his lips.

I licked my own in response.

His tummy growled.

I smiled.

"Okay, we eat, then we talk," he said, smiling a little as well.

I sniffed.

"How about a shower, then we eat, then we talk?" I offered.

"Deal." He went to get the room-service menu.

He *wants to talk? That's new.*

That's good.

☆   ☆   ☆

One shower, two cheeseburgers, and three chocolate shakes later, we sat at the table, across from each other. Over his shoulder I could see the lights of the Strip, the evening made the entire city sparkle.

"So . . ." he began, startling me a little bit.

"So," I responded.

You really should go back to speech writing . . .

"I don't really know how to start here. Not quite sure where to begin," he said, fiddling with the saltshaker, head down and not meeting my eyes. The tension was growing in him. I could feel it even with seven feet of polished oak between us.

"Hey, it's me. Just talk," I encouraged, wanting so much to go to his side of the table. It would be so very easy to go over to him, to crawl into his lap, to hold him close and feel his breath on my skin and make this okay for him. But I couldn't. He had a lot to explain, and he needed to get it out. Didn't mean the temptation wasn't strong, though, and I clenched the arms of the chair to stop from going over there and doing just that. Especially when he was worrying that saltshaker to death.

He grasped the shaker, held it tightly, then looked at me. "I hate my life," he said through clenched teeth, and I blanched. Seeing my reaction, he backed up. "No, no, see, that's the thing—parts of my life are amazing, *were* amazing, until I just fucked everything up. Dammit! I can't even explain this right!" he bit out, his frustration bubbling up. "Everything—it was all getting so close, you know? Everyone wanting something, not being able to make decisions just because they felt right. Everything had to be so calculated, so planned out, and it was just . . . Fuck, I hated it!"

I nodded for him to go on, watching as his fingers turned almost white as he squeezed the little glass bottle.

"And it was so *easy* to just go out, let loose, check out, and not care, you know? At first, it was just that. But then it became a regular thing, and my God, do you know what it's like to have people just bend over backward to get things for you? I mean, no one had a bloody clue who I was eighteen months ago, and then suddenly everyone wants to know you, wants to kiss your ass and get you whatever you want, and it's, like, normal, right? That's just how it is? How the *fuck* is that normal?" He yelled now, standing up and pacing around the room.

"And what happens? You fuck it all up, that's what happens. Christ, what an ass I was—to you, to everyone! It was just . . . God, it was like it was happening underwater, you know? I saw it happening, *you* saw it happening, but it was just so much easier to not deal with it! Not to admit it was too much, too soon, too fast, and too damned good. Just too much, too damned much." He continued to pace as he raged.

"And the drinking? That was one thing. I always held my own, but then it's like, the harder we partied, the easier it was to check out, to forget all the other bullshit. And the other stuff? The coke? I can see how people can let that get inside, get inside and take over. That shit's amazing. I only did that a few times—too much for me. The last time I did it was that night, the night your show premiered. That was the last night . . ."

I had tears streaming down my face at this point. I couldn't help it. The raw emotion that poured off him was staggering.

He whirled, saw my tears, and stopped dead cold.

"I can't even believe you're here, actually," he said after a moment, his voice no longer a yell. "After the way I treated you, why in the world are you here? Shit. I wanted to call so much. I wanted to apologize, but Christ, it was so messed up! And I hated the way people were treating you because of me! The things they wrote about you? The awful things that they said just because you maybe were dating a prat like me, because you didn't have the sense to get as far away from me as you could—"

"Jack!" I ran around the table to stand in front of him. "No way. You don't get to take that on, not on your own. Anything that was written about me, anything that any idiot on a website wrote, or a reporter gossiped about, nothing could be so bad that I would even *think* of not being with you. Don't you know that? How can you not know that?"

He was breathing hard, his own tears now shining in his eyes. "I watched your show, you know. I watched it every week," he said, his voice rough as he struggled to get control. "I read every article, watched every interview, saw every picture. My God, Grace, do you know how much I wanted to call you, talk to you? You seemed like you were doing so well. You seemed happy, and I was here and so messed up. And so much time had passed. I didn't think I could come home . . . I didn't know if you still loved—"

"*I was going out of my mind!* Are you kidding me?" I cried, slapping at his chest. "I went to bed every night wondering where you were and what you were doing, and I woke up every morning to go online to check and make sure you were okay, to see what kind of trouble you'd gotten yourself in the night before. And the mornings there wasn't any news, I spent the day trying not to panic, hoping I wouldn't get a call like the one I did the other night saying something had happened! That you'd been in an accident or any of the other million terrible things I dreamed up in my head because I didn't know, Jack! I didn't know what was going on, and the worst thing was, I couldn't help you! So don't give me 'I looked happy' or 'I seemed like I was doing well' when you of all people should know, it's not always how it looks." I paused, shaking. "And of course I still love you, Jack. Of course I do."

We stared at each other, both with the tears and the sniffling.

"I'm so sorry, so damn sorry," he whispered.

Thank you.

"C'mere," I whispered, prying the saltshaker out of his hand and tangling my fingers with his own. Slowly I stepped closer to him, and he opened his good arm to me. I pressed myself into him, a new wave of tears showing up as I breathed in his scent and nuzzled my face into his neck.

God. Damn. I had missed this man. I sighed into his skin as he clutched me closer, a deep throaty groan coming from him as he held me as tightly as he could. Tilting my head up, I let my eyes travel the column of his neck to his soft lips, to the strong jaw and the cheekbones for days, which now bore the scars of his troubles. And finally to his eyes, that green that swirled and deepened, forecasting his thoughts.

"I'm so in love with you, Grace." He looked down at me, my sweet, broken, wonderful boy. "And I'm dying to kiss you."

I raised up on my tippy toes as he leaned down. "I'm kind of dying for you to kiss me."

His lips feathered against my own, tentative, gentle, but warm. I smiled against his mouth, knowing this would not be the last conversation we had about everything that had happened, but knowing this wouldn't be the last kiss either.

☆ ☆ ☆

We kissed. We kissed for two minutes or two hours, I haven't the foggiest. We kissed long and deep, sweet and wicked. We kissed until my leg cramped and his arm fell asleep in the sling. And then we kissed some more. I fell in love with his mouth all over again, wanted to crawl inside and live there for an indeterminate amount of time.

Would be humid, like living in Florida.

Don't spoil this. I've earned some schmaltz.

And when his mouth began to move, tracing the tiniest of kisses along my eyes, fluttering against my eyelashes, sneaking over and nibbling on my ear in a way designed to make me come unglued, I knew there was not, could not ever be, another man who would know my body so well. And I knew where this was heading. And it would be good, so very, very good. Which is why I was completely surprised when he whispered in my ear, "Let's go home, Crazy."

My eyes popped open, my neck snapped up from its position somewhere behind me, where it had fallen when he turned my spine to goo. "You want to go home now? Drive all the way back to L.A.?" I asked as he nuzzled at me.

"Mmm-hmm," he told the spot *just* below my ear.

266

I looked around, looked behind him, out the window. The entire city was still laid out before us, the lights so bright they burned. He was right. We could do the bright lights, the big city. We lived in a town that was built on lights, on stars. But we were a canyon couple.

"Yeah, let's get out of here." I nodded, holding his hand and pressing one more kiss on his now love-swollen lips.

It was almost midnight, but we packed up his things as quickly as we could, settled up his giant bill downstairs, and were back in my car before one. He drove, and we rolled the windows down and let the wind blow in as we headed home.

I chuckled as we sped down the darkened highway, thinking about a movie I'd seen a long time ago.

"What's funny?" he asked, bringing my hand to his lips.

"I was thinking about the movie *Less Than Zero*, ever seen it? Robert Downey Jr.? Andrew McCarthy? They're best friends. Robert's character gets in trouble in Vegas, and Andrew has to drive out there in the middle of the night to bring him home," I answered getting giggly.

"Nope. Never saw it." He shook his head as I laughed again.

"Well, let's just say I'm glad I didn't find you sucking dick to pay for your crack habit." I snorted as the car swerved.

"Grace!" He swore as he brought the car back between the lines on our side.

He was quiet for a moment while I cackled.

"I'd never do crack," he deadpanned as I laughed again.

It felt good, to laugh with him, to crack up and giggle and be silly.

"How'd the movie end?" he asked when I was under control again.

"Um, not well." I looked out the window to the desert, cold at night.

"Not well?"

"Nope." I rolled up the window. "He died. Drug overdose."

We were both quiet.

"You know that's not what happened, right? I mean, I just went a little crazy. No one's addicted to anything. You know this, right? I went on what I think your generation would call *a bender*." He illustrated with quote fingers.

"My generation?" I scoffed, rolling my eyes. I sat for a moment, then turned in my seat to face him. "So you don't think you have a problem? I'm not pressuring, just asking so I understand what we're dealing with here." I held up my hands in a nonjudgy way.

"No, I know why you're asking. You have every right to ask. And the answer is no, not a problem, just a shitty way of dealing with what's been going on. I need to learn to handle this better, without partying so much. I can't promise I won't be a little hard to live with from time to time, but I'm willing to try handling this in a different way."

"Well, hell, I could try handling this a different way too. I'm no expert."

"I don't know. You seem to be doing pretty well with all this. Don't think I didn't notice how my girl went and got all famous on me. I'll need to get your autograph sometime soon," he teased.

"Autograph this. And keep your eyes on the road," I warned as he tried to lean in for a kiss. "Just promise me you'll talk to me next time you're feeling it, okay? The pressure? Just tell me. We'll work it out, but you have to talk to me, okay?"

He was quiet, watching the road. A slow grin crept over his face, and he looked back at me. "You know you're the mature one in this relationship now. How the hell did that happen?"

"I'm a girl, Jack. We're born more mature," I said primly, settling back into my seat.

He huffed, muttering something about maturity and age as we passed a sign that said:

LOS ANGELES 100 MILES

I stole his hand from his lap and held it the rest of the way home.

☆ ☆ ☆

It was almost dawn when he pulled into our driveway, the sky just beginning to tinge pink at the edges. We grabbed our bags and made our way to the front door. I turned the key and stepped inside, but he hovered just outside, on the doormat.

"What are you, a vampire? You need an invitation to come in?"

He looked at his feet, shuffled a bit. "Thanks for coming to get me."

I took his hand and pulled him inside before he tugged back.

"Really, Grace. Thank you," he said again before stepping in and locking the door.

"You're welcome." I leaned into his side as we took our bags and headed back to the bedroom. The room was in disarray, just like I'd left it. "I kind of took off the other night when Holly called me. I actually had to come back inside when I forgot my shoes." I chuckled, taking them off now and throwing them into the closet. I was so tired, my brain hurt.

He followed my lead, taking off his shoes, and sat on his side of the bed. With comforting familiarity, we slipped into our normal routine. I crawled into the bed on my side, he on is, and we met in the middle. Pulling me into his nook, he cradled me on top of him, his arm around me, nose in my hair as he kissed my head.

"Love you, Grace."

"Love you too, Jack."

With my head on his chest, rising and falling softly as we both slipped toward sleep, I offered up another silent thank-you that I had him back where he belonged. And when the dawn finally broke, we were asleep in our bed. Jack was back.

☆ ☆ ☆

I woke up sometime in the afternoon, based on the way the light was streaming in through the windows. I smiled as I stretched under the sheets, feeling the warm body next to mine and knowing who that warmth belonged to. Turning over, I was met with green, green, green. My sleepy eyes met his dreamy eyes, those dreamy green eyes that were full of love. Oh, hello, and something else.

"Hi."

"Hi, yourself," he murmured, dipping his head down to nuzzle me with his nose, drawing a path up my neck, then replacing it with his lips. I drew in a breath at the feel of his mouth on me, my fingertips tangling into his hair, which was now just long enough that I could dig in. Feeling a tickling just below my chin, I giggled as his mouth began to move lower, down toward my collarbone.

"Hey! Hey, you!" I pulled his head back up and held his face in my hands. "Can you do this?"

"Can I do this?" He rolled his eyes, humphing as he went back to his original path.

"No, no, no. Not *can* you do this. Can you do this, *with your arm*? Don't you need to be careful?"

In answer, he rolled over, taking me with him. As the covers drifted down and I perched on top of him, I felt his answer pressed exactly where I needed him. "You'll just have to be on top, Crazy." He pulled apart my shirt, button by button, as I nestled my hips into his.

"I can see you've thought this out, George."

"You have no idea how much I thought about this." His gaze smoldered as he parted my shirt and revealed me. And the green goes dark . . .

"Hello, girls, I've missed you." He grinned wickedly, ghosting his fingertips over my breasts, taunting and clearly delighting in the feel of his hands on me, on my skin.

Arching into his hands, with my shirt hanging down low on my arms, I let my fingertips come down and move across his body, reacquainting myself with his long, lean torso, the sprinkle of hair on that blessed happy trail, the muscles that flexed as I moved closer to Mr. Hamilton.

"Mmm, Grace . . ." He moaned as I brushed against him, scooting backward on the bed and away from his hands. He leaned up on his good arm as I tugged on his boxers, lifting up just enough so I could pull them down. I sucked in a breath at the sight of him, smooth and firm and exactly what I needed.

I trailed my hand up the inside of his thigh, listening to his breathing change as I got closer. I leaned down to press the tiniest of kisses on the very tip of him. He bucked off the bed, groaning at the slightest touch. I smiled to myself, then put us both out of our misery.

As I took him into my mouth entirely, the words he uttered through clenched teeth were equal parts obscene and nonsensical. Nice to know I hadn't lost my touch. His hand buried itself in my hair, urging me as I took him in again and again, swirling my tongue and paying special attention to that area riiiiight there . . .

"Fuck, Grace. Fuck."

Exactly.

Slipping out of my panties faster that you could say "Get it," I crawled back up his body, straddling his hips as he grabbed my curves and guided me down onto him.

Jack. Inside. Perfect.

Frozen in place at the exquisite, I let him fill me, took him in and felt him touch every part of me. We were both still, just letting the moment wash over us. His eyes bore into mine, his hand tightening on my hip as he slid deeper, inch by perfect inch, to penetrate me completely.

"Brilliant," he whispered, his accent breaking the silence and sparking me back to life.

"Brilliant," I agreed, and began to move.

Rocking over him, letting the sounds he made guide me, I slid him in and out, pressing and pulling into me. I matched him groan for lusty groan, arching my back as I rode him, first slow and then faster as the tension built. His hand snuck down between us, twisting and seeking and making the dots behind my eyelids begin to blur into a firestorm.

"You. Feel. Incredible," I panted, his fingers now holding

steady with that luscious pressure that detonated somewhere deep inside me, rocketing me forward onto his chest as I split into a thousand pieces and fell apart. And as I fell, I saw the face I loved, that beautiful face set tight in passion. Jaw clenched, forehead furrowed, lips chanting my name over and over again as he exploded inside me.

Jack. Inside. Perfect.

When I could lift my head again, my body spent and deliciously sleepy, he rolled me over onto my side, snuggling in behind me and throwing his arm over top, creeping out of the sling just enough to grab a handful.

"I missed this," he whispered in my ear, letting out a contented sigh.

I burrowed deeper, wrapped up and warm. "Me too."

Now Jack was back.

twenty

*J*ack was back, but all was not roses and tidy strings neatly tied up. He'd made an ass of himself but good, and he had some work to do. Over the next few days, all the chickens came home to roost, and he had more problems than he'd bargained for.

He had to start with Holly, who, while glad he was safe and seemingly off his bender, had gotten the brunt of his nasty while in Vegas, and she let him have it. She came over the night after we got back, and I hightailed it right out of the room when I saw how this was going to go. But he needed to hear it; he needed to know how his actions had affected people. And he did know it. He told me later he was okay with her yelling at him because he knew he deserved it. He also knew she wouldn't yell if she didn't care.

They came to an agreement about future promotions: that he would have more control over events and interviews he agreed to. He would do what he needed to do to promote his projects, but he'd have final say in how extended he was.

The conversation with Lane went much easier, in the way conversations between two guys almost always do. Lane came over a few days after Jack was back, took one look at the now barely there black eye and bruises, and started laughing. Slapping him on the back, Lane followed Jack out to the patio, and I could hear them trading insults within minutes. Honestly.

The real trouble Jack had got himself into was legal, and there was a lot of it. The club owner, that guy's partners, and at least half of the people who were there that night were suing for damages. Hospital bills, loss of income, property damages—they saw the opportunity to go after a celebrity, and go after him they did. But he handled it. He met with his lawyers and began the process of settling out of court for most of the charges. He didn't face any criminal charges, and for that we could be thankful. No embarrassing trial, no media circus. It could be managed as privately as possible.

The media? They had a field day. They printed accounts from people who were there that night and posted as many pictures as they could from all the nights when Jack looked drunk and disorderly. Most of his fans stuck with him, however, posting letter after letter in chat rooms and on messsage boards. They told him how much they loved him and how they hoped things were getting better.

It was funny how people who had never met him, would probably never meet him, felt they knew him. And while there were always going to be fans who thought he belonged to them somehow, that they were entitled to know everything about him no matter how personal, most of them just adored him and wanted him to be happy. They loved their Super Sexy Scientist Guy, sure, but it now became clear they loved Jack Hamilton just as much. Not all celebrities get a second chance the way he seemed to be. Fans could be fickle and turn on a dime. But they loved him, and they rallied.

And speaking of celebrity, Adam was everywhere: still out every night, always where the cameras seemed to be, and always just available enough for comments. Jack had spoken to him a few times, and their lawyers had spoken a few times as there was a shared responsibility for some of the actions of that night, but Jack hadn't seen him since we'd been back in L.A.

One night, flipping through channels before bed, Jack stumbled onto a gossip show, and there was Adam, outside a club in Hollywood with three girls and a bunch of cameras, totally in his element. He watched it for a few minutes while I stood in the doorway, not saying a word. He glanced at me, then back at the TV.

"That guy's kind of a dick," he said, then changed the channel.

He didn't even see the pillow coming when I threw it at his head.

Jack stuck pretty close to home during this time, not quite cocooning but just . . . breathing. He read scripts, he helped me run lines, and he eased back into a tentative friendship with Michael, which had always been tenuous at best. Michael continued to be quite protective of me, and he didn't go as easy on Jack as Lane did. But as a week passed, and then another, things began to get back to normal.

But it was us after all, and the normal was never actually normal. A point proven once more by a phone call from Holly one afternoon. A call she asked us both to be on.

Perched on Jack's lap, I took the call with him from the patio. In the shade of the lemon trees, we exchanged pleasantries with her until she cut right to it.

"So, Jack, I got a call today asking if you'd be interested in presenting an award at this year's Emmys."

I felt Jack freeze underneath me. He hadn't been out since that night in Vegas, had declined every interview request, and essentially hadn't been seen since everything had exploded. I scratched at his scalp a bit, letting him feel me. He patted my leg absently, taking a deep breath.

"Hmm, well . . . I'm not sure that's such a good idea. You?"

"Actually I think it's a brilliant idea," Holly countered. "It's a good way for you to be seen again. You're a film actor, and the Emmys always has a few movie stars. They'll be thrilled if you say yes. You can wave to fans, the red carpet is always an easy line to work—no tough questions. Plus you look pretty great in a suit."

He looked at me. I shrugged to say, *It's up to you.*

"I'll think about it. When do I need to let you know?"

"Soon. It's kind of a last-minute thing, but it could be a great way to get you back out there."

He rolled his eyes at that, but in a good-natured way. He'd stuck close to home, but he was getting a little stir-crazy, I could tell. It was time for the movie star to head back into Hollywood. But on his terms. He drummed his fingers on my thigh, thinking it over. "You know what? Fuck it. I'll do it." He smiled.

"Well, hold on there, Brit boy. There's something else to consider." She paused, and the drumming on my thigh stopped. "They want Grace to present as well."

Come again?

"Sorry, Holly, they want me?" I'm amazed I remembered how to speak.

"Sure. Your show's a fucking hit. I'm surprised it took them this long to ask, but that's showbiz."

Holy shit. I drummed my own damned thigh.

"But wait, so Jack and I'd be at the same awards? This isn't the same as us being at a party, same-place, same-time kind of thing,"

Jack started to fume. I put a finger to my lips to shush him. I wanted to hear this. It was something we had to consider.

"Well, that's the real question, isn't it?" Holly said. "How do you want to play this off? You know how I feel. I still don't think it's a good idea for you two to go public. Jack is a huge draw, and girls want to know anything and everything about him. Knowing that he is officially off the market? Won't go over well."

Jack was about to come out of his seat. Good thing I was sitting on him.

"And for the record, Jack, because I know you're about to come out of your seat, I'm thinking about Grace too. Coming out publicly as your girlfriend affects her as well. You saw how much hate she got when people first just started thinking you weren't single. You let everyone know she's your main squeeze? That opens up a whole new level of bullshit for her."

Jack came out of his seat. I signaled for the phone.

"Hey, Holly, let us call you back, okay?"

"Sure, sure. Is he pacing?"

"He's pacing."

"Are his nostrils flaring?"

"A bit. Let me call you back."

"Grace, this is huge for you. You two do whatever you want, and you know I'll support it. I work for you. Don't forget that. But if you're asking me my professional opinion, it's to not go public. Pure and simple."

"I hear you."

"The Emmys, Grace. They want you to be a presenter. Next year? You'll be nominated. I promise you that."

My heart left my body, flew around the backyard, and starting picking lemons off the tree. Holy shit, this was big-time.

"Call me back and let me know, fruitcake."

"Yep," I breathed, and hung up, not taking my eyes off Jack, who had stopped pacing and stood before me, tense. "What are you thinking?" I asked.

"I think you should go. One hundred percent you should go," he said instantly.

"And you? You still in?"

He shook his head. "I don't know. I think maybe this is one you should do alone."

"Now wait a minute. We both need to go." I pulled at the bottom of his shirt and moved him in between my legs as I sat on the back of the love seat. "I bet Holly has a plan already of how we could both go and still keep up appearances. You know she's thought this through from every angle."

His hands went automatically to my hips, and he played with a loose string at the end of my skirt as different arguments were fought across his features, all without saying a word. "How do I say this without sounding like a pompous ass?" He took a breath. "I don't want to make a night like this—a big night for you—about me. And if I'm there, I'm afraid that's what it will be. That's what they'll make it into." His eyes were sad.

"Oh, is that all? Pfft, I can handle that." I took his hands and wrapped them more snugly around my waist. "I'm going to the Emmys, George, like, on purpose. Going to the Emmys. Presenting. At the Emmys—did I tell you that part?"

He smirked, letting me draw him in. "You mentioned something about that. I suppose I'll have to go too, make sure you don't get into any trouble."

"Trouble. Ha. Not *me*," I teased, raising my eyebrows as he wrapped his strong arms around me and picked me up, my legs crossed behind his back. "I'm glad you're doing this. In fact, I think I'll even wear a slutty dress for you that night, just to drive you crazy."

"Fucking Nuts Girl," he growled, racing me across the yard and into the house.

"I need to call Holly back. Wait, wait, slow down, slow down, slow— Mother-of-pearl, that feels good . . ."

☆　☆　☆

True to form, Holly had indeed had a plan ready to go in the event we both said yes. Reluctantly (some of us more reluctant than others), we all agreed it was best for all involved if Jack and I continued to keep our relationship private and not for public consumption. Jack didn't like it. He didn't like it at all, but when he looked at it objectively, he knew it was still the best course of action.

The plan was remarkably simple: We'd take Michael and Holly as our plus ones. Holly would arrive with Jack, which made sense. Actors took their managers to premieres and award shows all the time, and this way she could be by his side to help manage the questions he'd be asked on the red carpet, just in case a reporter forgot their manners. Michael would go with me, which was again something totally within the realm of the possible. As the creator and head writer of a hit show—a show I starred in and had been invited to the Emmys as a representative of—not to mention being lifelong friends, his walking the red carpet with me would not only make perfect sense, we'd also give them a great story.

We could both go. Separately. And together. Kind of?

And so we found ourselves together in the line at the biggest awards show in television—just in separate limos. We texted each other.

Nervous?

I smiled down at his words on my phone.

A little, you?

I looked out the window at the line of cars, wondering how close to the front we were.

Jack and I had spent the day at the Peninsula hotel getting ready, and by that I mean it took me all day to be buffed and sprayed, teased and twisted, then poured into a dress and sewn in place while he stepped into his suit ten minutes before we left.

And damn did he look good. He ran a hand through

his hair, called it good, and was ready to go. Every female in the room sighed when we saw him. It was impossible to be that close to sex incarnate and not need to steal an extra breath or two.

But it seemed all he could see was me, in my not-so-slutty dress after all.

Dressed by a new designer who delighted in working with an actress with curves, I was draped in green silk that shimmered and slithered with every step. I was old Hollywood meets the twenty-first century, and my earlobes sparkled with emeralds that hadn't been outside a vault since Eisenhower had been in office, on loan from Van Cleef & Arpels. The gems were big enough to choke a horse, and they hung heavy, dripping with sprays of diamonds and barely dusting my shoulders. An emerald the size of a quail's egg sat on my left hand, catching the light.

And while I could've hung a rope of the same around my neck and played *Dynasty* with the big girls, I kept to what I knew. As Jack's eyes moved over me again and again, I traced the necklace he'd given me, feeling the words he'd had engraved there.

After a moment, he grinned that wicked grin. "Brilliant," he pronounced, taking my hand and bringing it to his lips for a kiss. My glam squad sighed in chorus behind me. "Quite a rock you've got there," he remarked, his fingers pressing around the ring, feeling the band. He turned my hand over and pressed a wet kiss in the center of my palm, still fingering my ring.

"There's a guard over there who came with the jewelry. He'll have you up against that wall in seconds if you try to steal my bling," I joked as his eyes flicked over my shoulder. Looking back at me again, he said in a voice low enough for only me to hear: "Speaking of up against that wall . . ."

I must have moaned louder than I thought, as the entire room burst into embarrassed giggles.

"Okay, you two, get it out of your system now," Holly warned, breezing into the room, all business but dressed in a red sequined gown that said the opposite of business. This was the likely reason Michael's eyes were bulging out of his sockets.

I shook my head to clear it, still swimming in the images Jack had planted in my brain. Me up against the wall, his hands slipping beneath my skirt, sliding down my body and pressing his tongue against my—

Ding dong.

Gross.

The doorbell brought me back to the present, a present where Jack chuckled, knowing exactly where my brain had been.

"Okay, people. First limo is here. Michael, you'll take Grace. Jack and I will follow in a bit," Holly instructed, moving efficiently through the room toward the door.

With this schedule, I'd be arriving well ahead of Jack. I'd likely be through the press line and inside before he even arrived, almost completely negating the possibility of us being photographed together.

Moving as quickly as I could in my dress, which was literally only a breath bigger than I was, I went to say good-bye.

"See you there but, you know, not see you there." I pressed a kiss on his cheek.

"Can't wait to see you on that stage, Grace. You look stunning," he replied, kissing me square on the lips.

"She's gonna kill you." I laughed as Holly came running over.

"Ack! You smudged her lipstick! And you, with a big kiss mark on your cheek? It's like you people have no idea what I'm trying to do here." She fussed over both of us, surprising Jack when she licked her fingers and started rubbing his face.

"Ew!" he exclaimed.

Laughing out loud, I let Michael lead me away from the room and down to the limo.

Which is where I now sat, moments away from walking the red carpet with my very good friend, who had written something so amazing it actually led to my being here. This was as much an acknowledgment for him and his work as it was for me.

My phone buzzed again, another text from Jack.

Not nervous. Just wish it was later tonight. When I have you all to myself again.

My tummy whooshed, going silly once more at his devil words. If the world only knew—seconds before stepping

286

out on a red carpet—the dirty texts that were flying back and forth.

My face grew hot, and I glanced up at Michael, who was texting as well.

"Holly?" I asked.

He nodded. "Yep. They just got here, probably twenty cars behind us in line." He put his phone away and inclined his head toward the car door. "Looks like it's our turn."

I took a deep breath, or as deep as I could in my green skin suit, as he opened the door. Stepping out first, he turned to take my hand and help me out of the car as the sounds of the crowd broke over me.

Wow.

A smile I didn't have to fake spread across my face as I looked down the red runner that cut through the beautiful chaos. As my dress swirled around me, caught in a sudden breeze, I saw flashbulbs pop everywhere. Me! They were taking pictures of me.

I could hear my name being called from all directions, and I turned to see the stands of fans, people who had come to watch and cheer on their favorite stars. They said my name! They were screaming for me, *for me*.

I felt the energy wash over me, tugging from all directions. It was heady. Feeling Michael's hand at my back, friendly and grounding, I willed myself forward and we made our way through the crowd. I smiled at faces I recognized—faces I realized I recognized only because they were famous! Holy shit! Everywhere I looked I saw someone I knew. Either I grew up with them on television, or I watched them on my favorite shows now.

I took Michael's arm, squeezing it, trying to keep my face in check and resisting the wild urge I had to jump up and down, dance and twirl and shout, "Christ on a crutch, how is this my life?"

He totally seemed to get it, and he squeezed back, enjoying this moment with me, totally on the same wavelength. I think we handled it well. We mingled and met, stopping periodically for pictures with some of the biggest names in entertainment.

Handlers ushered me on to the step and repeat to pose for pictures. I stood there, the light from hundreds of cameras popping and snapping from every direction, and relished in the feel of silk whispering against my skin. I felt good, I looked pretty, and I was out of my mind happy.

Once I took my turn, I stepped back into line with Michael, who accompanied me farther down the red carpet. It was like a sparkly but well-oiled machine, with reporters and cameramen lined up and waiting to talk to everyone as they made their way inside.

Taking a deep breath, I stepped up to the first reporter.

"Grace Sheridan, so nice to see you tonight!" she oozed. "You look fabulous. Who are you wearing?"

I smiled and nodded and played the game. I answered questions about my dress, my jewelry, the weather, who I was excited to see tonight, what award I was presenting, what was coming up on the next season of *Mabel's Unstable?*, who I was here with. Who was I here with? That was the question they asked as craftily as possible. One even went as far as to ask, "We see that Jack Hamilton is also presenting tonight. Anything you want to say about that?"

I smiled big, showing my teeth. "I'm excited to see all the stars here tonight. The more the merrier."

I was getting really good at this.

Michael moved with me down the line, some reporters asking him a few questions when they realized he was the writer behind *Mabel's Unstable?* We were almost done when he stepped away from me to take a call. One last reporter in the line, and then I was free and clear to head inside. But just as I stepped in front of her, I heard the crowd roar louder than they had all night. I turned around and saw him.

In front of his limo, there was Jack Hamilton. He waved to the crowd, and the orchestrated chaos became like a sonic boom. Girls screamed and yelled, bounced and shimmied, and those who had signs for him waved them frantically. He laughed, and the photographers went ballistic, flashes popping as he sauntered over to sign some autographs. Alone.

No Holly.

I turned to where Michael had gone, and when I caught his eye, I raised my eyebrow. He came back to my side, still on the phone.

"Sweetie, it's fine. No, really, it's fine. They'll be okay. It's not like you have any control over it," he said into the phone, then covered it to lean over to me. "She got sick in the limo right before they pulled up, so she had to stay in the car."

"Oh no. Is she okay?" I said, wrinkling my nose at the thought. Getting sick in a formal dress? I bet she was not very comfortable.

"She's fine. She's more pissed than anything, but what are you gonna do? Leave it to my girl to get morning sickness only in the afternoon." He grinned and returned to his phone conversation with Holly. "Yep, there are saltines in your purse. I put them in there just in case . . ."

If you were watching at home that night, here's what my interview sounded like, seventeen seconds after getting this news:

"We've got Grace Sheridan here with us tonight, star of the new hit *Mabel's Unstable?* Grace, how are you?"

"Um, what?"

"Grace, how are you tonight? You look great. Excited to be here?"

"Excited? Wait, what?"

"Um, yes, well, you *look* excited. Overwhelmed even a bit, maybe? Happens to the best of us, right? So, who designed your dress?"

"What? Oh, they're from Van Cleef and Arpels."

"Okay, that was Grace Sheridan. Go ahead and head on inside. Grace Sheridan, everybody!"

I stumbled off the pedestal and back over to Michael, where he was just hanging up the phone. "Holly's pregnant?" I asked. My mouth was still hanging open, so it came out in a slur.

He stopped in his tracks. "Dammit, I thought she told you! She told me she was going to tell you. Oh, I'm dead." He shook his head as a giant grin split his sweet face in two.

I could feel tears burning as a lump formed in my throat. "She's going to have a baby?" I could feel my own grin springing up. *A baby?*

"Well, yeah, we are." He nodded. Proud papa already.

Oh my. Before I could say anything else, a woman with a clipboard approached and began ushering me toward the entrance. "This way, Ms. Sheridan."

A baby. And look how happy Michael was. He was with the one he loved.

The world narrowed, focused down. The crowd quieted to a dull roar in my ears. I saw Michael's face, still smiling. I saw the woman with the clipboard waving me forward. But I spun, catching sight of Jack at the other end of the red carpet. There were countless people between us: handlers, stars, reporters, cameramen, awards-show staff with their clipboards, but through them all, I could see Jack.

With a reporter. He was only in profile, but I could see him. His jaw was clenched, and he was running his hand through his hair repeatedly, worrying it. He looked flushed, on edge.

Holly wasn't with him. No one was running interference.

The reporter leaned in, a vapid grin on her face. Her body language was predatory, eager. Every reporter after her was also looking at him, jockeying for position. Jack moved on to the next stop, smiling nervously, but almost immediately he looked defensive again. He crossed his arms over his chest and rubbed at his face.

What the hell were they asking him? He looked miserable.

I looked back at Michael, glowing at having let the cat out of the bag, happiness oozing out of every pore. The look on his face was every bit as dazzling as all the borrowed bling on this red carpet. I looked back to Jack, unglued and under attack.

I took off, my feet carrying me as fast as they could move in my fancy shoes, dodging famous faces and hungry hangers-on. I could see photographers take notice, and several began moving along with me as I got closer. I was close enough to hear the reporter ask, "So, Jack, we've heard about the drinking, the gambling, the wild nights out on the town, and now you've been hit with numerous lawsuits. What's going on? What can you tell us?"

Just as he flinched, his entire posture tightening as he fought between fight and flight, I reached his side. I placed my hand on his shoulder, then ran it down his arm. As I reaching the crook of his elbow, I turned him toward me ever so slightly. When he realized it was me, his eyes widened, eyebrows raising in surprise. Taking the opportunity,

I slid my hand farther down his arm to thread my fingers with his, and I grasped his hand firmly. Dropping my gaze from his for only a second, I smiled at the reporter. She seemed to be just now realizing who I was and what she'd gotten on tape.

Stifling a laugh, I looked back at Jack, who was now biting down on his lower lip, his entire face lit up. I winked at him, tugged on his hand, and led him away.

We walked down the red carpet together, and the fans in the stands lost their minds. As the cameras whirled and photographers almost fell over one another, I looked up at him, grinning as he relaxed and squeezed my hand. We stopped in front and let the press get their shot.

"Grace! Jack! Jack and Grace, look over here! Over here!"

For three solid minutes, I saw nothing but flashes—except when I looked to my left and saw Jack. And each time we looked at each other and smiled, the photographers went even more crazy. Their shouts growing even more frenzied. I laughed as Jack tucked me in to his side. The smile on his face bloomed even wider as his arm went around my waist. In public.

He leaned in to whisper in my ear. "Do you have any idea what you just did, Crazy?"

I grinned as he brushed a curl behind my ear. "Pretty quick thinking for a girl who isn't even wearing panties."

The shot on the cover of almost every magazine for the next week was me laughing, with Jack's mouth hanging wide open.

twenty one

Entertainment Tonight

The stars were out in Hollywood last night at the annual Emmy Awards show, but it was one couple in particular who stole the night. Perennial are-they-or-aren't-they couple, megastar Jack Hamilton and newcomer television actress Grace Sheridan, silenced all questions about the status of their relationship last night when they walked the red carpet together, surprising everyone as they acknowledged themselves as a couple for the first time anywhere.

So how did this happen? Let's break this down for you.

Grace arrived before Jack, walking the carpet with Michael O'Connell, the head writer and creator of her hit TV show *Mabel's Unstable?*, which is now in production on its second season. Scheduled to present an award, the seating chart showed Grace sitting several rows behind Jack, who was also scheduled to present. On an earlier broadcast we were able to show you where he would be sitting, which was to be in the front row next to his manager, Holly Newman, who happens to be Grace Sheridan's manager as well.

Cut to last night when Jack Hamilton arrived just before the show began. Speculation had been that he would do just that—arrive close to the beginning of the show so he could skip most of the press line, avoiding questions about his recent legal troubles. But when he arrived, he arrived solo, signed a few autographs, and was ushered into the press line.

And shortly after that is when Grace suddenly appeared at his side and the two of them posed for pictures. Holding hands, whispering to each other, after that moment the two appeared to be very much a couple. They smiled for photographers as they walked inside, and Grace sat next to Jack in the front row for the entire show.

Even as the show began, the couple remained the topic on everyone's lips. The evening's host even remarked that it was great to see Jack back out on the town, and with such a sexy redhead. The two each presented an award and stayed close together the entire evening. The pair were later spotted heading into an after-party accompanied by O'Connell and their shared manager,

Holly Newman, who turned heads of her own by wearing a white oxford over what appeared to be a designer red sequined gown.

So, ladies, your Super Sexy Scientist Guy seems to be spoken for . . . what say you?

Hamiltoned.com

He's back! He's back! He's back! After being out of the limelight and off the radar for weeks now, last night we got to see our favorite boy, Jack Hamilton, and even got to see him being sweet with his now finally confirmed girlfriend, Grace Sheridan.

Jack looked amazing in a black suit and black tie. He's still handsome as ever. *He can never go away for that long again!* And even hotter was his arm around Grace. We think we got a shot where you can see him alllmost touch her butt! OMG!

We love . . .

JackedOff.com

Once again, Grace Sheridan has made sure she is all over our boy, just when he was trying to talk about what's been going on! After being gone for, like, ever, our sexy Englishman showed up at the Emmys last night, and that cow made it all about her, *again*!

She was all over him, holding his hand, draping his

arm around her. He looked so uncomfortable. You could totally tell he was just trying to be nice.

Let it be known, now and forever, that we will never buy it. He could never love someone like her. And even if they are together, which we don't believe for a second, it would never last. What could he possibly have in common with a woman so much older than him?

Glad you're back, Jacky boy, but lose the redhead. Seriously.

Fashionwatch.com

As you knew we would, we have your annual best and worst fashions from the Emmy Awards, and making her first appearance on this year's Best Dressed list is actress Grace Sheridan. Sure, everyone was talking about who she was with, but we were just as interested in what she was wearing! Stunning in green silk, her curves slinked down the red carpet. Her hourglass figure is an inspiration.

TMZ

After stunning everyone at last month's Emmy Awards, Jack Hamilton and Grace Sheridan have been spotted everywhere in Los Angeles, and we mean everywhere. Our cameras have captured them at Whole Foods, Fatburger, Century City Mall, the movie theater—they've been everywhere. Whether holding hands or snuggling over ice cream at Top of the Glen, the formerly shy couple suddenly has no problem showing their affection for each other.

Jack is set to start work on the newest *Time* film on location in both Vancouver and Berlin, while Grace is wrapping up production on the second season of *Mabel's Unstable?* here in L.A. We'll see how long they can make it as a couple once they have to start traveling for work. Will they be a long-distance love?

CurvyGirlGuide.com

Starting this month, Grace Sheridan will be hosting monthly chats with readers of *BodyChange* magazine, a new magazine aimed at curvy women who want to live a healthier life. Bolstered by the interest in her own struggle, Grace has partnered with the magazine in an effort to illuminate the struggles women have with self-image, confidence, their sexuality, and everything else facing a modern woman. We couldn't be happier to continue to support organizations who elevate the discussion about health in America and what healthy looks like.

CelebTracker.com

Adam Kasen was fired from the set of action movie *Private Dick* after weeks of tension between cast and crew. The production company said only "We needed to go in another direction."

☆ ☆ ☆

Once more I found myself on a beach, beside an ocean, without a top on.

Laying back in the warm sand, I let my fingers sift through, centering down to the thin edge of a shell. I plucked it from the grains and examined it in the strong sunlight. It was swirled through with gray and iridescent pink and spiraled down in circles thin enough to see through. Over my shoulder, a shadow took shape on the sand.

"You can't take every shell home with you. I hardly have any room in my suitcase as it is with all the stuff you bought for the baby."

"Hey, that kid's gonna need everything I bought," I protested as he flopped down next to me.

"You don't think Holly's going to buy everything under the sun for her? As soon as she found out it was a girl, there was nothing pink left in any baby store this side of Mulholland! Michael said it was like a pink explosion at their place." He laughed.

"Good point." I grinned as he peeked under my big, floppy hat.

Jack's sun-freckled nose presented itself first, then those sweet lips. I kissed those very lips, and they kissed me back. I fell back onto the towel, pulling him with me. Sticky with sweat and salt, our skin stuck together, hot and twisted.

Hungry lips met mine again and again, halting only when I heard a telltale motor.

"They're close," I warned, reaching for my bikini top.

"So was I," he sighed, reluctantly tying me up and hiding my boobies—from him and the cameras.

On vacation again in the Seychelles, we learned quickly that things had changed since the last time we were here. We could no longer frolic naked on a beach in the Indian Ocean without a care in the world. Well, we could, but then my boobies would be splashed across every gossip rag in the Western world, and Jack wasn't quite so ready to share them.

Luckily, our island was isolated enough that they could only approach from the water, and we could hear them coming.

And they could hear me coming, something Jack was also careful about keeping under wraps after a particularly wicked session in the outdoor shower had me screaming his name over and over again. I tried to keep quiet, I truly did, but mother-of-pearl, it was hard.

And so was he . . .

And so was he.

I grinned at him, letting him pull me up off the sand to stand next to him and look out over the deep blue. Knotting my sarong more securely around my waist, I squinted at the horizon, searching.

"I hear them, but I don't see them."

"They're out there. We should head in." He settled me

in front of him with his hands around me, flat against my tummy. Tucking his chin into my shoulder, he held me tightly.

We were enjoying our last little bit of time together before he left to work on his next film. There was just enough time for a little break before the holidays, and when he asked if I wanted to take a trip, I agreed immediately. I wanted to come back to our lovely beach house.

Hearing the roar of motorboats a little closer now, he slapped me on the ass and hustled me toward the house. "Come on, Crazy. They already got enough shots of you in your bikini."

They really had. In the past, I would have been horrified to see pictures of my bathing suit–clad backside as I dug for shells in the sand next to my boyfriend, who had his hands all over said backside. But now? Eh. It was just how we rolled.

He paused as we shuffled across the beach on our way back to the house and began tracing his feet through the sand.

"You writing me another message, George?" I laughed as I stood on the steps, shaking sand off my legs.

"Uh-huh."

"Another grand gesture?"

"Uh-huh." He grinned, his tongue poking out of his mouth as he wrote with his big toe.

"You gotta come up with something new. That's old material. You need a new grand gesture," I teased, taking off my hat and letting my curls run wild in the ocean breeze.

He finished and extended his hand to me. "Why don't you shut up and come read it," he challenged, mischief in his eyes.

Wicked wanton man.

I kicked back down the steps, the sand hot between my toes, and took a running leap at the last minute to pounce on him. Catching me in midair, he let out an *oof*, a very British sounding *oof*, mind you, and let me monkey-crawl around his torso to perch on his back, wrapping my legs around his waist.

As I nibbled at his ear with my hands in a choke hold around his neck, he wobbled over to his masterpiece. Which he'd crafted with his toes.

"Okay, let's see this grand gesture." I giggled, peering over his shoulder and slapping at his hands as they tried to raise up my sarong skirty thing.

I could see one letter, then another, and then it all became so very clear.

Marry me?

I froze, no longer slapping. My legs, however, tightened.

"Ow, ow! Crazy, hey, ow!" he cried, unlocking my legs and pulling me off his back. With me in front of him now, he tilted my chin up and chuckled at the look on my face.

I was shocked.

Reaching into his pocket, he pulled out a box. Small, black. This was real.

He took my hand and opened my fingers, which were frozen into some kind of terribly romantic claw. Placing the box inside, he opened it up to showcase a perfect, round, brilliant diamond. Just one perfect diamond on a platinum band. Giant. Sparkling. Wow.

He leaned down to nuzzle me, pressing kisses across my face—eyelids, nose, cheeks, that damnable spot just below my ear. And in the Queen's English, in that very ear, he said, "Marry me."

I looked into his eyes as tears spilled over and down my face. They had to go around a giant smile to make their way to the sand below.

Yes.